HAWTHORN WOODS

Thank you, Marya

PATRICK CANNING

ISBN 979-8-66348-797-9

CHAPTER 1

The party was roughly divided into the same-sex groups of a grade school dance, both sides seeming to enjoy the break from their significant others. The women, most of whom seemed to be named Carol, laughed explosively, touching one another's forearms in agreement or emphasis as they sucked down wine coolers and long, skinny cigarettes, while men with mustaches cradled koozie-swaddled Miller Lites and rushed punchlines to dirty jokes under clouds of cigar smoke.

Francine stood alone in the kitchen, digging her thumbnail into the wood of the door jamb as she studied the residents of Hawthorn Woods. There was a time when she could have guessed professions, habits, personalities. But not anymore. She could see only a party of question marks, mingling on the cement patio under the glow of porch lights.

Yellow dust gathered on the linoleum floor below as splinters of wood chipped at her nail polish, revealing details only visible once they'd been separated from the whole.

Like the way Ben used to roll her toothpaste tube.

He had always used mint toothpaste, only touching Francine's cinnamon flavor when it was almost out, crimping the ends so the last of the paste was ready to go. Now Francine had to roll the empty tube herself, but she could never get the crimp quite right. One detail in a thousand, and such a stupid one to miss, but that's what stuck.

"Ow!" She jerked her hand back and flapped it in pain. A splinter had lodged deep under her thumbnail. She bit at the spot, watching as a head of strawberry blond hair wove its way through the crowd.

"There you are!" Ellie said, yanking open the screen door. "C'mon, you need to meet more of the neighbors."

"Ellie, I'd really rather—"

But Francine's sister had already pulled her out into the dizzying carousel of suburbia.

She took it all in as best she could, smiling and shaking hands while trying to look happy. The marathon of introductions was doing a number on her already exhausted psyche, especially since she was without her once-keen ability to read people.

Her ex-husband had taken a lot: a good chunk of her thirties, her faith in one half of the human species, and her favorite Whitney Houston cassette. Worst of all, though, was the theft of her confidence. How could anyone pretend to have good sense after marrying a man who'd turned out to be…what Ben had turned out to be?

"Ellie, I need a break," Francine said after meeting yet another Carol and her mustachioed husband.

"Ooh wait, just one more. Laura Jean!" Ellie towed Francine toward a short, blond woman whose waist-length ponytail swung as she spun to face them. Hair was always the first thing Francine noticed about someone; the curse of the stylist, she supposed.

"Best friend, meet big sister," Ellie announced. "Laura Jean, Francine. Francine, Laura Jean."

Please let there be at least one genuine person here, Francine prayed. Every woman she'd met that night had taken great trouble to appear welcoming, but never quite managed to transcend constipated pleasantries.

"You make us sound like a couple of Muppets when you say our names together," Laura Jean said to Ellie. Her voice had a faint twang, not a Southern accent so much as Diet Southern. "Francine. So very nice to finally meet you, even in seventy-percent humidity."

The woman's perfectly put-together look was a touch intimidating, but her words seemed sincere, her smile warm. Francine decided to risk being herself.

"Really wish I'd remembered how tropical Illinois is in the summer." She wiped a strand of sweaty brown hair from the sun-bolded freckles on her cheeks. "I'm starting to smell like a locker room."

"Oh boy, I'm right there with you." Laura Jean made a show of sniffing her own armpits. "I'm getting notes of eighth-grade boys, post-gym class, pre-deodorant."

The exchange sparked a smile from both of them, and Francine wondered if they'd decided to be friends at the same moment.

Still in auto-introduction mode, Ellie tugged on Francine's elbow. "Okay, we should keep meeting people. Ooh, you still have to say hi to the coupon club ladies and you gotta meet the Chief, of course—"

"Ellie, I just remembered." Laura Jean bumped her palm against her forehead. "Pete said to tell you the ice is running low in the beer tub."

Ellie's eyes went wide at the scandalous thought of warm beverages, and she ran for the garage. "I'm on it. Keep her company!"

Laura Jean plucked two bottles from the beer tub—already overflowing with ice—and handed one to Francine with a wink. "Looked like you could use an Ellie break. I adore your sister, but *mercy*, she is a treadmill jammed on High."

"Thanks. And thanks for not dying of surprise that we're related. That's the normal response from people, usually after they gush over how pretty she is."

"Oh, please. My older sisters had legs for days and nobody ever let little ol' me forget it. You and Ellie look plenty related to me."

Francine shrugged. "She took the aggressively-petite approach, which has its advantages. But I suspect the day you become a size zero is the day somebody makes off with your sense of humor at gunpoint. Though that may just be my rationale for finishing a pizza by myself."

Laura Jean gave a wry grin. "In any case, you're on vacation now, so you can eat as much of whatever you damn well please."

"Yeah. This is kind of a vacation, I guess." Francine wondered how chummy she should get in the first thirty seconds. They stood in silence for a moment, watching barefoot children chase each other around the patio's ring of citronella candles. "Did Ellie mention why I'm here?"

"Well." Laura Jean studied her beer bottle. "Since this feels like a feet-first-into-the-deep-end kind of friendship to me, I won't feign ignorance. She did say you were having a hard time."

Francine nodded. "That's polite-speak for a runaway train headed for a bottomless pit. Also the train is on fire or something."

They both laughed. Francine took a swallow of her beer and pinched at the faded daisy sundress sticking to her skin.

"My husband and I got divorced two years ago. The paperwork was easy enough to sign, it's just the moving-on part that's been tricky. Not one of my strengths, I guess."

"Oh please, when the grocery store stopped selling my favorite ice cream flavor, I wrote a letter to the CEO. 'Where's my rum raisin?'" Laura Jean gaveled the air with her fist.

Francine laughed as Laura Jean continued the ice cream story, but her attention had caught on a middle-aged couple across the patio.

A barrel-chested man, his pomade-drenched hair combed into im-maculate lines of gold, was quietly arguing with a waif of a woman with a black pixie cut. Their body language was a unique brand of tenseness Francine expertly recognized as marital discord. Apparently she could still read people if it was both obvious and marriage-related. Less obvious, however, was the meaning behind the occasional glances Pixie Cut seemed to be sending in Francine's direction. Something about them seemed...hostile.

Francine brought her attention back to the conversation at hand as Laura Jean wrapped up the ice cream epic. "'Read my lips,' I told 'em. 'No. New. Flavors.' In the end, they politely told me to get over it. Not the same thing, I know."

"Hey, ice cream or divorce, problems are problems."

"You sound pretty put together to me," Laura Jean said. "Maybe you're being hard on yourself."

"I can fake put-together when I'm meeting people. I just...are you sure you want to hear all this?"

"Absolutely! Feet first, deep end, remember? Let's have it."

"I guess I still haven't figured out a way to sort through everything that happened. Most of 'our' friends sorta turned out to be 'his,' so there really hasn't been anyone to talk to. Not like I'd have the time, either. I've been working double shifts at the hair salon to pay for an apartment that's somehow both shitty *and* expensive."

"Hmm." Laura Jean tapped her beer bottle against her lips.

"I don't feel like myself," Francine said, with a sigh. "That's why I came here. Ellie and I grew up in a place like this. I'm hoping a bit of relaxing nostalgia can help fix whatever's broken. Two weeks of shady trees and friendly neighbors to help get my mind right. People seem nice enough so far."

"Oh, everyone's plenty nice, and half of them might even mean it."

"And the other half?" Francine's eyes flashed back to Pixie Cut, who was definitely staring at her over the rim of her red cocktail.

Laura Jean smirked. "The other half might be a little nervous at seeing a total babe dropped into a sea of bored husbands."

"No, no, no. I'm no homewrecker. And thanks for calling me a total babe, but I don't think you can legally use the term for someone fast approaching forty."

"Hey! I'm *in* my forties, so watch it. And you're a certifiable catch. Got a sort of…Phoebe Cates-all-grown-up thing going on, and it is working. I am worried about this change-your-life-in-two-weeks business, though. I've been trying to cut down on that rum raisin for a decade and counting. Why the harsh deadline?"

"It was hard enough getting just two weeks off from work. Plus, I don't want to be the older sister crashing with the happy younger couple. It's embarrassing. July fifth, Pete and Ellie are back from their trip, and I'm back to San Francisco."

Laura Jean frowned, but breathed out resolutely. "Very well. I agree to your terms. My sympathetic ear and unparalleled matchmaking services are at your disposal. We're gonna put what's-his-name—"

"Ben."

"—soon to be what's-his-name once more, squarely in the rearview mirror where he belongs. I take payment in coffee and gossip. And rum raisin ice cream if you can find it. Summer 1989 is going to be the summer of Francine, no ifs, ands, or buts about it. Unless it's the butt of some dashing summer fling, of course."

Francine smiled. "Thanks, Laura Jean."

"Good. In the meantime, I'm gonna go check on my darling husband, wherever he is. Will you be all right on your own a sec?"

"I'll try to stay out of trouble."

Laura Jean squeezed her shoulder, then disappeared into the slow churn of polo shirts and perms.

Francine bit at the tiny splinter under her thumbnail as she gravitated toward the party's makeshift bar: a card table hung with glittery letters that read, "Bon Voyage!"

An elderly man examining the bar's spread of liquor bottles would've made a picture-perfect dictionary entry for "grandparent": tortoiseshell spectacles, handsome blue blazer, and gray hair the papery texture of a hornet's nest.

"Hi," Francine said.

"How do you do?" he returned, with a distinct accent.

She pointed at him. "German?"

"I am Swiss. It is a common confusion." He smiled. "My name is Roland Gerber. You are Ellie's sister, yes?"

"Yes. Francine."

Roland Gerber sized her up. "A fine, strong woman. I can see this plainly. Superior to that which you left behind, there is no doubt."

Francine blushed and shook her head. "I probably should've just saved Ellie some time and worn a neon 'divorcée' sign above my head."

"Your sister asked us all to be especially considerate. Perhaps I wasn't meant to disclose this. I'm normally a discreet confidant, but drinking causes me to act out of character." He held up a half-empty bottle of apple schnapps as the culprit. "In any case, welcome to Hawthorn Woods, Francine. You belong already."

"Thank you. Nice to meet you, Mr. Gerber."

She bummed a cigarette from a nearby Carol and stood alone among the candles at the patio's edge, watching fireflies bob weightlessly above the lawn. After a dry spell of quality meetings all night, she was feeling better, having gone two for two with a sincere Southern belle and a flattering Swiss expat. Maybe her luck was finally turning.

The orange tip of another cigarette joined hers in the fireflies' galaxy of yellow.

The man sat in a lawn chair, watching the party closely as he smoked. Wonderfully messy spills of jet-black hair stopped just below his ears, where began one of the worst outfits Francine had ever seen. A cheap tweed jacket covered a pink dress shirt and a pencil-and-paper-patterned tie, the whole ensemble anchored with brown corduroys the man was probably regretting in the night's heat. He was younger than the rest of the husbands, and without the gold stripe of a wedding band, maybe not a husband at all. His eyes were focused intently on the patio, like he was looking for someone in particular.

"Hey, everybody!" Ellie's husband Pete stepped onto the back stoop, hands cupped around his salt-and-pepper mustache. "It's getting kinda late, so I just wanted to say a few things real quick."

After a few good-natured jeers, the party quieted down.

"First, thanks for welcoming Francine, who will be keeping an eye on the homestead in our absence."

Embarrassingly marooned on the outskirts of the party, Francine gave a faux bow to the crowd's applause.

"Total babe!" Laura Jean shouted.

Pete held out a hand for Ellie to join him on the stoop. "Four years ago, when Ellie and I got married, we couldn't afford a honeymoon. Yes, we took a weekend up in that mecca of romance called Wisconsin, but Ellie's always wanted to go to Paris, and I've always wanted to take her."

Awws from the crowd.

"As excited as we are," Ellie said, "travel is nothing without a good home to come back to. I'm sure by the end of the first day, we'll be homesick for this special place and the special people in it."

She put her arm around Pete's waist, he put his around her shoulders. Treasured friends, gathered before them, a beautiful little house behind, a delayed honeymoon on the horizon.

A deep sting found Francine's heart. *This* was what she'd wanted with Ben. A place to call home with someone she could count on. The inertia of a mature relationship unassailed by lies. A future that looked brighter than the past...

But she didn't have any of that.

What she had was a rare, two-week opportunity to turn her life around. Fresh air and rosy memories to bounce her out of a rut that was starting to feel alarmingly familiar. Catharsis through nostalgia. Looking back to move forward. Whatever she called it, it *had* to work.

Because if it didn't, if she couldn't fix what was broken, Francine knew exactly what would happen. She'd slink back to San Francisco and find someone safe, someone she'd love out of pure will because waiting for the right person was too risky. She'd settle, and wilt, and in quiet but important ways, die, living the rest of her days as someone she didn't recognize.

A shiver of activity pulled her attention from the domestic bliss on the stoop to the center of the patio where Pixie Cut was threading the narrow gaps of the motionless party. A flicker of light came from the star pendant necklace on the woman's chest as it repeatedly caught and lost the porch light. Maybe what Francine had initially read as hostility in the woman's face was just frustration at her husband, in which case she and Francine would have plenty to talk about.

Francine wiped a sweaty hand on her equally sweaty sundress as she prepared to meet the umpteenth neighbor of the night.

"Cheers, Hawthorn Woods!" Ellie and Pete said, in unison.

They raised their glasses in a toast as Pixie Cut reached the edge of the patio and threw her entire cocktail into Francine's face.

CHAPTER 2

In most marriages, one or both partners are unhappy.
[x] TRUE   [   ] FALSE

S huffling sleepily into the kitchen, Francine plucked a note from the busy assortment of coupons on the fridge.

Hiya!

Left early for O'Hare to get a jump on traffic.

Don't know what the hell happened last night—SO weird, but please don't let it trip you up. Hawthorn Woods is a good place, and it will be good for you, I know it.

We'll call when we're by a phone, but we'll be on the move a lot, too—lots to see! *O-rah-vwa!* (spelling?!)

Love love love,

Ellie (+ Pete)

Sleeping in hadn't been a great way to start what were supposed to be—what *had* to be—the most productive two weeks of her life, but between a few too many nerve-calming beers and the cranberry vodka facial, Francine wasn't about to give herself too much grief.

She focused instead on a much more pressing problem: finding coffee, and fast. In your twenties, hangovers were annoying. At thirty-five, they were a life and death medical condition, and caffeine was an important part of the cure.

Her bare feet padded across the linoleum floor, its pattern of blue cornflowers worn away in the high-traffic areas of fridge and sink. She dug around the back of the pantry until her fingers found the ribbed tin of a Folgers can, which she extracted with religious reverence. Waiting for the Mr. Coffee machine to brew, she had time to take in all the sentimental accents of her sister's cozy kitchen. Spine-wrinkled cookbooks earmarked with sticky notes. Wooden countertops edge-rounded from a thousand instances of human touch. A flower-bordered cross-stitch that read, 'Home Sweat Home,' the sewn-in typo now a running joke.

Then Francine's gaze found a small chalkboard stuck to the freezer door.

milk
peanut butter
I'm sorry
me too
good luck today!
love you
love you more
raisins

The mundane minutiae of a shopping list layered with apology and forgiveness was just one of many signs of Ellie and Pete's still-breathing relationship, providing constant contrast to Francine's own failed attempt at love.

Now it seemed she might be failing in her attempt at recovery too, given the events of the previous night.

The cheer building at the end of Pete's speech had strangled awkwardly, save for a woman on the other side of the patio who had been oblivious to the drink throw, and continued to clap loudly.

Francine had stood there, dripping, not understanding what had just happened.

She'd never met the woman with the pixie cut before. Hadn't met her husband either. Hadn't done anything to anyone that night except shake hands and smile.

The voice that cut the silence had been loud and diet-Southern.

"Ex*cuse* you, Magdalena!" Laura Jean had thundered. "You apologize right this minute!"

Pixie Cut had muttered something in Russian and stormed off into the night, leaving her excessively muscled husband to stumble through an apology to Francine before hurrying after his wife.

And while the cranberry vodka had washed off easily enough (and tasted pretty good, to be honest), the effect had definitely lingered. Lovers quarreled and siblings squabbled, but such a random, ugly action from a complete stranger had left Francine disturbed. Neither Ellie nor Laura Jean had had anything bad to say about Magdalena beforehand. So, why?

Francine's fragile belief that the future held anything good wavered.

"Aunt Francine?"

She jumped, feet actually leaving the ground, before she turned to find her seven-year-old nephew sitting at the kitchen table behind a box of Lucky Charms.

"Charlie!" she gasped. "You scared the shit out of me."

An awed smile crept onto the boy's face.

"Shit, I shouldn't have said that. Or that," she quickly added. "Don't tell your mom, okay?"

He pretended to zip his still-smiling mouth.

Francine poured the available coffee into a mug and joined him at the table, careful not to bang her head on the low-hanging Tiffany lamp.

Unlike her and Ellie, Francine and her nephew actually looked related, sharing dark blue eyes, a surplus of freckles, and copious amounts of messy brown hair.

"Are you hangovered?" Charlie asked, through a mouthful of Lucky Charms.

Francine snorted. "I'm *hungover*," she corrected, and used the steaming mug of coffee to down twice the recommended amount of aspirin. "Did you say goodbye to your mom and dad this morning?"

Charlie nodded. "They said if I give you any trouble, it's no allowance, no dessert, and no TV for the rest of the summer."

"Yikes. Well, I've never taken care of a kid before, so how about this?" She held out a pinky. "You be cool for me, I'll be cool for you. We'll help each other out. That way, your parents will come home and find you in one piece, and we can have some fun along the way. Deal?"

Charlie hooked her pinky with his own. "Deal." He spooned a final bite of cereal into his mouth and ran for the back door. "'Kay, bye!"

"Hey! Hold up, mister. What's the agenda for the day?"

"What's agenda mean?"

"It means, what are you going to do all day? And don't give me any substitute teacher runaround. I'm sure you're allowed to play with fireworks and smoke cigars, but just know, aunts have special powers that let them smell nephew lies a mile away."

Charlie jittered with anticipation in the doorframe, an inch from total freedom. "I go out to play after breakfast, then I come back for lunch, then I leave again, then I come back when it's dark."

"Okay. I'll make you a sandwich and leave it in the fridge in case I go for a walk or something. And it's milk with lunch, not pop. *Capeesh,* Bubba?"

"What's that mean?"

"I dunno. You're just supposed to say *capeesh* back."

"*Capeesh.*"

"Okay, just go before you explo—"

Charlie darted across the backyard.

Francine downed a handful of the colorful marshmallow cereal, wincing at the sugar as she watched her nephew race toward the willow tree in the middle of the block, laughing in easy joy as he went. She could remember the feeling well: a buoyant pull that made running more natural than stopping. It was one of the many marvelous sensations that hadn't quite survived her trip to adulthood.

What did she have instead?

Little anchors. Little anchors called regret, and loss, and almost. They were light when she picked them up one by one, but then came the day she'd picked up so many she couldn't shake them off, and she was left longing for what she once was: a child in summer, weightless and full of hope.

$$\ast \quad \ast \quad \ast \quad \ast$$

At least fifty Precious Moments figurines lined the shelves of a long bookcase in the guest room, a.k.a. Francine's room for the next two weeks. The porcelain children, which Francine had always found a little creepy, shared shelf space with Pete's antique clock collection, a hobby so boring even stamp collectors made fun of it.

The clocks mercifully didn't chime on the hour, but their softly ticking second hands gave the room a just-tolerable white noise.

Francine peeled away the blanket she'd collapsed onto the night before, revealing the orange-and-yellow, butterfly-patterned sheets beneath like a pair of embarrassing underwear. Ellie had a penchant for buying wacky bed sheets to show how fun and spontaneous she was. Being married to an antique clock collector did funny things to a person.

Upending her suitcase, Francine spilled her clothes and few material possessions out onto the bed at about the same speed with which they'd been packed. If anyone in Hawthorn Woods needed to know how to flee the West Coast in a hurry, she would be only too happy to enlighten them.

1) Ask the landlord of your shag-carpeted and stucco-ceilinged apartment to hold your mail. Try not to be offended when he asks for your name and unit number, even though you gave him a Christmas card last year.

2) At no point should you cry, as it only serves to slow things down.

3) Strongly demand, reasonably ask, then desperately beg for an immediate two weeks off from your busy job, putting you on thin ice with the boss.

4) Sell your expendable possessions in a beyond-depressing yard sale that quantifies your existence into a specific monetary value. Hint: It's less than you think.

5) Use your yard sale profits to buy the best San Francisco to Chicago flight money can buy, or at least the best flight *you* can buy. Turns out three connections make for the cheapest option, so you're off on an involuntary tour of the contiguous United States.

6) Do not let the fact that you are alone and carrying nearly your entire life in a single suitcase trick you into violating Rule # 2.

7) Board your first flight and immediately violate Rule # 2, drawing the doting concern of the Swahili-only, elderly lady in the window seat next to you.

8) Don't spend the next three connecting flights calculating how behind you are in the race of life and how you have absolutely no idea how to fix what needs to be fixed, including how to politely wake the Kenyan grandmother snoring on your shoulder.

Francine examined her worldly possessions scattered unceremoniously across Ellie's butterfly sheets: a worryingly-thin wallet, a tangle of cheap necklaces, half a box of dollar store tampons, half a roll of Lifesavers (mostly pineapple-flavor), an essential army of bobby pins, an issue of *Vogue*, her favorite scissors and comb from the salon, a bright yellow Nancy Drew hardcover, a VHS tape labeled with a tiny skull and crossbones, and a stack of papers bound by a red rubber band.

Francine picked up the papers. The Minnesota Multiphasic Personality Inventory: an exhaustively thorough, hundreds-of-questions-long personality test. Ben had given her the pages a few weeks after they split because he was just so damn thoughtful (after they'd split, anyway). Francine refused to fill the papers out, but also refused to throw them out, leaving the neat rows of true and false boxes forever unchecked. She did, however, answer the occasional question in her head, and perused a few for fun.

I like to read newspaper articles on crime.
True.
I believe that women ought to have as much sexual freedom as men.
Oh, you betcha.
People say insulting and vulgar things about me.
Pixie Cut might have a few choice words.

If I could live my life over again, I would not change much.

False, false, a thousand times false.

In Francine's mind, living without regret was nothing more than the ultimate coping mechanism, one that dictated a person was supposed to learn from mistakes and move in a direction that was exclusively and unrelentingly forward. Because people ended up together if they were meant to, and there were plenty of fish in the sea, and blah, blah, blah.

She wrangled the rubber band back around the papers and chucked them under the bed. The empty scoring page landed face up, showing the abbreviated categories of D, Hy, Pd, Pa, Pt, Sc. A personality type wouldn't tell her anything. The MMPI was just a *Cosmo* quiz wearing fancy pants, one she should have left in California with the rest of her mistakes.

This was bad.

Hawthorn Woods wasn't supposed to be a place for recursive thought and self-judgment. It was supposed to be Francine's last-ditch, Hail Mary, damned-if-I-don't shot at becoming her once-vibrant self again.

She picked up the Nancy Drew hardcover from the bed.

She'd read the fictional teen investigator's mysteries for as long as she could remember, even walking around as a kid herself with a magnifying glass. Later she'd entertained the girls in the salon by tracking down stolen combs or guessing customers' professions. A keen ability to read people was one of Francine's best qualities, something she enjoyed and prided herself on. At least before the skill had become a casualty in Ben's careless exit.

She studied her beloved heroine on the cover. Nancy was resolute and brave, and in no universe would she come undone just because someone stopped rolling her toothpaste tube, or a nasty neighbor felt like throwing a drink on her.

And right then and there, Francine rewrote her own prescription, from one of relaxation to one of investigation. Out with cucumber slices on eyes and cocktails before five, and in with flashlights and following clues wherever they led.

Francine Haddix and the Airborne Vodka? The title needed some work, but the reason behind Magdalena's drink throw was definitely a mystery. And even though the offense was a little pedestrian, something in the woman's eyes, a glint of hate or fear, had spoken to something much deeper than a tipsy misunderstanding.

But to follow the yet-to-be-found clues, Francine would need a lay of the land and a detailed who's-who. She needed a tour guide. Someone honest, but gossipy, and definitely on her side.

She had just the person in mind.

CHAPTER 3

I gossip a little at times.
[x] TRUE [   ] FALSE

"I am *so* glad you called," Laura Jean said, stepping out her front door. "I apologize for not offering a proper welcome tour myself."

Francine shrugged casually as the two of them started down the driveway. "I figured I should know who lives where, given the surprise at the party."

"I have been dying to talk to you about that. Should've dumped my beer right on Magdalena's head. Mutually assured destruction and all that."

Francine laughed and pulled a pack of Camel 100's from her yellow shorts. "Okay if I walk n' smoke?"

"Walk n' smoke. I like that."

"That's what Ben used to call it."

"What's-his-name," Laura Jean corrected. "And please, I'm not some pearl-clutching housewife. Smoke your damn cigarette. And how is it this hot out already?" She put on a big pair of sunglasses, long ponytail swishing as they walked. "Okay, tour time. The block is basically a rectangle, and Mark and I are at the bottom right corner."

She pointed behind them at the tidy red-brick split-level with a Notre Dame flag waving beside the garage.

"Did you guys go to Notre Dame?"

"Us?" Laura Jean laughed. "Hell no, we'd never get in. We've got twin girls there, going into their sophomore year. They decided to stay on campus for the summer, Mom's heart be damned. Hawthorn Woods is apparently a bit too sleepy for girls their age. I'm still adjusting to the empty nest, so if you start to feel like my pet project, it's probably because you are."

A woman driving by in a boxy white minivan made little attempt to hide a curious stare at Francine.

"I was kinda hoping people would've forgotten about last night's little incident," Francine said.

"Some people around here have nothing better to do than mow the lawn and fantasize about their children's potential. Oh God, I think I just described Mark and me. Anyway, do *not* take last night personally. I know they say a full moon makes people squirrelly, but Jee-sus. Okay, back to the tour. As you may know, we are now passing your lovely sister's house. I miss her already. Pete's a good one, too. Bit of a blink-and-you'll-miss-it personality, but that makes him a good foil for your hummingbird sis."

A gaggle of boys wearing toilet paper on their heads rode past on mismatched bikes, narrowly missing Francine as they mimed karate moves and shouted the names of Renaissance painters. Someone's little sister tried to keep pace, complaining about having to be a news reporter.

"Teenage Mutant Ninja Turtles," Laura Jean explained. "Kids' shows are so damn weird. But okay, this here's Del Merlin." She gestured at the house to the left of Ellie's: a one-story ranch with gray siding. The open garage showed off a cherry red sports car, a true unicorn among the neighborhood's uninspired stable of mostly brown and blue sedans.

"Del's basically married to that car. He's well into his sixties, but if you're willing to date up, he is widowed..."

"Thanks, but I don't think I'm desperate enough to date retirement age."

Yet, Francine added to herself, hoping she was joking. The first cigarette hissed in surrender as she put it out on the bottom of her shoe and pocketed the butt. She lit another and offered it, half in jest, to Laura Jean.

"No, thank you. I haven't smoked since high school, and don't you go asking how long ago that was. I will say, though, my sister-in-law is a pack-a-day woman and she's got skin like a cowboy boot. Ditto her personality."

"I'm pretty far from a pack a day, but it has picked up since the divorce."

"Since you brought it up," Laura Jean said, "how about giving me something more to chew on?"

"Something about my divorce?"

"Yeah. If I don't ask now, I'll have to wait for another natural transition. That could be *minutes* from now."

"Hmm." Francine dragged on her new Camel. "How to encapsulate the joy that was being married to Ben? First he was a stranger, then that cute guy who got his hair cut every other Thursday, then my boyfriend, fiancé, husband, ex-husband. Now he's just a stranger again, but one who insists on a permanent place in my thoughts. Exes are weird like that, you know?"

"God and the devil, packaged into one person."

"Bingo. I think Ben had fun at first, and he really did like me. But I don't think I ever rose past the rank of accessory. I always used to shake my head when I heard about people getting divorced after less than a year.

That was for teenagers or celebrities. Or teenage celebrities. Now it's me."

"Best almost-year of his life, the son of a bitch," Laura Jean grumbled supportively. She nodded toward an old man playing fetch with a big white husky in the backyard of the next home. "Next up, we have Roland Gerber. He's our resident expatriate from Switzerland, and that's Ajax, his dog."

The house could have been the cover of a fairy tale book: a brown and white Tudor cottage nestled into an abundance of spruce trees, cardinals fluttering from one branch to the other like living Christmas ornaments.

"I met Mr. Gerber," Francine recalled. "Super nice."

"Sweet as pie. Him and the dog. Roland practically built the neighborhood back in the fifties. Eighty-two years old and still comes to all the parties, how do you like that? I hope I'm still moving that well at *sixty*."

Francine watched a blue jay swoop out of an oak overhead and soar between the modest split-level homes across the street, adding a nice brushstroke to the living Norman Rockwell painting. All around, garage doors and windows were open, letting in the warm air and sunshine. Children, already on their first popsicle of the day, sprinted across expansive gradients of green grass littered with the colorful plastic of Fisher-Price. Three pigtailed girls singing Madonna songs in the rear-facing backseat of a station wagon squealed as their father sprayed the window with a hose.

Despite a rocky start, it was safe to say Hawthorn Woods held all the sentimental junk Francine had hoped to find during her stay, and even on her second cigarette she breathed a little easier.

"I can't get over how gorgeous this place is," she said. "I keep wait-ing for the Keebler Elves to pop out of one of the trees and chuck a Fudge Stripe cookie at me."

"It's cute, right? Oh hell." Laura Jean looked ahead to the first house on the other side of the block. "I wish we didn't have to go by this next one."

✷   ✷   ✷   ✷

The single-story ranch showed signs of disrepair all around, gutters sagging above siding the color of scrambled eggs. A sun-bleached lawnmower sat next to a shed in knee-high grass like an ironic art installation.

In the gravel driveway, a scrawny and shirtless teenage boy leaned across a lime green dirt bike, using a wrench on the engine. He straight-ened up and pushed his greasy orange hair out of his face, then started the bike up. It coughed bluish smoke out of its tailpipe for a few moments, then sputtered and died. The teen cursed and leaned back across the bike to try something different.

Laura Jean sighed. "Okay, I might have to get a little gossipy here, and I hate that, so let me just gossip on myself real quick. I got pregnant with the twins before I got married, I cheated on every single math test in eighth grade, and my mother-in-law still thinks Mark and I go to church every week but I'm pretty sure the last time we went was two Popes ago."

Francine gave Laura Jean the sign of the cross with her cigarette. "I absolve you of all your sins."

"Thank you. This is the Banderwalt family, they moved in last year. The place was a fixer-upper when they bought it and, well, they didn't fix it up. The mother's nice enough, a bit checked out, to be honest. She's technically an invalid, I suppose. Father's out of the picture. I think they split right before the move. There's a little girl, Diana, but she's a rare sight outside the house."

"And our young mechanic friend here?"

"That's Eric. In cowboy-speak, he's the troublemaker 'round these parts. Mischief maker. Steals beer out of garages, sneaks around with a BB gun, you can see it leaning against the shed there. I will say, however, being the mother of two teenage girls tends to make me a little wary of teenage boys, so, you know, grain of salt."

The gangly teenager gave up on the bike and chucked his tools inside the shed, securing the door with a rusted bike lock. Turning toward the street, he noticed them walking by, and delivered a thick oyster of spit into the gravel.

"Real charmer," Francine noted.

"Yeah, well, back to Francine-gossip. Knocked any boots since the divorce?"

Francine grinned as they continued on. "What kind of depraved tour company are you running here?"

"Hey, don't make me feel like a pervert. I just need to know what I'm working with."

"What you're working with is, no, I haven't been with anyone, and haven't wanted to be, either. Ben may have killed sex for me forever."

"Don't you dare say that! Are you still using his last name?"

Francine nodded. "Orthine."

"*Francine Orthine*? Hon, you sound like a Twinkie ingredient!"

"I never liked it either. It's just...a lot of paperwork," Francine said, unconvincingly. "I do want to change it back to my maiden name, Haddix. I'm getting there."

Laura Jean gave her arm a supportive squeeze. "I'll call you whatever you like, but holy hell, Haddix is *much* better. Sounds to me like a French name, and French is sexy, which makes my matchmaking job that much easier."

"I don't remember hiring you for that."

"It was in the fine print. Ugh, our next stop is my least favorite of all. Lori Asperski. She's the self-appointed dictator in our little corner of the world."

"The only two-story on the block," Francine observed as they passed the bleach-white New England Colonial. Its immaculate side yard was edged with a low fence that contained a tidy chicken coop and a brown goat lazily chewing long strands of grass.

"Lori's gotten even prissier since the Banderwalts moved in," Laura Jean said. "She tried to get thirty-foot hedges put up next to the farm, but they would've touched the power lines so the village said no. That put Lori in a bad mood, but only for the last year or so. Remember that woman in the minivan?"

Francine nodded.

"One of Lori's Hens. That's what I call her army of sycophantic mommies. They never miss a chance to blow things out of proportion. I've been on their shit list lately too, because I got chosen as director of the Fourth of July parade. It's a pretty big deal around here.

"Let me guess. Lori usually does it."

"Correct. I'm sure she's been going stir crazy and driving her husband, Dennis, nuts as a result, though you wouldn't hear it from him. About as conversational as drywall, that man. Ah." Laura Jean perked up as they left the Colonial behind for a brown split-level at the top of a long driveway. "Soviet territory at last."

Francine noticed the house's backyard met Ellie's at the huge willow tree in the center of the block. Magdalena Durham lived a lot closer than she liked.

"Well? Don't clam up on me now," she prodded, eager to get some information for her detective case.

"Magdalena is Russian—which is totally fine. I'm just sayin', when it comes to manners, you can definitely tell Baltic from Midwest. The woman's not a hugger, but before last night I never had a problem with her."

"She's married to the big blond dude?"

"She is, indeed. Hollis is our police chief." Laura Jean smirked. "So you noticed him, huh?"

"Don't make this worse. I just saw them together at the party. They seemed troubled to me."

"Okay, normally this would be too gossipy even for me, but since your safety could be at stake…"

"What?"

"Well, I don't know how else to say it other than 'mail-order.' I'm not saying we saw a receipt, but Hollis has all but explicitly acknowledged it."

"The guy looks like an American Gladiator. Why would he need a mail-order bride?"

Laura Jean shrugged. "Who knows? I feel for her, though, just a teensy bit. Imagine, you get crated up in Moscow, then, days later, someone crowbars the lid off and you walk out into the middle of American suburbia. Next thing you know, my annoying ass is bringing you welcome cakes and what-not. Speaking of which, I owe you a welcome cake. God, what are all those parade preparations doing to my manners?"

Francine wasn't sure, but she thought she saw a pixie cut silhouette peering at them through the blinds of an upstairs window. The sight made her taste cranberry vodka all over again. She tried, with Laura Jean's new information, to figure out how she could have offended Magdalena, but still came up empty.

"Aha." Laura Jean interrupted her thought process. "We've saved the most interesting house for last."

The final house on the block was another single-story ranch, with mint green siding and no distinctive features Francine could see.

"This is the most interesting house?"

"Tut tut," Laura Jean teased. "Didn't anyone ever tell you it's what's on the inside that counts?"

"Okay, so what's inside?"

"Two words. Mister. Mystery."

"Mister Mystery?"

"The previous owners moved to Michigan a few months ago and the new owners aren't moving in until mid-July, so they rented it out." Laura Jean's excitement peaked. "It's the right bowl of porridge at last, Goldilocks. He's not too old, not too young, quiet but sweet, and more or less handsome-ish, assuming one takes the time to look. His real name is Michael Bruno, but I think Mister Mystery is so much cooler, don't you?"

Francine thought back to the man she'd seen smoking in a lawn chair. "Messy black hair?"

"Ooh! You met him already?"

"I didn't meet him, just saw him at the party."

"Lucky for you I'm so persuasive. That was the first social invitation I've been able to get him to accept all summer. I'm gonna try to go two-for-two and invite him to my barbeque tomorrow night."

"Are you inviting me too?"

"You never need an invite from me," Laura Jean scolded. "But yes. With bells on, please."

"Is Magdalena going?"

"Well...yes. Close-knit community etiquette demands that I invite everyone. Maybe the two of you can bury the hatchet in a nice, fat brat-wurst."

"I don't know..."

"I'll have a poncho on standby, just in case she gets the itch to drench you again. Please, please, please."

"Okay," Francine surrendered. "Couldn't turn out worse than last night, right?"

"God, I hope not!" Laura Jean took a moment to calm herself. "My girls have mentioned that I can be a touch overbearing at times. The name 'Smother Goose' may have been tossed around once or twice. So while you are definitely coming tomorrow night, no argument there, I'll leave it up to you whether we invite Mister Mystery or not. Fair?"

Francine looked over her shoulder at the mint-colored house. Each dwelling so far seemed to be a kind of brick and mortar facsimile of the people inside. The plain, detail-free ranch fit the pattern well, giving away little about the not too old, not too young, quiet but sweet, more or less handsome-ish inhabitant.

She'd gotten a curious thrill upon seeing Michael Bruno the first night, but what if he was just another Ben? That wasn't the impression she'd gotten, but of course she'd been wrong before.

"I'll think about it."

CHAPTER 4

I often think: "I wish I were a child again."
[x] TRUE   [   ] FALSE

"Alley-oop!" Francine knifed her hands under Charlie's armpits and lifted him into the sink. The boy had become impossibly sticky and grimy in the last ten hours, but she was taking the cool-aunt route of letting him wash his black-bottomed feet in the sink in lieu of a full bath.

Ellie had been so engrossed in her travel itineraries, party planning, and a thousand other things, she'd failed to give Francine a crash course on childcare. Even the cursory spiel normally given to a teenage babysitter would've been nice: Here's the number for pizza, don't overwater the zinnias, Thursday is garbage day, and oh, here's how to keep a seven-year-old alive.

That same seven-year-old was excitedly prattling on about how he'd had the "most amazing day ever," though Francine suspected that was basically how Charlie saw every day in summer.

"...and I raced a Lego boat down the stream by the park and somebody carved a bunch of swear words under the slide there and then I used my allowance for the ice cream truck which I almost didn't catch in time but then I did and I got a Bubble Play. That's the cherry-ice baseball glove and the baseball in the middle is gum and it's like hard as a rock but you can use it as a marble so it's still good. And I got brain freeze but if you put your tongue on the top of your mouth it goes away."

"Mmhmm..." Francine nodded as she scrubbed the soles of his feet with a sponge and some dish soap. It was fortunate the conversation wasn't dependent on her responses, because her mind kept wandering back to San Francisco. And Ben. And all the little details of their life together. The memorized cocktail orders. The cologne he wore only on weekends. The birthmark on his left hip she said looked like a shooting star.

"And then I caught tadpoles at the pond. Oh, there are three ponds at the front of the neighborhood. Tadpole Pond, Snapping Turtle Pond, and Haunted Pond. Then I pretended there were ninjas and a robot attacking me but I got away, but then I fell and skinned my knee for real."

"Mmhmm..."

Their mutual dislike of movies that let a phone ring for too long. The understanding that she'd eat any pickles that came with Ben's sandwiches and he'd eat whatever olives came with her salads. The lullaby of his beating heart as they fell asleep together.

"Aunt Franciiiiine," Charlie complained. "My feet are clean now."

"Right, sorry." She dried his feet with a dishtowel and hoisted him out of the sink. "Wanna do the honors?"

Charlie nodded, and eagerly dumped a packet of cheese powder into the waiting pot of macaroni.

"Mac and cheese is the fanciest, best food in the world," he announced, stirring the yellow-orange goo.

"Fancy food for our fancy dinner." Francine plated the rest of the meal. "We also have pan-fried beef cylinders, you might call them hot dogs, and a seasonal offering of, um, garden candy."

"Veggies." Charlie stuck his tongue out in disgust as he carried the plates over to the table.

Francine joined him with two glasses of lemonade. "All paired with a Minute Maid frozen concentrate, 1989. A fine vintage. It might not be the pinnacle of fine cooking, Bubba, but it's definitely the pinnacle of mine."

Charlie however, had no complaints, as he began to devour his hot dog.

Francine tried her mac and cheese, which, she had to admit, was pretty fantastic. One undeniable perk of babysitting was getting to dive back into the comfort foods of her own childhood.

"Being here with you makes me think of when I was a kid," she said.

"*You* were a kid?" Charlie asked, while hiding some lima beans behind his last bite of hot dog.

"Yes, you little smart aleck. A lot like you, actually. I loved summer and hated lima beans." She picked a pale bean from her microwaved vegetable medley and flicked it out the open window. "They're almost as bad as green olives."

"I hate green olives, too. So much."

Francine smirked, ninety-nine percent sure the boy had never tasted an olive in his life. "Go ahead."

Charlie enthusiastically chucked his own lima beans out the window.

"You will, however, have to eat *some* green things while I'm here. I have to be the adult every now and then. So what do we do with the rest of the veggies on your plate?"

Charlie thought hard. "What if we eat them real fast, then eat the mac and cheese to get rid of the taste?"

"Love it." Francine held out a pinky. "Together?"

Charlie hooked it. "Go."

They scarfed the mixed vegetables, then packed their mouths with mac and cheese. After they'd washed it all down with a gulp of lemonade,

Charlie let out a loud burp, and Francine couldn't stifle a laugh. "Okay, my little garbage disposal, I'll clean the plates while you go throw on some pj's. Giddy-up."

"'Kay."

He scampered off and Francine brought their plates to the sink, cranking open the window to let in the fragrant scent of a lavender bush. The nonsensical, sun-wearing-sunglasses thermometer clipped to the window shutter showed a temperature in the mid-nineties, even well after sunset.

While the wet, stagnant heat was inescapable, reminiscing with Charlie had offered Francine a brief respite from unproductive thoughts about Ben. But in the absence of interaction, she could feel the stormclouds gathering again. Not good.

"I get to explore at night," Charlie said from the doorway behind her.

"Charlie! You have to stop sneaking up on me like that."

"At least you didn't swear this time."

"Excuse you, mister. I never swore, and you're supposed to be neck deep in pj's by now."

"I'm serious." Charlie ran over to the sink. "I get to explore at night, just for a little bit. I forgot to tell you that when I told you my agenda this morning."

"And I told *you* that you can't substitute-teacher me on everything. Plus, I just scrubbed your feet clean," she added, realizing she'd have to redo the dishes with a new, non-foot sponge.

"I'm not tricking you," he promised.

Francine shut off the faucet and dried her hands. "Tell me with a straight face your parents let you do that."

Charlie adopted a serious face and tone. "They let me do it. Exploring is the best at night. It's not super hot and there aren't any cars. I run around, maybe play Tag with other kids, maybe say hi to Ajax, and then

I come home and I'm tired, so Dad can watch TV and Mom can drink wine without me bothering them."

"I don't know, Bubba."

"You said if I'm cool, you're cool. Remember?" Charlie held out his pinky for an emotional uppercut.

Francine narrowed her eyes at him, but hooked the tiny digit. "Five minutes, starting now."

CHAPTER 5

The only interesting part of newspapers
is the comic strips.
[x] TRUE   [   ] FALSE

C harlie exploded out the back door and rushed toward the willow tree, grabbing one of its whip-like branches to ride high into the night sky. Aunt Francine had only given him five minutes, but he wasn't worried. He'd always been able to squeeze ten minutes out of five.

Launching himself from the willow branch, he landed on an acorn and didn't mind the pain. A soft foot meant it was still June, a time of popsicles and stargazing and the certainty that school would never come again. July would bring camping in the backyard and running through sprinklers and collapsing on the grass to watch the big color bloom of fireworks. By the time August rolled around, a bare foot could withstand an honest-to-God nail. Arms and legs would be bronzed and faces wise with another summer savored. The adults might rule nine months of the year, but these months were for those who did a lot with a little, and never dreamed of more than a day well-spent.

He ran beneath the stretches of roadside oak trees, their leafy canopies punched with puzzle pieces of moonlight. He passed pet graves marked by cruciform twigs that wouldn't last the winter in the backyards of houses he knew by the quality of their Halloween candy. Ancient elms, stirred by the nighttime breeze, dropped seed pods that spun like tiny helicopters in their lazy fall. Even the ground had something to say, speaking to Charlie's still-tender feet with smooth carpets of clover, the chalky smoosh of dandelions, and the wet slide of a wild strawberry.

The night's heat wrapped back around his skin as he slowed to a walk, breathing in the sweet smell of a freshly cut lawn. An owl glided above the surface of Tadpole Pond, out for the hunt. Short summer nights always gave the animals a frenzied urgency, pulling them down from their trees and out of their holes earlier than usual. Charlie remembered he didn't have an abundance of time himself and veered back toward his block. Five minutes could only be stretched so far.

He was almost to the willow tree when he heard a phone ring in the mint-colored house. A new family was supposed to move in soon, but right now there was just some guy living there. Mister Mystery, the grown-ups called him.

Charlie knew the stack of firewood in the backyard was surrounded with spiky weeds and crawling with spiders, but it was right by an open window, making it the perfect spot to spy from. Some other kids had filled the cubbyholes of the log pile with Lite Brite pegs, crusty old Play-Doh, and even a little fire truck. Charlie pocketed a few of the Lite Brite pegs to play with later, then looked through the window.

The kitchen inside looked like someone had tried to turn it into a library. Both the table and countertops were covered with papers, folders, books, and black-and-white pictures. Charlie was creeping closer for a better look when Mister Mystery suddenly rushed in and picked up the phone.

Startled, Charlie fell backwards into the wall of firewood, but he was just quick enough to stick his arms out and keep the logs from falling.

"Hello? Ida, hi. How are you?" Mister Mystery tapped a cigarette stub into an ashtray and slid into a chair at the table, his back to the window.

Charlie's heart raced from the excitement of eavesdropping and the strain of holding up the logs. A bead of sweat rolled down his spine.

"Yeah, I went to a party last night. Lischka was there, but I didn't talk to him. I figured it's best to just keep watching for now. I tried not to talk to too many other people, but I guess everyone's a little curious about me, so I had to make some stuff up. They think I'm a writer..."

Now a bead of sweat ran *up* Charlie's back. Sweat didn't do that. But spiders did.

He screamed and shook his shirt, spilling a daddy long legs into the grass. The logs and toys he'd been holding fell and crunched noisily on the lawn.

The phone conversation inside the house stopped.

Charlie froze, and listened. He heard only the phantom whistle of a distant freight train, moaning over the low buzz of cricketsong. Slowly, he raised his chin.

Mister Mystery was peering out the window, phone cradled to one ear. Charlie and the firewood stack were just outside the kitchen's spill of light. He was safe, as long as nothing—

A teetering log fell onto the toy fire truck, triggering its light and siren.

Mister Mystery dropped the phone and dashed toward the back door.

Running with the speed of someone being chased, Charlie reached his house in record time. He quietly closed the back door, raced up the split-level stairs, and plunged into his parents' big bed, breathing heavily.

He heard Aunt Francine get out of her bed. A moment later, her head peeked into his doorway.

"Jump into that bed any faster and you're gonna leave a crater. Did you have fun outside?"

He nodded.

"You want to sleep in your parents' room?"

He nodded again.

"Okay. G'night, Bubba."

"'Night, Aunt Francine."

She went back to the guest room, leaving Charlie to think about what he'd heard at Mister Mystery's house. "They think I'm a writer." It seemed like a weird thing to say.

He carefully slipped out of bed and looked out the window.

Down by the willow tree, Mister Mystery was picking up the colorful Lite Brite pegs that had fallen out of Charlie's pockets. He looked confused, and extremely worried.

CHAPTER 6

I do many things that I regret afterwards.
[x] TRUE   [   ] FALSE

Francine rolled over on the butterfly sheets and groaned in the late morning light. Uninvited dreams of Ben had filled her sleep. Pushing someone out of your head was possible with tremendous discipline, but the heart healed on its own time and dreams were its favorite expression.

Her gaze found the skull and crossbones VHS tape lying by her suitcase. She shouldn't watch it. When had it ever helped?

Rolling onto her stomach, she saw a certain stack of papers below the bed. The MMPI had never helped much either, but Francine pinched the corner of a page and pulled it out into the light for a quick, mental Q & A.

I am very seldom bothered by constipation.

How was that relevant to a personality group?

It does not bother me that I am not better looking.

First, that bothered everyone on the planet. Second, weird phrasing. And third, rude.

I sweat very easily, even on cool days.

This was getting way too personal.

What had been Ben's point in giving her the ridiculous quiz, anyway? Did he think it would give her insight into who she was, and that would somehow make everything that had happened less painful? Would she be able to find someone new in a hurry, just like he had?

She tucked the page back under the bed and rolled onto her side to face the shelves of clocks, which made her think, unsurprisingly, of time. What if coming to Hawthorn Woods didn't change anything? What if she'd just given her problems a new zip code? What if the only progression in her life was one of dwindling time, draining her of looks, energy, and hope that a positive future was still possible? No direction, no vibrancy…

Nope. Francine hopped out of bed. She had to externalize her negative emotions in a productive way, get those dead-end thoughts out of her head and out into the open, where they could be identified and rejected.

She peeked into the master bedroom and found it empty. It was a good thing kids still possessed the special power of waking up early as long as they didn't have to go to school or church, because Charlie didn't need to see her like this. But she needed to talk to someone. Anyone.

Down in the kitchen, she grabbed the phone and dialed Laura Jean. It rang on the other end several times before going to an answering machine. Laura Jean and Mark were probably out getting supplies for the barbeque. Oh God, the barbeque. How was she supposed to go out tonight and look happy?

Francine hung up and tried the long international number Ellie had taped above the phone. A choppy back and forth with the impatient front desk clerk of a Parisian hotel revealed that Ellie and Pete were also out.

Who else could she call?

All of her connections in California either knew Ben or were more acquaintances than actual friends. Her parents, who had had her and Ellie in their forties, lived in a Florida retirement community. Both were hard of hearing and not so great on the phone.

Through the front screen door, she watched what looked like a fluffy white cloud trot contentedly down the street. It was the husky, Ajax. Francine never forgot a dog. But what was his owner's name?

The elderly man came into view a moment later, moving at a more leisurely pace than his four-legged counterpart.

Roland something. Gerber. Roland Gerber.

He'd seemed pretty nice at the party, and eighty-plus years were apt to leave a person with a healthy reserve of know-how and a wanting social calendar. Maybe Roland Gerber wouldn't mind playing therapist for the day.

There was one way to find out.

CHAPTER 7

I am so touchy on some subjects
that I can't talk about them.
[x] TRUE   [   ] FALSE

The elderly man answered her knock with a delay reasonable for his age. "Ah. Francine, yes? Nice to see you again."

"Hi, Mr. Gerber." Instead of following with, "I'm experiencing persistent, acute emotional trauma brought on by a divorce you know nothing about, and you don't know me at all, but you're old and sweet and stereotypes have taught me you probably have lots of advice to dispense in folksy tidbits, so I'd like some of that, please and thank you," Francine simply said, "I thought I'd come over and meet your dog."

Dogs were the best social shortcut on the planet.

"You may indeed meet Ajax, but only on the condition you join me for some mid-day tea and cookies."

Bingo.

"Sounds like a good deal to me."

"Excellent. With the day's fine breeze, I think the back porch would do nicely. I will meet you there with all the comforts I can manage. Ajax is around back."

Francine started around the charming little cottage, more excited than ever to talk with Roland Gerber. The guy spoke like he was from another century, which he technically almost was.

She spotted Ajax sleeping soundly in the crosshatched shade of a hammock. The husky roused at her approach and bounded happily over.

His clean white fur was absurdly soft, melting through Francine's fingers as she repeatedly reassured Ajax that he was, in fact, a very good boy. The two of them entered the porch, its old-person musk landing somewhere between mothballs and caramel. Francine sat on one of two identical loveseats patterned with gold and brown stripes. She thought the sofas looked a lot like the Samoa cookies the Girl Scouts sold, though it was possible Mr. Gerber's mention of cookies had influenced her thinking.

Luckily, he made good on his promise a moment later, dipping his head around a low hanging planter as he carried a tray of tea and cookies in through the double doors of the house.

"Your thumbs are definitely greener than mine," Francine said. And while that was true, she also figured it might not hurt to butter the guy up a little. "I only have one houseplant alive back in San Francisco, and it survives exclusively on accidental splashes of dishwater."

Mr. Gerber sat on the loveseat opposite Francine and set the tray down on the coffee table between them. "I admire a survivor. It is a quality easily appreciated when one reaches my age." He unbuttoned his navy blue sport coat, which was perfectly fitted and probably older than Francine.

Her breakfast-deprived stomach audibly grumbled.

Mr. Gerber smiled and gestured to the plate of cookies. "Please don't be shy."

"Never have to offer me a cookie twice." She bit into one of the tan cookies and tasted black licorice. Ugh. *Why did people this evil exist?* She threw down the cookie, then quickly picked it back up again.

"Is something wrong?"

"No, I just…I'm sorry, but this thing is disgusting," she admitted, wincing at her own rudeness.

Mr. Gerber, however, looked delighted.

"Aniskrabeli," he said with a chuckle, before biting into a cookie of his own. "A legacy of my Swiss heritage. They are made with anise, which tastes of licorice, a flavor not so popular in this country. I pray you'll forgive my test, but I often serve them to guests because it tells me something important." He poured fragrant black tea into cups accented with the gold outline of a mountain range. "The tea is strong and licorice-free, I promise."

She accepted the cup and saucer he offered her. "I wish all my tests were given in cookie form. What does it tell you?"

"It almost always produces a telling reaction. Usually politeness, which should be admired. But occasionally it reveals honesty, which should be revered. In that spirit, tell me your troubles."

Francine drank down half her tea to wash away the taste of the cookie. "My troubles? Just like that?"

"Allow me to return the respect of your honesty. It is clear to me you are a troubled woman. While an interest in Ajax needs no further justification, I suspect something more in your visit. Perhaps the idea that wisdom comes with age, which if true, would make me nearly prophetic."

It is clear to me you are a troubled woman. Damn. She'd come for insight, but hadn't expected to get it so readily.

Sharp and straightforward. Exactly what she needed.

$$\ast \quad \ast \quad \ast \quad \ast$$

Francine opened her mouth to tell Roland Gerber all, but abruptly stopped at the edge of the conversational diving board.

She and Laura Jean had spoken the same language right off the bat. But Mr. Gerber's manners and poetic vernacular left her with an odd desire to please, like she was in the presence of a friendly but imposing authority figure.

"Sorry. I kinda feel like I'm in the principal's office."

"Ah!" Mr. Gerber lamented playfully. "I have failed in my duties as a tea and cookie host."

"Mr. Gerber—"

"Please. Roland."

"Roland." Francine smiled. "I'm all for being direct, but I don't know if I should spill all my heartache on our first meeting."

"Ah, of course. A matter of the heart. They are among the most devastating."

"You're sure you don't want to start with something easier, like the weather?"

"Hot and humid, as it was yesterday, as it will be tomorrow. Let us leave the daily forecast to those with time to waste while we assault that which distresses you most." He brought out a marble ash tray from a drawer in the coffee table, set it in front of her, and sipped patiently at his tea. "Separated or divorced?"

Francine smiled at the ash tray. Either she smelled like a walking bowling alley, or Roland Gerber was as perceptive as a certain famous teenage sleuth. She pulled the Camels from her shorts pocket and tapped one out. "Divorced."

He leaned forward and lit the cigarette with a handsome metal lighter. "You still wear the ring. The name too, I presume?"

Francine exhaled deeply, hoping to create a smokescreen for her sudden feeling of vulnerability. "I still use his name, yes."

"A curious anachronism," Roland noted. "But who am I to judge? I still own a phonograph."

Annoyed at the deplorable lack of petting, Ajax nudged his snout under Francine's non-cigarette hand. She scratched the dog's wealth of snowy fur to delay a conversation she was still having trouble jumping into.

"Is he named after, um…" Francine couldn't place the reference she'd planned on making and wished she hadn't started the sentence. "The…Roman guy?"

"The Greek warrior," Roland corrected kindly. "A grand hero of the Trojan War. But this Ajax gets his name from the bleach powder I use on my kitchen sink. Perhaps you've credited me with too much cleverness."

"That's exactly the kind of thing smart people always say." Francine continued to pet the dog, who nudged her hand each time she stopped.

Roland snapped his fingers. "Ajax, *platz*."

The husky yawned and laid down, splaying himself flat in instant comfort.

"I guess I'm just confused," Francine said at last. "I was kind of cool on my ex when we first met. I had a funny feeling I couldn't shake that he was…off, somehow. But he won me over, and it was like the second that happened, he started to lose interest."

Roland ate another anise cookie and chewed thoughtfully. "We must remember that people are remarkably poor at harmony, and relationships are dynamic things tied directly to the heart. It should come as no surprise that they produce the grandest emotional fireworks. In an ill connection, you're either hurting or being hurt. I say this not to excuse the behavior of the other party, but rather as encouragement for you to allow yourself negative feelings. But be careful not to take the false bait of good and evil. We cause pain because we feel pain."

"Jesus." Francine dragged hard on her cigarette. "You're a fortune cookie with a heartbeat. But I am a little worried your advice might be…too polite to be useful."

"You'd prefer something a bit more raw."

"Yeah, maybe."

"Bed another man as soon as possible."

Francine coughed on her cigarette in laughter. "Bang a stranger? That's your raw advice?"

Roland smiled wryly. "Perhaps too raw, but yes."

"This better not be a come-on."

Now it was Roland's turn to laugh. "Goodness, no. I would recommend someone at least adjacent to your own generation. My point is only that the past is complex and sometimes inexplicable. The present, however, can be as simple as you allow it to be, and actionable goals can be marvelous crutches in the growth process. Your story is undoubtedly much deeper, but I won't be too nosy just yet."

Francine relaxed into her loveseat, feeling infinitely better than she had lying in her bed. The tea was tasty. The dog was soft. The toxic thoughts threatening her day had been waved away by a fragile, aged hand.

"Roland, if you didn't serve licorice cookies, you might've just become my favorite neighbor. Laura Jean still holds the coveted spot for now. Are you going to her barbeque tonight?"

"I am indeed. But if I may be so bold as to impose one last bit of advice before we move on to less strenuous topics." His face grew serious as he leaned forward in his loveseat. "The tortures of an unsettled mind carry tremendous weight. You would do well to expel them with terrific prejudice as expediently as possible."

"You mean talk to more people about this?"

"The specific method you choose is of no consequence. What is important is that you do what is required to survive."

"I will. Thanks, Roland."

"Now, then." He relaxed back into his loveseat, his tone light once again. "How is it said? 'Some enchanted evening, you may see a stranger across a crowded room.' Perhaps this evening will prove enchanted for you."

"Perhaps it will."

She smirked doubtfully, but was surprised when a certain stranger came to mind. One with wavy black hair who smoked in the company of fireflies. A stranger whose invitation to the party that night was dependent on whatever Francine did next.

CHAPTER 8

I enjoy gambling for small stakes.
[x] TRUE   [   ] FALSE

Francine had told Laura Jean the truth. She hadn't "bedded" anyone since the divorce. Hadn't even considered it. But on Roland's vague suggestion, she found herself crossing the middle of the block and knocking on a stranger's front door in the lingering heat of the afternoon.

"Hello?" The voice came from somewhere behind her.

Francine walked to the open garage and peeked inside.

Reading a book on a lounge chair in the middle of an otherwise empty space was Mister Mystery. He quickly put the book under the chair and stood to meet her.

"Hi," he said, almost as a question.

"Hi. Um, I'm your neighbor, kind of. I'm staying at my sister's place on the other side of the block."

"You're the one who got the drink in her face."

"Yep. That's what I'm known for around here."

"Sorry." He smiled. "Sometimes I talk before I think, if I think at all. I noticed you before that. I'm Michael Bruno. People call me Bruno." He shook her hand vigorously, spilling strands of black hair across a friendly-looking face.

Francine's mind had built the man up into a James Dean-esque loner who lived a rogue existence on the fringe of society, or the fringe of parties at least. The man before her was about as brooding as Mister Rogers.

"I'm Francine…Haddix."

"Is that French?"

"I don't know, actually. Are you suntanning in a garage?"

"I've been cooped up a while. Thought I'd go outside. I'm a city mouse, so I guess I didn't get too ambitious."

"Me too," Francine said. "I mean, I grew up in a place like this, but I live in San Francisco now."

"New York," he said. "Guess we met somewhere in the middle."

Francine decided he was indeed handsome-ish. And that was thanks mostly to having the hair of a Greek god, because the man's sense of style had not improved since the tweed jacket number she'd seen him in the first night. Today's outfit was one a person would only wear if they'd lost a bet: a short-sleeved, pale orange dress shirt with a bright green paisley tie, and the same ugly brown corduroys. The ensemble was eye-wateringly bad, but also sort of sweet in the innocence required to wear it.

"You're just visiting here, right?" he asked. "Housesitting?"

"Babysitting my nephew for two weeks," Francine said, leaving out any unnecessary divorce details that were decidedly unwelcome at a flirty first meeting. "It's kind of a steep learning curve to be solely responsible for another life, but I flip a mean pancake, and the rest I pick up along the way. Pancakes are my favorite food, since you were probably wondering."

"Oreos for me," he volunteered.

"An excellent choice. What brings you to Hawthorn Woods?"

For the first time, he hesitated. "I'm on vacation."

"You took a vacation here? Voluntarily?"

Another almost imperceptible hesitation. "I'm a writer. I like to work wherever it's quiet. This seemed like the perfect spot."

"I thought the same thing until the end of my sister's party."

"Yeah, what was that all about?"

"Don't know yet, but I'm working on it. So do I become a character in your story just by talking to you?"

"A couple of city mice meet in the country? Hmm. That could work."

She couldn't quite tell if he was flirting, but this seemed as good a time as ever to make her pitch. "Do you have any interest in coming to a barbeque tonight?"

"At Laura Jean's, right?"

"How'd you know that?"

"She invited me. Said I could only come if I brought you."

Francine smiled. "She can be quite persuasive."

"I was going to walk over to ask you after my tanning session in the garage here." He gestured to his lawn chair and Francine saw the title of the book he'd been reading: *Justice Not Vengeance*. The pages were riddled with tabs of yellow paper. She considered asking if it was a good read, but the way he'd rushed to put the book under the chair made her think he wasn't looking to chat about it.

"I accept your intended invitation," she said, instead. "See you tonight, Michael Bruno."

"Just Bruno." He smiled. "When you say the whole name, it makes me feel like I'm in trouble."

CHAPTER 9

Much of what is happening to me now seems
to have happened to me before.
[x] TRUE   [   ] FALSE

Francine found Charlie sprawled out in front of the house's air conditioner, wearing only his underwear.

"Dad never lets me turn on the AC," he confessed. "He always says, 'If you're hot, eat an ice cube.' But it's so hot this summer."

"Dads have to be cheap. It says so in the parenting rule book. Your secret is my secret."

She nudged Charlie over with her foot and joined him on the immaculate carpet of the rarely-used dining room.

"You're smiling," he said.

"I always smile."

"No, you don't."

"Okay Smile Police, it just so happens I had a good day. How 'bout you?"

"Most amazing day ever! I looked for sprinklers to play in, and then I caught bullfrogs."

As if on cue, a *croak* sounded from the direction of the kitchen.

"Charles. If that sink has any more frogs than the zero it had this morning, your desserts are in grave, grave danger."

The nuclear threat of dessert withdrawal had the desired effect: Charlie did a backward somersault up to his feet and dashed into the kitchen.

With visions of Pete studying the energy bill under a microscope, Francine turned off the deliciously cold air and trotted upstairs to the bathroom, ready to wash the day's heat off with a cool shower. She could even put Ellie's curling iron and hairsprays to use. This didn't necessarily mean Francine was fully on board with the prospect of a new romance—just that she was open to considering a possible conversation regarding the suggestion of the idea. Maybe.

This was all assuming, of course, that Michael Bruno was pining for a vacationing hairstylist in romantic freefall. His odd but cheerful manner made it hard to tell if he was interested or just friendly, especially in the span of five minutes.

The guy might not be postcard-handsome, and he sure as hell wasn't a sharp dresser, but there was something in the way he carried himself and the way he spoke, like he wasn't lacquered in the guarded cynicism most people acquired as they aged.

Feeling a little silly for her instant infatuation, Francine nonetheless allowed herself to enjoy the feeling of a new crush as she lathered, rinsed, and repeated. After wrapping herself in a towel, she opened the bathroom door to let out the steam and began to blow dry her hair.

She'd finished with her hairspray and moved onto the curling iron by the time Charlie crawled onto the creaky landing at the top of the stairs, breathing heavily.

"I took him all the way back to Haunted Pond and turned him around a few times so he wouldn't try and come back."

"I don't think he misses the kitchen sink, Charlie, but thank you."

"How come you're doing that?"

"Because I want to look nice for Laura Jean's barbeque. You're excited, right?"

"Yeah, I guess. Who's gonna be there?"

"Probably the same people that go to all the parties around here, Bubba." Francine moved the iron to a new strand of hair.

"Is Mister Mystery gonna be there?"

She looked at him in the mirror. Why had he asked about Bruno?

"Yeah, but don't call him Mister Mystery, it's not nice. He's a writer, maybe he can tell us a good story while we eat." She wrapped a new strand of hair around the iron.

When the questions noticeably stopped, she looked to find Charlie churning his hands in indecision, a look of worry on his face.

"Charlie?"

"He's not a writer!" Charlie blurted.

"What?"

"I heard him talking on the phone last night. He said, 'They think I'm a writer.' He's a liar and you shouldn't be friends with a liar."

Francine tried to make sense of the outburst. Bruno wasn't a writer? Why would he lie about that?

She swished the sentence around in her mind, hoping her nephew had misunderstood something.

They think I'm a writer.

Maybe he—no. *No.* She wasn't going to do it again. She wasn't going to give pass after pass until she ended up hurt. Why had she thought Bruno was so authentic anyway? Because he'd been nice to her for five minutes? Because of some vague quality in his face or voice? Jesus. She'd given the guy a shot less than an hour ago and already he'd turned out to be a dud. Usually people took their time in letting her down.

"Aunt Francine!" Charlie cried.

Smoke streamed from the hair wrapped around the curling iron. Francine yanked the curling iron free and slammed it onto the tile counter, swatting at her smoldering strands of hair as a noxious smell filled the bathroom. "Goddammit!"

She hung her head and tried to calm down.

Why had she expected Bruno to be any different than Ben?

"I'm sorry I yelled," she said softly to Charlie. "I'm not mad at you. Okay?"

"'Kay," he whispered.

"You really heard Mr. Bruno say that on the phone?"

"Yes."

"You shouldn't eavesdrop, Charlie. You know that, right?"

He nodded meekly.

"C'mere." She held her arms open and Charlie ran into the hug.

"I'm sorry I eavesdropped," he said with a quiver.

"It's okay, Bubba. Go watch TV downstairs for a little bit, okay?"

"Are we still going to the barbeque?"

"Absolutely," Francine decided. "We're not gonna let a stupid little lie ruin our night, are we?"

She hooked Charlie's finger, then watched as he hopped down the stairs, the drama already forgotten. Kids were so resilient, so quick to forget.

It was going to take Francine just a bit longer.

CHAPTER 10

I refuse to play some games because
I am not good at them.
[x] TRUE   [   ] FALSE

Ellie's Bon Voyage and Welcome Francine gathering had provided the minimum party requirements of beer, booze, and a mixing bowl full of pretzels. Perfectly serviceable. But it seemed neighborhood get-togethers were a bit more of an art form for Laura Jean Cunningham. While Charlie ran off to play with some of the other kids, Francine marveled at a suburban backyard transformed into a social meateater's paradise.

Thoroughly iced coolers offered an impressive range of pop for the kids and domestic beer for the adults. Circles of orange and lemon bobbed in a glass bowl of red liquid taped with a label that read "Down South Punch (Not for Youngsters)." Flower-centerpieced picnic tables dotted the lawn, close but not too close to a massive grill crowded with every cut of meat imaginable. And best of all? No sign of good hair and a bad tie. Maybe Bruno had decided not to come after all, which was just fine by Francine.

Laura Jean spotted her from across the party and quickly made her way over in a wonderful, cream-colored party dress. Francine looked self-consciously down at her own daisy sundress, which she'd only succeeded in ridding of cranberry vodka stains ten minutes earlier.

"In my rush to flee the West Coast I mostly packed t-shirts," she explained, as they shared a hug. "This is the extent of my formalwear."

"Are you kidding? It looks better than ever. Mine's about as comfortable as a lampshade. And where is the dashing Mystery Date?"

Francine decided Laura Jean was much too busy at the moment for her newest sob story, so she simply said, "Haven't seen him yet."

"Probably spending extra time in front of the mirror hoping to wow a certain someone."

Francine nodded. "Probably."

"Well get yourself a drink and relax, I'm off to hostess whatever needs hostessing, and I'll find you in a bit. And don't you two sneak off together without saying goodbye." Laura Jean winked and rushed off to welcome an arriving Carol and her family.

Francine exhaled and walked under the fairyland glow of Tungsten string lights hung between two huge oaks on either end of the lawn. She scooped herself a cup of Down South Punch, one hair-raising sip confirming the stuff was definitely not for youngsters.

Standing on the sidelines of a game of horseshoes, she studied what Laura Jean had previously called a sea of bored husbands. To Francine, it might as well have been a sea of green olives. All around, waistlines and hairlines raced away from each other to see which could finish off sex appeal first. Resigned clothing hung from soft-shaped bodies below faces with untrimmed mustaches and untreated rosacea.

Francine realized she was being overly hard on the men of Hawthorn Woods. They'd all been perfectly nice to her so far, even if a few friendly smiles hadn't quite matched the hungry eyes above. She'd just had a little too much Down South Punch and far too much experience to give them the benefit of the doubt.

Not that it mattered anyway, because every hairy ring finger showed the dull glint of a wedding band. It would just be nice to know there was something out there for her other than a buffet of compromise.

"Francine, right?" the man standing next to her said. His crew cut of white hair had a distinctly military look to it, probably trimmed and measured each and every morning. "I'm Del Merlin, I'm your neighbor on the other side."

Francine remembered Laura Jean saying Del was in his sixties, but he was probably the most fit-looking person she'd met in her life: an immaculately slender waist that said red grapefruit for breakfast, and impressively toned arms that said red meat for dinner. His copper skin stood out against the white undershirt he wore tucked into his jeans, where the keys to his beloved sports car dangled from an empty belt loop.

"Nice to meet you, Mr. Merlin," Francine said, knowing a correction was coming.

"Call me Del."

"Oh, come on. How often do I get the chance to say Mr. Merlin? I don't know if you're aware, but there was this wizard…"

"No, no one's ever mentioned it." He grinned. "How's the punch?"

"Deadly good," she said. "Can I get you one?"

"Not a drinker, but thanks."

He grinned again, and Francine didn't like the leering quality his expression seemed to be taking on. She adopted a businesslike tone to ward off any flirting the widower might have had in mind. "So I'm still putting faces to names on the block. Can you help me out?"

"Sure." Del looked around. "Well, just about the only people from the block not here are the Banderwalts. Not the party types, I guess. No, wait, that new guy's not here either. The renter. Bruno something or other."

"Mhmm."

Del pointed toward the blond police chief. "You know the Durhams, of course."

Chief Durham was standing with his back to them, Magdalena's pixie cut visible over one stocky shoulder. Before Francine could ask a probing question, Del had moved on.

"Over there we got Roland Gerber, talking to Dennis Asperski."

Francine watched her benevolent Swiss therapist scoop himself a big cup of Down South Punch. Drinking a beer next to him stood a frumpy, balding man with bad posture.

"I'm already a big Roland Gerber fan," she said. "Dennis is married to someone named Lori, right?"

"He is," Del acknowledged, with a note of fatigue.

He nodded beyond the two men, where a globular woman was enjoying her position in the center of four attentive women. At last, the famed Lori Asperski and her Hens.

Lori was tented in a black and white gingham dress, the chemically-brown hair atop her head bundled into a strange, clamshell fan shape. Her blue eyeshadow was a hue somewhere between pool chalk and a butane flame, and she wore a lot of it.

"Lori's supposed to be something of a hard case, right?" Francine said.

"She's a bitch," Del grumbled, then looked quickly at Francine. "Sorry. I don't say that lightly. Lori's...well, you probably just have to meet her."

The woman's sapphire-encased eyes noticed the two of them watching her, which she apparently took as an invitation to head their way, pushing unapologetically through her Hens and other nearby guests.

"Pleased to meet you, Francine," Del said quickly. "But you're on your own with this one."

He risked passing through the crossfire of horseshoes, leaving Francine wide open to the approaching checkerboard sphere.

"Why hel-*lo*, sweetie!" Lori Asperski tittered. Her mouth stretched into a smile that made Francine think of an overburdened suspension bridge, strained cables ready to snap and kill anyone nearby. "You're Ellie's sister."

Francine wasn't sure if it was a question or an accusation.

"Right. I'm—"

"You didn't do your proper rounds the other night. None of us got the chance to meet you, so we had to draw our own conclusions. That's how little whispers start, right?" The suspension-bridge smile drew even tighter.

"That or people start whispering," Francine said.

At even a mildly challenging response, a faint shadow seemed to pass behind Lori's eyes, though the rest of her expression stayed the same.

Not wanting any more enemies in Hawthorn Woods than she already had, Francine tried to make nice. "Laura Jean pointed out your house the other day. It's really pretty. I love your little farm."

"That was so nice of Laura Jean." Lori's face pinched in on itself. "So cute, this party of hers. It's a bit...*much,* you know? But God, ca-yute. So how's the stay been so far? Word is you're here for some R and R due to the pitfalls of love?"

"Just a little vacation," Francine said, already certain there was no one on the planet she'd like to share her private life with less than this woman.

The assumption was immediately put to the test as Michael Bruno approached with two plates of barbeque.

"Hi. I made you a plate," he said to Francine. "Well, Laura Jean kind of put it in my hands, but I'm the courier."

"Our other tourist," Lori announced, clearly spurned by Bruno's failure to show her proper deference. "Mister Bruno, isn't it?"

He nodded. "Just Bruno, for those in a hurry."

"Mmhmm." Lori feigned amusement.

"I saved some seats for us," Bruno said to Francine. "We probably don't want to lose 'em."

"Enjoy the party." Francine nodded over her shoulder, happy at the chance to vacate Lori's company, even if it meant joining Bruno's.

✴   ✴   ✴   ✴

They sat at a clearly empty picnic table and Francine gave a quick wave to Charlie, who was gnawing on a freeze pop as he bounded happily around the edge of the party in a fierce game of flashlight Tag. At least one of them was making good on the pledge to not have their night ruined.

"So bad news first," Bruno said. "There were no pancakes on the grill. Talk about poor barbeque etiquette."

"I'll get over it," Francine said.

Bruno stopped chewing his bite of potato salad. "Oh, hey. I hope I didn't interrupt anything with that lady back there. Laura Jean said you'd thank me. You did look kinda miserable."

"It's fine," Francine said. "Thanks for the food."

"Hey, what're friends for?" Bruno said, cheerily going back to his potato salad.

He'd changed his outfit, but succeeded only in shifting the flavor of bad. The short-sleeved dress shirt, white with burgundy stripes; the tie, a map of Bermuda. An attempt had been made to formalize the unruly hair, now combed into an italicized version of itself that somehow looked even messier than before.

They think I'm a writer.

The thing about being married to a liar was that it made you really hate lies: little-white, bold-faced, and every kind in between.

"You're a teacher," she said, suddenly.

Bruno's posture tightened. "Why do you say that?"

"The faded line on your corduroys, right where the chalk ledge is on a blackboard. You read and take notes like a teacher, And your ties…I'm not trying to be mean, but only a teacher has this many ugly ties."

"The kids give 'em to me as a joke."

"So you're not a writer."

A better liar would've been able to pivot between the two professions, but Bruno just stammered. "I…I don't—"

"'They think I'm a writer,'" Francine recited bitterly. "Like we're all so stupid for taking your word."

He frowned. "That was you outside my house last night."

Francine realized she probably shouldn't have been so specific in her accusation. "No."

"I don't believe this."

"Bruno, it wasn't me."

He shook his head. "I shouldn't have come tonight. I can't…get involved with people like this while I'm here."

"What?"

"Francine, I think we should be the kind of neighbors who just wave from now on."

"But you're the one—"

"Hi, you two!" Laura Jean trotted excitedly over and sat next to Bruno with a plate of barbeque. An amply-sized man who had been working the grill all night sat down next to Francine with his own piled-high plate.

"Mark Cunningham. Delighted to meet you, Francine," he boomed.

Francine pulled her glare away from Bruno, who had gone back to quietly eating his potato salad. She shook Mark's huge hand and made the effort to be present, reasoning she could always stew about Bruno later. "Nice to meet you, Mark."

Aside from a fluffy red beard, Mark's hair was aggressively unremarkable, suggesting generic brand shampoo, no conditioner, and no product. He wore an apron that showed a pig happily eating a pork chop, probably purchased from the same store that sold Ellie's sun-wearing-sunglasses thermometer.

"My wife's been talking about you for two days straight," he said. "So I insisted we join you to see what all the fuss was about."

Laura Jean blushed. "Oh stop, I mentioned her once or twice."

"Agree to disagree," he teased. "Michael, good to see you again. Really doing a number on that potato salad. You an Irish boy like me?"

Bruno gave Francine a quick, worried glance, but copped to the new tone of conversation. "I don't think so, but the milkman had red hair, so who knows?"

Mark chuckled. "I like that! I've got mick jokes for days."

"Mark Cunningham, don't you start telling jokes." Laura Jean playfully pointed a plastic knife at him, which he parried with his own.

The two of them had an effortless back and forth that wasn't just keeping up appearances. They truly enjoyed each other. Laura Jean had made the right choice.

Francine, on the other hand, had picked Ben. Now she'd blown it again by considering Bruno. It was all so obvious now: the dishonest way he chatted with the Cunninghams, the clearly deceptive smile, the…fraudulent way he…drank his punch.

Maybe she was being the slightest bit overreactive.

What did she even know for sure, anyway? Her "evidence" was based on the half-context of a phone call overheard by a seven-year-old who probably shouldn't have been outside in the first place.

"Let's color you in a little, Michael." Mark disappeared a bite of chicken the size of Laura Jean's whole portion. "How many trips around the sun?"

"Thirty-five."

"Francine's thirty-five too!" Laura Jean announced, perhaps having noticed the lack of sparks between her favorite new couple. She tapped Francine's foot under the table.

"What kind of writing do you do, Bruno?" Francine asked.

Bruno faltered, possibly trying to think of a good lie, possibly trying to swallow his latest bite of potato salad.

"You're a writer, right? That's what you told us," Francine pressed.

"Yeah. I write…history books."

"What are the titles of some of your books, Michael?" Mark asked, oblivious to the little drama unfolding before him. "I'd love to expand my library beyond Clancy comma Tom."

"Well, uh…I should've said I'm a writer of the non-published variety," Bruno managed. "Maybe someday."

"Maybe the story you're writing here in Hawthorn Woods," Francine suggested. "What's it about?"

She'd keep pushing him until he said something that didn't check out, and then everyone would see him for the fraud he was.

"Civil War," Bruno said, after a short pause.

Liar.

"I love Civil War stuff!" Mark said. "Which part are you covering?"

"Just some of the battles."

"Oh c'mon, don't make me beg for details," Mark chided, and Francine could have hugged him.

"Battles in Virginia, mostly."

"Which one?" Francine pounced, as Bruno continued to spool out more and more rope. Bad liars always hung themselves when their stories got too big.

"Shiloh."

"Shiloh's in Tennessee, isn't it?" Mark asked.

Busted.

"Right." Bruno said. "Mixed my states up."

"Ah, I do it all the time."

And Mark just went back to eating his chicken like nothing was wrong. Laura Jean hadn't noticed anything, either. Bruno was going to get away with it. Just like Ben had.

Francine abruptly got up from the picnic table, spilling her plate of food.

She mumbled something like "Excuse me" and walked shakily toward the house, bumping into Magdalena Durham by accident. She felt stares from the rest of the partygoers glued to her back as she passed into the Cunninghams' kitchen and pushed through Lori Asperski and her Hens, who were of course fascinated by the red-faced, wild-eyed woman from San Francisco. But Francine didn't care. She just had to get away. Deeper into the house, up the carpeted stairs, down the hallway, through the master bedroom, into the sanctuary of a bathroom where she flung the door shut, crumpled onto the edge of the bathtub, and stopped trying not to cry.

CHAPTER 11

The sight of blood does not frighten
me or make me sick.
[　] TRUE　[x] FALSE

A soft knock rapped on the door. "Francine? Are you all right? I'm comin' in."

Laura Jean slipped inside and joined Francine on the edge of the coral pink bathtub.

"I am a royal butthead. Inviting him without asking you, pushing you guys together like a pair of stuffed animals. I'm sorry."

Francine sniffed. "Everyone down there must think I'm nuts."

"Nobody thinks that."

Francine gave her a doubtful look.

"Okay, Lori and her brood might cluck about it for a while. We'll blame your spirited departure on my Down South Punch. I always make it too damn strong." Laura Jean spun off some toilet paper and handed it to Francine to blow her nose. "What happened?"

Part of Francine just wanted to be alone, to squeeze her glowing coal of grief, letting it burn her and no one else. But some of Roland Gerber's words came to her mind. Something about expelling the tortures of an unsettled mind.

"Ben's getting married next month," she said. "I ran into a friend of his at the grocery store last week and he mentioned it, thinking I knew. I pretended I did. Once the guy walked away, I just left all my stuff in the cart and went home. Then I freaked out for a few days and jumped on a plane to come here." She let out a deep sigh. "Ben moved on a long time ago, but our marriage is still all I can think about, even after everything that happened. And tonight I thought…" She stopped and shook her head. "It's stupid."

"What?"

Francine wiped streams of mascara from her cheeks. "I just got a feeling when I met Bruno. I liked him, and I haven't let myself feel anything like that for a long time, so I guess it came on strong." She tossed the mascara-smeared toilet paper into a trash can. "But Ben was a liar, and I guess Bruno is too."

"What did Bruno lie about?"

"It doesn't matter. Definitely nothing that should make me this upset. You should be outside with your guests. I'm sorry."

"Here's what I think." Laura Jean sat on the carpeted toilet lid so she was face to face with Francine. "Everybody is so focused on catching that first train. They want to catch it before they're some arbitrary age, and it has to be shiny and perfect, and they have to ride it forever. But things don't always work out like that. Sometimes that first train comes back to the station and drops you off, and you have to wait for another one. Jesus, does this train metaphor make me sound old?"

"Keep going," Francine said, with a slight hiccup.

"Another train will come around, I promise you. And yeah, maybe it's got a few dings in it and the paint is scratched, and the conductor might wear, excuse me, the ugliest damn ties on the planet. But that's okay, 'cause life's more interesting that way."

"You stayed on the first train."

"Yes, but it hasn't always been a smooth track. Mark and I have been through a lot. Like I said, I got pregnant before we were married. And that was down in Mississippi, mind you. Sometimes the tracks—oh, forget this damn train metaphor." She offered Francine the last of the toilet paper. "What I'm trying to say is, you get to a certain point in life and there are more damaged people than not, and that's okay. Shiny is boring. I like Bruno, but if he's not right for you, so what? You're both leaving soon anyway, like trains passing in the night. Hey! I brought it full circle."

Francine smiled in spite of herself, then noticed the black splotches of mascara she'd dripped onto Laura Jean's pristine outfit. "I messed up your dress."

"Oh, who cares?" Laura Jean swiped a bit of black from Francine's cheek and dotted it on the opposite side of the dress. "Now it's a fashion choice."

"Thank you, Laura Jean." Francine sighed. "I don't know how I'm going to tell my mom."

"About Bruno?"

Francine shook her head. "That she's been replaced."

"Oh, stop. You stay up here as long as you need to. We're winding down outside anyway. If you want to slip out the front door, you go right ahead and do it." Laura Jean squeezed Francine's knee, and headed back down to the party.

Francine sat on the edge of the tub a while longer. While she eventually managed to steady her breathing, the flow of tears wouldn't stop. This seemed to be as good as her emotional state was going to get for the moment, so she walked quickly down to the front door.

The game of flashlight Tag had migrated to the front yard, leaving the heavily chalked driveway crowded with children until an earsplitting whistle sounded from somewhere in the backyard. The kids moaned and groaned at the communal bedtime call, but slowly disbanded.

As she watched Charlie skip happily home, Francine decided to take a quick loop around the block to try and pull herself together.

Turning the corner, she walked parallel to the Cunninghams' backyard, where punch-happy neighbors thanked Mark and Laura Jean before wandering off in ones and twos. Among the lingering guests, Francine saw Dennis Asperski, looking remorsefully at an empty beer cooler, and Magdalena Durham, chatting with a Carol by the now dormant grill.

Francine almost lamented the lack of horn-locking between her and Magdalena that night. It seemed her lame, knock-off Nancy Drew investigation was fizzling before it had even started. So much for the distraction. No tranquil recovery. No pan-flash romance. No mystery—

She froze.

In the weak light of a lamp post at the bottom of the Durhams' driveway, a figure rose from where it had been crouching in the street and stared at her.

In the half-second it took Francine to wipe the tears from her eyes, the person backed completely out of the light and was gone.

Francine looked behind her. There were no party guests around. Heartbeat doubling with each step, she moved hesitantly toward the island of light, where a pool of red was slowly expanding on the asphalt.

The blood came from an animal. Lori's brown goat, its fur unnaturally dark around the neck. Someone had cut its throat.

Francine put a hand over her mouth. But something compelled her to keep walking closer. Her sandals touched the edge of the light. The goat's strange, hyphenated eye stared blankly up into the night sky. A large triangle had been lightly carved into the fur of the stomach. Small, jagged letters in blood on the asphalt next to the goat read: Get Off Our Block.

Then somebody screamed.

CHAPTER 12

```
I believe in law enforcement.
  [   ] TRUE  [ x ] FALSE
```

The phone rang early the next morning. Francine blindly slapped the nightstand a few times before finding the handset. "Hello?"

"Ms. Haddix?"

"Yes?"

"This is Deputy Martin at the Hawthorn Woods Police Department. The Chief is conducting interviews about the incident last night. We'd like you to come in at eight o'clock. Does that work for you?"

Pete's clocks told her that was in twenty minutes.

"Um, yes. I mean, I guess I can make it."

"Thanks for your cooperation, see you soon."

The inspiration of a police summons put a spring in Francine's step. She made Charlie some toaster waffles and brought them down to the family room, where he was watching a prison movie he swore he was allowed to watch.

"I'm going to lock the door when I go. Just stay down here 'till I get back. You know how to use the phone in an emergency, right?"

"Yes," he said, trying to watch the movie.

She looked for any sign of stress or concern in the boy's face, but he seemed completely fine, chewing syrupy waffles while the onscreen inmates planned a grand escape.

When Francine had gotten home the night before, Charlie had been understandably curious about all the screaming. She'd told him Brownie

70

had been hurt by accident, like when a raccoon got hit by a car. He had accepted the explanation and gone to sleep, saving Francine from having to explain a horrific act she didn't yet understand herself.

After double checking the lock on the front door, Francine briskly walked to the huge red barn at the front of the neighborhood that housed the police station and some municipal offices. She entered a door between two white globes stenciled with the word "POLICE," and waited in the station's small lobby until a cheery deputy led her back into the bullpen.

They walked on hard carpet colored with generations of coffee stains, passing dispatcher stations hung with red, white, and blue streamers for the upcoming Fourth of July holiday.

"Are you gonna be here for the parade?" the deputy asked. "It's a pretty big deal around here."

"Yep," Francine responded automatically, trying to keep her wits about her for the meeting. Or would it be an interrogation?

She waved to a familiar Carol, avoided eye contact with one of Lori's Hens, and soon arrived at a windowed office along the back wall with a door that read: *Hollis Durham, Chief.* The huge man with impeccably combed hair waved her in.

"Ms. Orthine. Thanks for coming in. Close the door behind you, if you would."

Thanks to the Chief's liberal use of pomade, the office smelled strongly of sandalwood, a much-preferred scent to the bullpen's odor of whatever was microwaved last.

"You can call me Ms. Haddix, or Francine if you want."

"Okay, Ms. Haddix." Chief Durham eased his action-figure body back down behind the desk and gestured to a chair in front. "Can I get you a coffee? Can't say it's gourmet, but it'll perk you right up."

She hadn't slept much and wondered if it showed. "I'm fine, thanks."

"You've had quite the eventful stay so far," he said, signing off on some paperwork.

The words sounded slightly accusatory, and Francine picked nervously at her already-chipped nail polish.

"I think it's safe to say I'm done with parties for a while. I don't know what comes next in the sequence of cranberry vodka and dead goat, but I definitely don't want to find out."

Chief Durham's chair squeaked in protest as he shifted his substantial bulk, filing away the papers before giving her his full attention. "I should've come over to apologize for that first night. My wife's not really the apologizing type. Northern people just have a more…pragmatic disposition, and Russia's damn near polar. Maggie really is a kind soul."

"I don't know if she thought I was checking you out or something. I wasn't," Francine made clear. "I just can't think of anything I might have done to her otherwise."

The Chief waved dismissively. "It probably has more to do with me than anything else."

Francine would've loved to ask what that meant, but he'd already moved on.

"Anyway, I'd rate it as unlikely that you flew halfway across the country to kill a stranger's pet goat, but I did hear you were the first to find the animal. Is that true?"

Francine had hoped her first-on-the-scene status might have been forgotten in the night's chaos. She wanted to help, but Hawthorn Woods was starting to seem like the kind of environment where being in the wrong place at the wrong time could earn you a wealth of whispers.

"Yes," she admitted. "I was walking home from Laura Jean's, and I saw someone standing over the goat."

"You walked around the whole block to go next door?"

"I wanted some fresh air before bed. I'm a big walker." She felt no need to sully the story with her personal drama.

"Mmhmm," he said evenly, jotting notes she couldn't see on a notepad behind the porcelain pig on his desk. "This person you saw. Tall, short? Fat, skinny? Man, woman?"

"I was kind of far away and they weren't totally in the light." Francine tried not to think about how, if she were an emotionally stable person, she wouldn't have had to wipe her eyes, and this would be an open and shut case. "I think I startled the person while they were making the triangle on the goat's stomach. They took off pretty quick. Then one of Lori's Hens—er, friends—showed up and started screaming, and everybody else came over to see what was happening. Then Lori herself showed up and really started screaming at everyone."

The Chief rubbed his temples as if he'd just remembered a headache. "I've had nearly the whole block in this morning. There's due diligence, and then there's…heavily inspired due diligence."

Francine relaxed, feeling they'd established the minimum requirements for a rapport.

"Does this inspiration rhyme with Schmori Schmasperski?"

"No comment." The Chief grinned. "Although Lori—the inspiration, I mean—is pretty disappointed I haven't locked anybody up yet."

"An animal getting killed isn't, like, normal here, is it?"

"Ms. Haddix, Hawthorn Woods may not be Times Square, but we don't slaughter livestock in the streets either. Technically, nobody in the neighborhood's even supposed to keep farm animals. If it were anyone else but Lori, you can be sure she'd turn them in, but nobody else cares. At least, I didn't think so."

"How about the triangle?"

"Could be a bad prank that got out of hand."

Nothing about the carving on the stomach or the words on the pavement said "prank" to Francine, but for now she'd give him the benefit of the doubt. He certainly knew the neighborhood better than she did. She found him friendly but coy, pretending this was a conversation when, in reality, he was only interested in extracting information. But that was what the police were supposed to do. Francine just had to keep the exchange going so she could do the same.

"Does anybody hate Lori enough to pull a prank this serious?" she asked.

"Oh, we have our fair share of wayward youths, just like anywhere else."

"Schmeric Schmanderwalt."

He looked amused. "You know the block pretty well."

"Do you think it might have been directed at you specifically, since it happened near your driveway?"

"Couldn't say. Though I do become particularly unpopular this time of year. People bring fireworks in from Wisconsin or Indiana, at which point I have to confiscate said fireworks. That makes a grudge against me unhelpfully unexotic."

"But just because the animal was found there, doesn't necessarily mean it was supposed to be, right? Like, maybe the goat was just too heavy for the person to drag much farther than next door." She thought about the figure she'd seen, and the chilling way they'd lingered over the goat, almost as if they were showing it off to her. "I keep thinking about the 'Get Off Our Block' part. Is there a chance…Do you think it could have been meant for me?"

"I promise you that Magdalena—"

"Oh no," Francine said quickly. "I didn't mean her. She was still at the party."

But you weren't, she thought. And while the scrawny Eric Banderwalt or frail Roland Gerber would've had a hell of a time killing a struggling animal, the man before her could probably dispatch a bull with a butter knife without breaking a sweat.

"You're more inquisitive than half my deputies," Chief Durham said, sounding more impressed than annoyed. "I know you've had an odd introduction to the neighborhood, but I can't imagine someone building so much animosity toward you in two days that they'd kill an innocent animal. I hope you won't worry about your safety. We're going to be running extra patrols and instituting an after-dark curfew."

"That's good to know," Francine said.

The Chief stood, apparently signaling the end of the meeting. Following his lead, Francine stood herself, and was reaching for the door when he cleared his throat.

"Listen, uh, it may not be my place to say anything, but Ellie mentioned you're here for...therapeutic reasons. With all this goat business and that unfriendly welcome on your first night..." He cleared his throat again. "Relationships can be difficult things. I hope your stay here helps more than it hurts."

Francine studied the uneasy mountain of uniformed muscle before her, looking for any of the simmering affection she'd thought she'd felt from Bruno, or the unwelcome lust she'd definitely felt from Del Merlin. But neither was present. And while she wasn't quite ready to cross Chief Durham off her emerging suspect list, his concern felt genuine.

She held out a hand. "Thank you."

The Chief shook it, and added an extra, reassuring pat. Francine turned to leave and gasped.

Standing on the other side of the glass, watching their brief but tender exchange, was a very unhappy looking Magdalena Durham.

The Chief opened the door and kissed his wife's cheek. "Hiya, hon."

"What is this?" Magdalena said, pointedly not looking at Francine.

"Rounding up the usual suspects," he said cheerily, taking a small Tupperware container from her hands. "What do we have here? Jell-O salad?"

"I bring you food thinking you are working, find you having fun instead."

"Honey, no. This is standard—"

But Magdalena spun around and stormed through the bullpen.

Francine wasn't thrilled about the spectacularly bad timing, but she also wasn't going to dwell on it. She was too excited.

After making it through her meeting with the Chief, it was now time for her to look into the mystery herself. Not the kind of mystery that could be wiped away with a washcloth and a change of clothes, or the kind that stayed harmlessly on the pages of her beloved Nancy Drews. It was a *real* mystery, just like she'd always wanted, and for once, it seemed she'd gotten what she'd asked for.

CHAPTER 13

I don't blame people for trying to grab
everything they can get in this world.
[   ] TRUE   [x] FALSE

Back home, Francine splashed cold water on her face, battled her messy hair with some trusty bobby pins, then yanked on her favorite yellow shorts and a rainbow-stripe tank top.

Down in the family room, Charlie was still watching his prison break movie, and seemed to be in the same high spirits as before. But Francine decided to give him a special surprise, just in case he was brilliantly hiding some goat-murder stress.

"You can pick our dinner tonight. Anything you want."

"Ooh, I got some ideas already," he said, with worrying enthusiasm. "Can I go outside and play now?"

Francine didn't love the thought, but Chief Durham had said they were running extra patrols, and it wasn't like she could keep Charlie locked in the family room for the rest of her visit.

"Yes. But don't talk to any strangers."

"There aren't any strangers here."

"Well, be extra careful anyway. Promise?"

He hooked her pinky and bolted up the stairs.

"I'll leave ants-on-a-log for you in the fridge," she called after him.

"Thank you!" came the reply from outside.

Once she'd made Charlie's snack, Francine stepped out onto the driveway and lit her first delicious 100 of the day. Smoking in the cheerful rainbow shirt made her look a bit like an edgy kindergarten teacher, she knew, but it was a good I'm-here-on-summer-vacation disguise.

It was time to begin Francine Haddix and the Dearly Departed Goat.

Every time Nancy Drew poked around following a crime, her attentions were starkly unwelcome. Francine hadn't exactly endeared herself to the good people of Hawthorn Woods in the first place, so she'd have to be inconspicuous and pleasant as hell. She wasn't looking forward to her first interview subject, but was going with the vegetable logic of just getting it out of the way first.

"Morning, Del!"

Del looked up from his beloved cherry red sports car. He wiped his hands on a terry cloth rag, his dark, muscular forearms rippling like tightly braided ropes. "Morning, Francine. How goes the vacation?"

"If nothing else, it's been interesting." Francine kept her voice light and chatty as she examined the showroom-ready convertible. "Mustang?"

"No." The answer came with palpable disappointment, and Francine knew she'd committed some grave automotive sin. "This is a 1960 Corvette. Roman Red. Not cherry red—lots of people think that."

"Pfff, no, that's Roman Red for sure. Sorry I said the M-word. I just figure whenever anyone's working on an old car, it's a Mustang. This thing's spotless. Do you ever drive it?"

Del shook his head. "Rarely. Some guys drive, some guys tinker. I tinker."

"This might be a dumb question, but why?"

"Number one killer of men my age is a disease called retirement. People stop doing things and resort to alcoholism, or worse, golf. My baby here keeps me busy."

"Not to brag, but I used to hold the flashlight for my dad as a kid, so I'm basically an automotive genius. Mind if I join in?"

Del shrugged. "Put out that coffin nail and we'll get to it."

Bingo.

Francine extinguished and pocketed her cigarette, then joined Del at the rim of the Corvette, a miniature city of engine between them.

"We're gonna take out the carburetor for a cleaning," Del said. He waited. Clearly an unspoken test.

Francine scanned the several dozen engine components, none of which looked in need of a cleaning. On a prayer, she pointed to a shiny circle.

Del nodded in approval and gestured to an immaculately organized workbench. "Grab yourself a socket wrench."

Francine approached the tools on the workbench, but her attention immediately went to a rifle mounted on the wall above, its polished wooden stock and sleek black barrel gleaming in the garage's fluorescents. She flicked at a padlock that secured the gun to the wall.

"Eric Banderwalt's got a rifle kind of like this," she said.

"This one doesn't shoot BB's," Del said. "Wrenches are on your left."

Brownie hadn't died from a gunshot wound, but it was good to know which suspects were armed. Francine grabbed a socket wrench with a rubber grip, hoping the insulated handle would save her from getting shocked if and when she poked something that wasn't supposed to be poked. Electrocution would probably hurt her claims of being an automotive genius.

"Should be six bolts on that side," Del said as she leaned deep over the engine to reach the carburetor. His eyes lingered around the scoop of Francine's rainbow tank, and she suddenly wished she'd taken the time to put on a bra that morning.

"No pot of gold there, Del."

"No, you're just gonna want to be careful of the hood prop." He nodded at the metal brace next to her chest.

"Oh." Feeling stupid for flattering herself, Francine found the first bolt, and began her real work. "Did you have to meet with the Chief this morning?"

"Sure did, though I didn't have much to say. I went straight home from the party. Out like a light. Didn't hear about everything that happened 'till this morning when the deputy called."

"So what's your theory?"

"About the goat? Oh hell, who knows? Probably some kids messing around who took things a little too far. Not that hard to believe. At least it was quick. Having your throat cut is one of the more painless ways to go."

That was an interesting bit of knowledge for someone to have…

"I heard people aren't technically supposed to have farm animals here," Francine said. "Do you think someone could've been mad about that?"

Del shrugged again as he decoupled a thing from another thing. "I don't think anybody cared enough to off the goat. Plenty of better reasons to hate Lori Asperski than her farm."

"Like what?"

"You met her. Pick one."

They laughed and Del moved to the front of the car, perpendicular to Francine.

"Plus, I don't think she'll ever forgive me for my crime." He sighed.

Francine's wrench stopped. "What was that?"

"I was born Puerto Rican."

She rolled her eyes and went back to work.

Del shook his head as he torqued against a big bolt. "I'm not saying she's got a pointy hood in the closet, but Lori likes for more than just her Christmas to be white." He jiggled the bolt free and it clanked into the guts of the engine. "Ah, dammit. Didn't hear it hit the floor, did you?"

"Nope."

Del wormed his arm down into the engine, probing for the bolt. When his hand came back up, it just so happened to brush against Francine's right breast. "Sorry," he mumbled.

"No problem," she answered, but took half a step away. It might've been unintentional, or he might've seized an opportunity and wanted to make her think she was crazy for noticing. In Francine's opinion, the ninth circle of hell was reserved for gaslighters, the lowest of the low. Ben was definitely in for a sweltering afterlife, and it seemed like Del Merlin might be angling for the spot next to him.

"Does Lori really give you a hard time about being an immigrant?"

"It's all in the eyes," Del said. "That glint of entitlement, or superiority, maybe. I guess nobody told her America is the world's experiment. People magnetize here precisely because it's not the old country. You can make something new and better, if you do it right. Lori acts like she crawled out of a bald eagle's ass and got squatter's rights. I don't think it works like that. And I certainly don't remember her digging bullets out of teenagers along the Mekong."

"You were in Vietnam?"

"Yes, ma'am. Field medic. Sixty-nine to seventy-two."

Del pulled up his sleeve to show a faded tattoo on his shoulder: snakes twisting around winged medical poles jammed through a fractured skull. The somewhat contradictory imagery was framed inside a shield...in the shape of a triangle.

Francine's inner Nancy Drew was about to do a backflip before her concentration was broken by a high whining sound as Eric Banderwalt raced by on his dirt bike, leaving a cloud of bluish-black smoke in his wake. Francine watched him go, her eyes slightly narrowing. The rogue teenager was definitely one of her favorite suspects, but a casual drop-in would probably be a little tougher in his case.

She turned back to the car to find Del watching her with a frown. He plunged his arm back into the engine.

"I hope you're not like her," he said.

"Who?"

"Lori. She believes the neighborhood demands a certain class of people. Decided by her, of course. I grew up in a house like the Banderwalts'. They're a family that's trying. The kid gets into trouble now and then, but nothing too bad."

"But you said it might have been kids messing around who killed Brownie."

"You really want to know who did it, don't you?"

"I'm curious about—"

Del's hand came up from the engine and found her breast again—palm first.

Absolutely wonderful.

Marriages came and went, and hair styles changed with the weather, but Francine could close her eyes and trust-fall into the arms of unwanted sexual attention, because they would always be there for her. Del was just another gaslighter after all.

A leering grin hooked his face. "Sorry about the grease."

"So am I." Francine pulled the hood prop with her finger, dropping the polished slab of metal down onto one of Del's hands.

He wailed and fumbled at the Corvette's grill for the release. "*Shit! Ah, shit!* Pop the hood. Pop the hood!"

Francine calmly found the release latch and popped the hood.

Del slid to the ground, cradling fingers that were cherry—no—probably more of a Roman Red.

She chucked her wrench onto the workbench and strolled out of the garage, brushing at the grease stain on her shirt.

Scotland Yard would probably balk at a correlation between boob grabbing and goat killing, but it took a Grade-A dickhead to kill an innocent animal. Del Merlin had just proven himself certified prime.

CHAPTER 14

I am afraid when I look down from a high place.
[x] TRUE   [   ] FALSE

Popcorn and chocolate milk. On the roof. That's why you didn't let a seven-year-old make the dinner plans.

Francine opened the window in the master bedroom that looked out on the roof. "If I don't win Aunt of the Year, the system's rigged."

"They give awards for that?" Charlie asked.

"Never mind. Ugh, I am not loving this idea."

"Do you have a height phobia?"

"Your knowledge of words is so random. No, a phobia is an irrational fear. My fear of heights is very rational."

"It's not *that* high up," Charlie said.

Francine stepped gingerly out onto the roof above the garage. The grade was shallow, sloping gently down to acorn-filled gutters at the edge, but she white-knuckled the windowsill and closed her eyes anyway.

"What're you doing?" Charlie asked.

"I'm trying not to think about what it would be like to fall off the edge."

"That's called vis-ua-li-zation." Charlie stumbled through the word. "Dad says basketball players do it to make free throws."

"Terrific. I'm gonna visualize not falling off."

When she hesitated a second longer, Charlie scrambled out the window. "Do it like this!"

"Charlie, get back inside!"

But he was already out on the roof, walking around the grayed shingles without a care in the world. "C'mon, I'll help you." He held out a tiny hand.

Francine let go of the windowsill and, with Charlie's help, stood freely on the roof.

"Hey, this isn't so bad."

"It's great!" he corrected.

They set up some plastic-weave chairs from the garage facing the backyard, put a huge mixing bowl of popcorn between them, and poured chocolate milk from a Thermos into two Dixie cups.

"Do clouds taste like cotton candy?" Charlie asked once they were settled and looking skyward.

"No. They're mostly just rain waiting to happen."

"I think they taste like cotton candy," Charlie decided. He pointed at the grease splotch on her chest. "What happened to your shirt? Were you playing by the ponds without me?"

"I would never. I just got careless with some trash, nothing to worry about," she said, envying the boy's innocent world for the millionth time. Feeling partially in that world now, she allowed herself to relax, enjoying the fatty butter of the popcorn and the sweet finish of chocolate as stars came to life in the night sky.

"Can you tell me about the consternations?" Charlie asked, his nose underlined by a brown milk mustache.

"Constellations. And sure, that's um…Orion, The Bear."

Francine was pretty sure the stars she'd pointed at weren't Orion, and that Orion wasn't a bear at all, but that was the nice thing with kids. You could make stuff up and not get called on it.

"Do you want to make a few of your own?" she asked.

"Yeah, um, that one's kind of like a tiger. Ooh, that looks like a tiger too."

While Charlie rattled off made-up constellations, which were probably as accurate as Francine's official ones, she mentally evaluated all of her suspects, starting with those accounted for at the time of Brownie's slaying.

Magdalena Durham—Soviet Instigator.

Laura Jean Cunningham—Kindred Spirit.

Mark Cunningham—Jolly Giant.

Dennis Asperski—Personality TBD.

Then came the more odds-on picks: individuals whose whereabouts after the party were unknown.

Del Merlin—Retired Marine. A confessed dislike of the goat's owner and a boob-grabbing prick.

Roland Gerber—Swiss Expat. A longshot, but didn't cops say it was always the person you suspected least? Or was it the most?

Hollis Durham—Police Chief. Significant physical prowess, victim found practically on his property.

Lori Asperski—Busybody Supreme. Her grief and anger had seemed real, but maybe she just liked the attention.

Eric Banderwalt—Teenage Troublemaker. Had the reputation for mischief, but as of yet, no direct connection.

Michael Bruno—Transient Fibber. Hadn't seemed like the animal killing type, but how could he be trusted?

"What are your neighbors like?" Francine asked, suddenly realizing she had a pint-sized bank of information in the lawn chair next to her.

Charlie finished a handful of popcorn. "Mr. and Mrs. Cunningham are nice. Mr. Merlin's got a cool car. Mr. Gerber's okay, and Ajax is nice. Eric Banderwalt's scary. I don't really see his mom or sister much. Chief

Durham has a cool walkie-talkie. Mrs. Durham talks funny. Mr. Asperski's boring and Mrs. Asperski's super mean."

"Good stuff," Francine mused, loving the cut and dry perspective of a seven-year-old that classified people as nice or cool or super mean. Sometimes that told you everything about a person, with any further detail only muddling the picture. "Keep going."

"I said everybody already."

Francine couldn't help herself. "What about Mr. Bruno?"

"Mister Mystery? He's just visiting. He's not a real neighbor."

"Neither am I, then," said Francine, pretending to be offended.

Charlie groaned. "You're different." Then he looked at her curiously. "Are you instigating?"

Francine laughed. "Did someone call me an instigator? Was it Mrs. Durham? Wait—it was Mrs. Asperski, wasn't it?"

"No. Mom called today and I said you were out on a walk, talking to neighbors."

"You didn't tell me she called."

"Oh yeah, I was supposed to write it down. I told her you were out instigating. Like the guy with the funny hat." He duck-billed one hand in front of his head, the other behind.

"Is that Sherlock Holmes? Oh, an *investigator*."

"That's what I said."

"Yeah, I suppose I am an investigator," Francine said, after a pause. "You live in an interesting neighborhood."

They watched one of Chief Durham's deputies drive slowly down the other side of the block, a precautionary patrol and gentle reminder of the curfew.

"He's looking for who hurt Brownie," Charlie whispered. "And you are too."

"I…"

"You said it was an accident."

Francine looked at the boy's eager face and decided he had a right to know what was going on around him. "Nobody knows yet."

"I can help."

"No, Charlie."

His face wrinkled into a pout, but Francine shook her head. "We're eating popcorn for dinner on the roof. Good luck making me feel guilty."

"Why would someone hurt Brownie?"

Francine sighed, wondering how best to answer. "My grandma always used to say, 'This world just keeps gettin' stranger and stranger.'"

"What's that mean?"

"There are some things we just don't understand. At least not right away."

Charlie tried out the expression. "Stranger and stranger."

"I know I let you go out that first night, but from now on you have to stay inside after dark. Daytime is okay if you're careful, but it's just too dangerous right now."

"'Kay," Charlie mumbled.

"Charlie. I really need your help, okay? How about a *capeesh*?" She held out a pinky.

Charlie sighed and hooked it. "*Capeesh.*"

His thumb bumped hers and she winced in pain.

"What's wrong?" he asked.

"Nothing. Just a stupid splinter I got from your kitchen."

"Here, I'll get it."

"Charlie, no—"

But he had already dragged a finger firmly across the tip of her thumb.

Francine felt a short stab of pain, then relief.

"Got it," he said proudly, blowing the sliver off his finger into the night breeze. "See, I can help."

Francine looked at him in amazement. "You certainly can."

Charlie brought his gaze skyward once again. "Can you tell me more consternations?"

"Behold." Francine pointed to a random plot of sky. "Gemini, the Crab."

Far below this unofficial constellation, she watched two people walk through the side yard on their way home. Eric Banderwalt was carrying his BB gun and holding the hand of a little girl with blond-white hair. That had to be Diana.

But Francine was more interested in the neon green backpack hanging from Eric's shoulders. It was hard to say for sure, but it looked like the bottom of the backpack was wet. And a familiar shade of red.

CHAPTER 15

I have had very peculiar and strange experiences.
[x] TRUE   [   ] FALSE

Charlie waited for the light in the hallway to turn off and began to count to a hundred. He'd successfully argued his way into sleeping in the master bedroom every night, telling Aunt Francine it would help him miss his parents less, which was sort of true.

But it was also the only room with a window that opened out onto the roof. That was valuable because the carpet at the top of the stairs was loaded with so many hidden creak spots that even if you crossed it like a frozen pond in spring, it always got you in the end.

…Eighty-two Mississippi…eighty-three Mississippi…

Yes, he was going to have to break his pinky promise and whatever the heck *capeesh* was, but if Aunt Francine was trying to find out what was wrong in the neighborhood, he was just the person to help.

…Ninety-eight Mississippi…ninety-nine Mississippi…one hundred.

He leapt out of bed and packed pillows under the blanket so it would look like he was still asleep. The prison movie he'd watched that morning had been entertaining *and* educational.

The mirrored closet door rolled easily open, unleashing the great smell of Mom and Dad's clothes. Charlie pulled a bed sheet with a frog pattern from the linen shelf and twirled it until it turned into a long rope. The prison movie had taught him a lot of great things.

He sat on the windowsill, enjoying the nighttime breeze as he looked around the roof for a place to tie the sheet. The gutters were made of thin metal that would bend in a second. The chimney was strong, but too close to the middle of the roof. The TV aerial was too skinny and too close to the middle of the roof, so a double loser.

What about the rooster weather vane?

The bird's iron base was big and solid and bolted pretty close to the edge of the roof.

Bingo.

Charlie crept across the shingles and tied one end of the frog sheet rope around the weather vane using his dad's advice of, "If you don't know a knot, tie a lot." Then he let the rest of the sheet fall and bravely looked over the edge.

The sheet only reached the top of the yew bushes on the side of the garage. That might be okay, though, because yew bushes were some of the softest you could fall into, even though their squishy red berries got juice all over your clothes.

Legs wrapped around the sheet, eyes tightly shut, Charlie took a few breaths for courage and started to slide slowly downward. After what felt like forever, his toes grazed the top of the bushes. He let go and the yews did their job, cushioning his short fall and getting berry juice all over his shorts. Crawling quickly out of the bush, he listened.

No siren. No yelling guards. No barking dogs. The escape had been a success.

Charlie skipped to the front of the garage and found the driveway still warm with memory of the day's heat.

Next door, Mr. Merlin was standing in his front yard, repeatedly throwing a tennis ball up into the sky. Bats, thinking the yellow orb was a bug, continually chased it up and back down again, zooming away in smooth curves like tiny black hang gliders. Charlie thought this was pretty cool, but Mr. Merlin didn't seem too impressed with his own trick. He just kept throwing the ball higher and higher. Charlie wondered if he'd been doing it so much he hurt his own hand, because a few of his fingers were wrapped in a bandage.

The triumphant aluminum crunch from a game of Kick the Can echoed from two blocks over, where the older kids liked to play. Apparently they didn't feel like following the curfew either. They'd never play with someone as young as Charlie, but that was okay. He wasn't out for fun. His job was to help Aunt Francine get rid of the trouble in the neighborhood, so he ran in the direction Trouble lived.

✴   ✴   ✴   ✴

Every yard in Hawthorn Woods was an infinity of little surprises—some good, like peacock-tail sprinklers and never-found Easter eggs, and some bad, like landmines of dog poop and chipmunk holes that loved to twist an ankle. The yard Charlie ran through now had plenty of bad surprises, all hidden by tall grass that never got mowed. He tried to avoid the anthills, patches of gravel, and crushed aluminum cans with sharp corners, and eventually made it to a window that glowed red, almost like the bedroom inside was on fire.

Peering inside, he saw that the red light came from a lava lamp on top of a dresser crowded with empty Pepsi cans. A boombox playing Guns N' Roses sat atop a fish tank of cloudy water where a Grow-a-Frog swam in tireless circles. Grunts sounded from the floor, and a second later Eric Banderwalt stood up, swinging his skinny arms.

Charlie dropped to the grass just in time.

Eric was doing push-ups. The scariest kid in the neighborhood was getting even stronger. Just great.

Charlie decided to keep moving and snuck along the house's dirty yellow siding, crawling around a broken rocking horse, its mane thick with the cobwebs of things best left alone.

The next bedroom window glowed faintly yellow-orange. Peeking over the sill, Charlie saw Eric's little sister, Diana, curled up on a mattress with an illuminated Glo Worm. The pajama-clad toy was feared by kids everywhere because it had a hard rubber head, so if someone swung the thing at you, it was basically a nunchuck. You had to squeeze a Glo Worm to make it glow, so Diana must've been squeezing it now, even though she was asleep.

The girl's skin was almost see-through, kind of like the animals that lived at the very bottom of the ocean. Instead of sheets and a blanket, her mattress was covered with a plaid sleeping bag that looked like it could use a good wash. Charlie had camped out in his family room before, but this didn't seem like the same thing.

Diana stirred as muffled, angry shouting came from somewhere else in the house. She squeezed her Glo Worm tighter, but the weak light flickered, the toy's batteries almost dead.

Charlie army-crawled toward the front yard.

Through the broad window, he saw Mrs. Banderwalt in her wheelchair, parked in front of a TV playing a static-fuzzed game show. Eric was standing next to the TV, and he looked pretty upset.

"Sorry, honey, what?" Mrs. Banderwalt said.

"I said I'm pretty sure he's been coming around. I've seen tobacco stains in the street. He's waiting for the right time."

"I haven't seen him."

"He doesn't come into the house. He sits in his truck and watches."

"But…what do I do?"

Eric sighed. "Forget it, Mom."

Charlie hugged close to the house as Eric came out the front door and crunched across the driveway. He used a key on a string around his neck to open the bike lock on the shed, then went inside.

Charlie peeked back at the window. Mrs. Banderwalt was still just looking at the TV, like she hadn't even heard Eric. It didn't seem like she was watching the game show at all. It was almost like she was staring right through it. Her face was empty, but somehow sad too.

Sounds of scraping metal inside the shed made Charlie crouch down again. Moving quickly across the front of the house, he took care to step over the plastic covers of the window wells as he snuck up to the shed.

Through the half-open door, he saw Eric standing at a piece of plywood laid across two construction horses, dragging the rectangular blade of a butcher's knife across a flat stone. The light bulb blazing above his head was filthy and surrounded by a growing number of bugs, but Charlie could just make out a big pile of something white against the back wall. He squinted to try and see better, pushing closer to the open door.

Thwack.

Eric's knife chopped into the plywood.

He wrenched the blade out and brought it down into the wood, again and again.

Thwack. Thwack. THWACK.

The table broke, spilling a bag of tools that knocked the door fully open, bathing Charlie in light.

Eric spotted him and froze. "What are you doing here?"

Charlie wanted to run, but his legs wouldn't move.

"*What are you doing here?*" Eric demanded, and started toward him.

Charlie's legs released at last and he flew across the yard, almost slipping on a grainy anthill mount. He couldn't let Eric see him go home so he changed course at the willow tree, eventually diving into a crop of boxwood shrubs on the side of someone's house.

Slowing his breathing while trying to keep it quiet, he counted to a hundred-Mississippi and finally relaxed, satisfied that Eric hadn't followed him.

Peeking inside the window above his head, Charlie found a bedroom, or at least a poor attempt at one. An open suitcase and full ashtray lay on the floor next to a long, flowery couch made up with bedsheets and a pillow. Almost every available space was covered in papers and folders.

He heard the house's front door open, and a moment later Mister Mystery walked into the bedroom wearing dark clothes that were way too hot for the night. He took a pair of binoculars—the expensive kind you had to order from a magazine—from around his neck and dropped them into the suitcase.

The only people Charlie knew who used binoculars were spies. So who had Mister Mystery been spying on? He tried to think back to the phone call he'd heard, and the name of someone Mister Mystery had seen at the party. Something with an 'L.' Lischka? There was nobody in the neighborhood named Lischka.

Mister Mystery switched off the light, lay down on the couch, and lit a cigarette. The tangerine coal glowed and faded in a slow pulse, like a tiny lighthouse at sea.

After a long while, a hand ended it in the crowded ashtray, and all was dark once more.

CHAPTER 16

Someone has it in for me.
[x] TRUE   [   ] FALSE

Francine cracked one eye open. A dozen clock faces informed her it was nearly ten-thirty in the morning. So why did she feel so tired?

It might have had something to do with the slew of Ben dreams that had roundhoused her psyche all night.

She hauled herself up to a sitting position and was rewarded with the sight of Lori Asperski powerwalking down the street outside with her loyal Hens in tow. Each wore matching athletic shorts and ankle weights.

The day was off to a rough start.

Francine trudged downstairs and found Charlie eating his daily helping of cereal in the kitchen. She ruffled his hair. "Morning, Bubba."

"Morning, Aunt Francine."

The phone rang.

Charlie perked up. "Ooh, can I answer it?"

"It's okay, I got it," Francine said. "Hello?"

"Francine!" Ellie's voice crackled through on a terrible connection.

"Hey! How's the trip? *It's your Mom*," she added in a whisper to Charlie.

"Great! Paris is beau…never wanna leave. Miss…so much! How's everything going?"

"So far so good. Plenty of veggies at every meal." Francine winked, and Charlie signaled locked lips.

"And?" Ellie said leadingly. "How are *you* doing?"

"Good. Mostly good."

She wanted to tell Ellie that Laura Jean was a saint, Del was a creep, and her self-therapy had been derailed by a gone-nowhere romantic prospect and a suspiciously slaughtered farm animal. But Charlie didn't need to hear all that while he browsed the back of his cereal box.

"Francine?...I'm losing you..."

"Ellie?" Less and less of Ellie's voice made it over the Atlantic, and Francine finally gave up. "The house is on fire. I crashed the car. Charlie's smoking much more crack than usual."

"You're garbling hon...hate Parisian phones! We...soon...love..."

The valiantly struggling connection died.

"What's crack?" Charlie immediately asked.

"Nothing. Forget I said that. Go ahead, go do your thing."

Charlie raced out the back door and the phone rang again.

"Ellie? Can you hear me?"

"Francine?" The voice on the other end of the line was crystal clear, and definitely not Ellie's.

The breath in Francine's chest grew stale. "Ben?"

"Hi. I stopped by the salon today, and the girls said you were visiting your sister. I still had her number, so I thought I'd call."

Francine had lost the power of speech. She put a hand on the counter to steady herself.

"I hope it's okay that I called," Ben said.

"How are you?" Francine spouted finally.

"Good, real good. Things at work are busy, but everything else is going great. A lot of people still ask about you."

"That's great," she forced. "Tell everyone I say hello."

"I will, I will. I, uh...I don't know if you heard, but I'm engaged."

"Yeah, I heard." Francine gave a short laugh. "Congrats."

"Oh. Okay. Thanks. Um, how's everything with you?"

"Just visiting my sister right now. But you already knew that. Enjoying a little vacation, y'know? I'll be back in San Francisco soon. Everything else is…the same."

Francine tried to think of something, anything, to say. She felt like a debt of a person, completely devoid of experience and identity. What could she offer up against "engaged"? What had she done in the time since she and Ben had parted, except degrade?

"I, um…" Ben faltered again. "Katie's pregnant."

And there it was: the final prong in the engaged-married-baby trident pushed neatly into the soft of Francine's heart.

"That's really neat," she managed, much too casually for her words to be believable. "I actually have to go, though. Thanks for calling."

"I wanted to ask—"

But Francine had already hung up, gripping the counter even tighter as the room funhouse-mirrored on her.

Why? Why would he call to tell her that? To keep her from hearing it from someone else? To gloat? Had he sniffed the coastal air that day and decided that somewhere, two thousand miles away, his ex-wife was doing just a little too well for his liking?

She'd moved to San Francisco for cosmetology school, and had been looking forward to an exciting new adventure in an exciting new city. And it had been fun, part of the time. But eventually she began to feel lonely, and lost.

Then she met someone. A California native with a bright smile who came in for haircuts a little more often than necessary. He had a solid job in finance, putting together money for new high rises. Construction was booming in San Francisco, which was great news for him and his co-workers. They were nice enough, she supposed, though they only ever called her "the hairdresser," even after the wedding. Maybe because Ben never corrected them. But she tried to grin and bear it, because the next step of their relationship was the one she'd been looking forward to most.

Francine had never been baby crazy, exactly. They'd always talked about having kids "someday," and that had been fine. But it soon became clear that Ben's "someday" was much more indefinite than hers, some undefined future point they never reached before the marriage crumbled and revealed two very different people.

But now his "someday" had come. He was going to have a baby. But not with Francine.

And where was she? Trying to solve a pet murder. Being felt up by geriatric gearheads and suffering the cold stares of a mail-order bride she'd never even met.

Francine could feel the emotional venom building inside of her. She wasn't going to run crying into Laura Jean's bathroom again or play phone tag with Ellie, but she had to do something. The answer was obvious.

✳ ✳ ✳ ✳

Ajax ran over and flopped onto his back at Francine's feet as she walked up the driveway.

"Hello, hello!" She scratched the dog's belly. "Oh, and I guess hi to you too, Roland."

"Good afternoon, Francine." Roland jabbed his shovel into one of the many piles of mulch that had been dumped around his tidy cottage. "Everything all right?"

"Yep, just out for a walk."

A cheek-packed squirrel, completely ignored by Ajax, scampered past Francine's feet and up a nearby oak.

"The squirrels are going crazy for this stuff. What is it?"

"I pay a local nut company to dump their leftover pecan shells on my lawn, then I spread them out as mulch. Some nuts are inevitably missed in the shelling process, and so it is a major holiday on the woodland creature calendar. I find the work very freeing, though I wish I'd not scheduled it for the days following Down South Punch."

"Oh yeah, I had some of that stuff. Maybe we should both stick to beer next time."

"I've never cared for the taste. Normally a strong drink causes me no ill, though on occasion I'll have a sip too many."

"Yikes," Francine sympathized. "I'd like to go all my days without knowing what a hangover feels like in my eighties. It may surprise you to learn I've overdone it on one or two occasions myself."

"Nonsense. A lady always drinks exactly as much as she intends. It falls to her company to adjust accordingly."

"Everything you say could be embroidered on a pillow, I swear."

Roland smiled as a squirrel scampered up and stole a pecan from his shovel. "Usually there are quite a few more of our little friends here. Something's thinned them out this summer."

"I doubt it's canine intimidation," Francine said, as the furry bandits continued their raid around a sleeping Ajax. "Want a hand with the mulch?"

Roland tsked. "I don't intend to have a woman do my labors."

"The twenty-first century is damn near here, Roland. We're gonna have to get that attitude right. How about I shovel, you spread?"

"Yes, boss." He handed her the shovel.

Francine began to heave mulch from the pile Roland had been working on and was surprised at how quickly she was out of breath. Too many
cigarettes lately.

"Did you have to talk with the Chief yesterday?" she asked. "About
Brownie?"

"Indeed I did. The poor beast."

"Looked like she went quick, at least."

Roland winced. "Let us not add weight to our task with any unnecessary, heavy conversation. Tell me, dear. How is your heart?"

"You think that's a lighter topic? Well. Other than running from the
barbeque in tears, I'd say I'm pretty stable."

"I admit, I witnessed your urgent departure. Was it our bad apple who
antagonized you further?"

"Lori?"

"Magdalena."

"Oh. No, she was fine at the barbeque. It was just a classic ghosts-of-
my-romantic-past kind of thing. My ex is getting married soon. I just
found out he's having a baby too."

"I see." Roland nodded solemnly. "Troubling, no doubt. Though if a
darkness in your past grows yet darker, of what concern should it be to
you now?"

"Come on, it's not that easy to just drop the past. I'd down a cement
mixer of green olives if it meant getting Ben's ghost out of my head, but
part of living seems to be collecting lots of stuff you wish you'd never
seen or said or gone through." She flung a load of mulch on a row of
cornflowers with a little too much force.

"And yet we demand of ourselves that we remain bright and positive," Roland said. "Whatever wisdom you believe I can give, it will be
only words. Easy for me to say, difficult for you to do."

"I know I'm taking a long time with this, but I wish people would just admit that some injuries make you weaker, and some failures don't come with a baked-in lesson."

Roland stopped working and indicated for Francine to do the same, then inhaled deeply and closed his eyes. "Let us abandon the theoretical for the moment. Breathe, listen, and feel."

Francine followed his lead and closed her eyes. As her breathing slowed, she felt the wet heat on her skin, heard the summer drone of bull-frogs and the liquid grind of bike chains. The children of Hawthorn Woods were in the full flow of midsummer, thinking neither too far forward, nor too far back.

She enjoyed a long exhale and opened her eyes, thinking much more clearly than before. "I thought I'd maybe met someone interesting. I was excited. That hasn't happened in a long time."

"But it is not meant to be?"

"He lied to me." She stirred the mulch with her shovel tip. "That was Ben's favorite hobby, so I guess you could say it's a sore spot for me. I just thought it would be nice to underestimate someone for once."

"Mmm." Roland leaned pensively on his rake.

"I don't do manual labor for 'mmm,' Roland," Francine teased.

"Cars travel at high speeds, in completely opposite directions, sepa-rated only by a few inches of yellow paint. Roads intersect and we pass through, trusting others will stop based on the hue of a light. I do not drive myself, but perhaps there lies the lesson."

"Meaning?"

"We live perilously, within small margins of error, and somehow still survive. The way we accomplish this is with understanding."

Francine felt slightly irked he hadn't unquestionably taken her side. "You're saying I should just let the lie go?"

"Perhaps it is the case that this 'lie' is nothing more than a simple confusion. It would be a tragedy for a misunderstanding to disallow what might otherwise be."

"See, though, it's all about honesty for me. If he'd lie about something that's not important, you can be damn sure he'll lie about something that is. Secrets have weight. That's why people write tell-all autobiographies and murderers secretly want to get caught."

Roland looked at her strangely.

"Surely your new interest is guilty of nothing as heinous as murder."

"I don't think Bruno killed anyone. I'm just saying, truth is patient and there when you need it. And you always do."

"So." Roland smiled and went back to raking. "It is Mr. Bruno who's caught your attention?"

"You met him?"

"Very briefly, on the day of his arrival. I said hello while I was walking Ajax. I found him to be odd, but pleasant."

"He is. Both of those things. I don't know, maybe I'm way too sensitive about it all." She carried a load of mulch to the base of a spruce tree and stopped to catch her breath.

"Perhaps a period of silent work, in consideration of the heat," Roland suggested. "I must warn you, however, on our next meeting I will endeavor to pull at larger thorns."

"I have thorns?"

"You are still wounded. But take comfort in the fact that wounds can have tremendous value."

"Hell of a way to be rich," Francine grumbled.

They worked in silence, occasionally stopping to watch the question marks of squirrel tails sailing the grasses around a snoring Ajax. Soon all the spruce trees and flower beds were uniformly dressed with pecan mulch. Roland brought out big glasses of iced tea which they wasted no time in drinking as they admired their work. After promising she'd come back soon to complain about her love life again, Francine headed home, feeling physically exhausted but mentally uplifted.

Wanting to avoid any chance of running into Del, she took the long way back and didn't stop until her feet reached the penny-brown stain at the bottom of Magdalena's driveway.

Someone had tried to wash the blood away, but the dark shape and its sour, metallic odor remained. It seemed part of that night wasn't ready to leave just yet.

Francine looked up and saw Bruno watching her through a window of his green house. Should she go talk to him? Should she—

A dark shadow raced across the stain as Magdalena rushed into Francine and punched her on her right ear.

"You stay away!" Magdalena screamed. "Stay away, slut!"

Francine shielded her face, seeing only flashes of pixie cut as the flurry of punches continued.

"Hey. *Hey!*" Bruno's voice grew louder as he ran over and sliced an arm between the women. One of Magdalena's wild fists popped Bruno on the nose and she backed off in surprise, breathing heavily.

"Stay away from my husband! Understand, slut? Stay away or get hurt!" She stormed back up the driveway and slammed her front door.

"Jesus. What the hell was that?" Bruno put a hand on Francine's shoulder to steady her. "Are you okay?"

"She's nuts! She thinks I'm trying to steal her husband or something. *I'm sure he's quite happy with his purchase!*" Francine yelled up the driveway.

The adrenaline brought on by the attack subsided, and she remembered she didn't like Bruno. The thought seemed to occur to him at the same moment, and he quickly pulled his hand away from her shoulder.

"How…how are you?" he asked.

Francine's cheerfulness from her latest Roland meeting had been completely punched away. "Hmm, how am I? Well, let's see. In the last twenty-four hours I had my tit grabbed, I got a call from my ex just so he could tell me how amazing his life is, and I just got punched in the ear, which I now know is a very painful fucking place to get punched."

She was beginning to walk away when a piece of relevant Roland Gerber advice glittered in her mind.

It would be a tragedy for a misunderstanding to disallow what might otherwise be.

She stopped and turned.

"Okay, Bruno. This is a moment you won't get back. Here and now is your last chance. Why'd you lie to me about who you are? And don't tell me I'm making it all up. Don't make me think I'm crazy."

Bruno wiped blood from his nose. "I want to tell you. I just…"

"Then tell me. I liked you, Bruno. I thought we—"

"Is it too early for a drink?" he asked.

CHAPTER 17

I enjoy detective or mystery stories.
[x] TRUE   [   ] FALSE

Francine followed Bruno down narrow stairs covered in carpet the color of Barbicide. Given the context of walking into a near-stranger's basement, she tried not to think about how much the brand of blue, comb-disinfecting liquid also sounded like the murder of a hair stylist.

Nose plugged with twin tufts of toilet paper, Bruno passed a pool table and disappeared behind a nautical-themed bar bathed in the light of a neon Budweiser sign.

"I think the previous owners kept a bottle down here somewhere," he said. "They left a lot of teddy bear stuff in the kitchen too. They were obsessed with teddy bears."

Francine took a seat on one of the cracked-leather bar stools and re-adjusted the bag of frozen peas she was holding to her ear. Bruno reappeared from behind the polished dark wood of the bar with two dusty highball glasses and a half-full bottle of Cutty Sark scotch.

"You might wanna rinse those out—" she started, but Bruno was already pouring into the glasses.

He slid a glass of dusty scotch across the bar, held up his own, and exhaled deeply.

"I trust you. You trust me. Agreed?"

Francine clinked the glasses and kept her eyes on him as they drank, feeling the dry scotch cut through the pain in her slowly-numbing ear.

"I'm not a writer."

"No shit, Bruno."

"I'm a teacher. You were right. The writer story was because I needed an excuse to be here."

"So what's the real reason?"

"I'm…kind of a detective."

"Holy shit." Francine looked at him skeptically. "Seriously?"

"Not officially. I don't work for a police department, and I'm not licensed or anything. It's more like freelance work."

"A hobby."

"Yeah, I guess. I haven't been doing it long, and I'm not great at it, but even I know that when you're working a case you can't just go around telling everybody about it. So that's why I lied." He stopped abruptly, awaiting her judgement.

"You're really a teacher?"

"Ninth and tenth grade history at St. Anastasia High School in the Bronx. Go Eagles."

Francine thought it over. "So, what? Paper grading by day, crime fighting by night?"

"I pick up cold cases, stuff the cops have moved on from. Sometimes a new look or beginner's luck can crack a case. It happens."

"Holy shit," Francine repeated.

"I pick a case and do my research during the school year." He pulled the twists of toilet paper from his nose. "Over summer break, I hit the road in my car and investigate in person. I have to be back in New York by mid-July to prep for the school year. If I haven't figured out the case by then, I move on."

"How many cases have you had?"

"This is my fifth."

"You've solved four cases?"

Bruno's blush was visible, even in the crimson glow of the Budweiser sign. "Just the last one, actually. I didn't solve the others in time."

"Okay. So why the deadline? What if you're close to figuring something out?"

He thoughtfully spun his empty glass. "The whole reason I started this was to stop obsessing. The deadline is the deal I made with myself, so I stick to it."

He was clearly holding something back, but for the moment Francine let it go. "And people pay you for this?"

"I should've emphasized the 'free' in freelance. Can't exactly point to my track record and ask for money, so it's all been pro bono so far."

Francine's head was starting to spin from the alcohol, the cold of the peas, and the fact that her initial, trusting opinion of Bruno might have been on-target after all. But before she let herself get carried away...

"Did you like me when we met? Or did I imagine that? Are you even single?"

His brow furrowed on a pretty simple yes or no question. "Kind of."

"*Kind of?* Jesus, Bruno. Don't be slimy."

"I'm not single."

"Are you married?"

"I'm...not single."

Incomplete, but enough. Romance wasn't in the cards. Francine was more disappointed than she wanted to admit, but maybe they could thrive in a different way.

"All right," she said. "I just needed to know how to handle myself in our partnership."

"Partnership?"

"I'm going to help you with your case."

"Oh, no." Bruno shook his head fervently. "I only told you all this so you wouldn't hate me, not because—"

"You don't have a monopoly on amateur sleuthing. I've been investigating this spooky little neighborhood, too. The Mad Russian. The dead goat. The bloody backpack."

"Bloody backpack?"

"Belongs to Eric Banderwalt, the kid who lives down the street from you, Mr. Shut-In. I know a bit about everyone on the block, because I snoop around, and I talk to people."

"I'm not so good at that part."

"Yeah, no kidding. That's why you need me." Francine drained the remaining bit of scotch in her glass. "I'm social concentrate."

Bruno frowned. "I don't think—"

"You know what hairdressers have to do? Talk to people. A lot. All while using scissors a centimeter from eyes and ears. And if you get an angle wrong, it's tears from kids or angry housewives demanding to see the manager. Some people want to be flattered and some don't want to talk at all. And you have to instinctively know who wants what, or the tip suffers. The humble beautician is therapist, artist, and flawless actor, all while keeping hair out of the shirt collar."

"So being a hairdresser makes you a good detective?"

She shrugged. "Does being a history teacher?"

"Fair point." He swirled the green and yellow bottle of scotch between his fingers for a moment. "What would you get out of helping me?"

"What do you care?"

"Let's say I do."

Francine evaluated his face. He'd been honest with her...

"Three reasons. One, I have a lifelong obsession with Nancy Drew that partially informed who I am. As of late, that part of me has been in limbo." She shook her glass for another hit of booze and Bruno gave her a splash.

"How come?"

"For reasons we don't need to get into just yet, if ever."

"Okay. Two?"

"Two, I think there's a natural detective gene in everyone that yearns to carve a tiny slice out of chaos and try to make sense of it. The scenery is nice around here, but some of these folks are hiding bad things, I can feel it. There are guns in garages, and petty rivalries, and I think maybe a good deal more."

"And three?"

Francine exhaled. "Three is, I could really use a win right now. You either understand that or you don't. No explanation available."

For a moment, she thought she recognized a simmering romantic flair in his eyes. But he blinked it away, possibly out of consideration for whatever girlfriend or wife waited for him back in New York.

He extended his hand across the bar. "A professional partnership, even though neither of us is a professional."

Francine smiled and shook the offered hand, feeling a little anchor lift inside of her.

"Okay," she said. "I showed you my case. Now show me yours."

Bruno's expression sobered.

"What do you think of Roland Gerber?"

$$* \quad * \quad * \quad *$$

For a moment, Francine didn't say anything. Then she burst out laughing.

"*Roland?* What'd he do? Steal the Lindbergh baby?"

"He's a man of a certain age, from a certain part of the globe."

"Switzerland?"

"So he says. I think Germany. He arrived in the US around 1950. As for his activities in the forties and thirties…I have some theories."

Francine clued into the implication and almost slipped off her bar stool.

"You think he's a fucking Nazi?"

"My client thinks he's a fucking Nazi," Bruno corrected. "But I think she might be right."

Francine paused, then laughed again, so hard she dropped the bag of peas from her ear. The brittle bag burst on the bar, spilling wrinkled green orbs onto the Barbicide carpet.

"Bruno, maybe you should be a writer, 'cause that is creative. Have you *met* Roland Gerber? I have afternoon tea and cookies with the guy. He's an old softie. Totally harmless."

"And what about fifty years ago? What if everything—the frail movements, the genteel attitude, the Swiss upbringing—what if it's all an act? If he's the guy I'm looking for, he's been hiding for half a century. The routine's probably pretty seamless by now."

A sharp corner of the cracked-leather barstool dug into Francine's thigh. Her amused doubt was wearing off. "Why do you think he's…that?"

"I'm working for a woman named Ida Nussbaum. A Holocaust survivor."

"Holy shit." The amused part of Francine's disbelief evaporated completely.

"She's looking for a Brigadeführer, an SS commander. Nasty guy, even for a Nazi. No death certificate, no trial at Nuremberg, no indication he stayed in Europe. But there are a few suggesting he left. Possibly came to America. Possibly to Hawthorn Woods."

"Holy shit," Francine said again. A long silence followed. "What's his name? The SS guy."

"Oskar Lischka."

The mysteries in Hawthorn Woods kept leapfrogging one another in magnitude, but this felt like the big one at last. Of course it would involve someone who'd been quickly becoming one of Francine's favorite people on the planet. How could she go after Roland?

But there was always the chance that Bruno's suspicion was incorrect. Maybe it was nothing more than a simple misunderstanding. If that was the case, she might be able to help prove a friend's innocence.

"I don't want my nephew around any of this stuff," she said. "Can we work here at your place?"

"I've been working out of the kitchen. All the research and Oreos you could ever want."

"Okay. Nine o'clock tomorrow morning." She swallowed the last of her scotch. "And you'd better not be lying about those Oreos."

CHAPTER 18

Francine passed under the willow at an enthusiastic pace, her arms full of books and a Welcome-to-Hawthorn-Woods coffee cake Laura Jean had left on her doorstep. It was Day One of her and Bruno's official joint investigation. So far this morning, she'd been nervous, excited, then nervous again.

Would her hobbyist detective skills make the grade? Would Bruno be a rigid taskmaster or an encouraging teammate? Would there be an air of forbidden romance hanging in the room? She knocked on the front door to start Francine Haddix and the Case of the Fugitive Nazi.

Bruno opened the door and smiled. "C'mon in."

Francine walked into a house that had the empirical requirements of floors, walls, ceiling…and practically nothing else. "Haven't unpacked the chandelier yet, huh?"

"It's pathetic, I know," Bruno admitted. "My bed is a wonderfully uncomfortable sectional."

"Ah, the bachelor aesthetic."

Bruno only grunted, neither confirming nor denying his bachelorhood as they moved into a kitchen with a strikingly singular motif. The wallpaper, drapes, tablecloth, dishtowels, cookie jar, and even a little radio on top of the fridge had the pattern or shape of a teddy bear.

"I tried to warn you," Bruno said.

"It's cute. In a terrifying sort of way."

She set her books and coffee cake on the table, gawking at the amount of research in the room. South American newspaper clippings covered the backsplash, while tomes about the Third Reich rested on the stovetop and a booklet on extradition law poked out of a toaster slot. Francine relocated the last two items to mitigate the worst of the fire hazards, adding them to the esoterically organized manila folders, legal pads, photographs, and maps on the table.

Bruno grabbed a piece of coffee cake and took a bite.

"Holy cow, this is really good. You made this?"

"Uh, sure. If Laura Jean tries to take credit, don't believe a word she says," Francine said, still taking in the skyscrapers of research around her.

She flipped through books on the Maginot Line, blitzkrieg warfare, and the Red Ball Express, each of the subjects vaguely familiar to her. "Since I haven't been in a history class for a decade or two, can I get a quick refresher on the war? Any relevant broad strokes, I mean."

Bruno took another bite of cake. "Sure. 1939, German army invades Poland, does army things like kill enemy combatants and commandeer strategic locations. Standard warfare type stuff." He brushed some crumbs from his purple plaid tie. "But the Nazis also had a plan called The Final Solution, their answer to 'The Jewish Question.' Since the military was a little busy, they established the Einsatzgruppen—SS Death Squads tasked with killing political leaders, nobility, and of course Jews. Some Jews were sent to the ghettos before being deported to labor or extermination camps. Some were killed on the spot. My client, Ida, lived in a town called Trnów that was too rural for the ghettos. But eventually, an Einsatzgruppen battalion showed up. That battalion was commanded by Oskar Lischka."

"Okay, I gotta ask. If Lischka is such a bad dude, how come there aren't more people chasing him?"

"You mean, why does it fall to a history teacher to try to crack the case?"

She returned his grin. "No, ass, that's not what I asked."

"Lischka was still alive at the end of the war," Bruno explained. "That much is documented. So in early spring of '45, when the cracks start to show in the roof of Hitler's Berlin bunker, Lischka exits stage left to South America. There were escape routes called ratlines that got some of the Nazi brass out of Europe. I think Lischka took the one that went from Germany to Spain to Argentina." He dropped a finger onto a folder. "In 1951, a man believed to be Lischka is tracked down in Puerto Lobos, a tiny fishing village on the coast. By the time agents from the freshly formed Mossad arrive to investigate the tip, it's too late. The small home on the edge of the town where Lischka is suspected to have lived is burned out."

"Was there a body?"

Bruno nodded. "But because of the skeleton's condition, and the fact that rural Argentinian autopsies in the fifties were less than perfect, the corpse's identity could only be guessed. But an immolated Nazi was a satisfactory end to one of many active threads, so Lischka was pronounced dead and apprehension efforts were shifted to other fugitives."

"So whose body was it?"

Bruno shrugged. "Probably a merchant fisherman or a vagrant. Someone who wouldn't be missed. Lischka lures them into his little *casa,* and—" Bruno clucked his tongue. "Knocks them on the head with something heavy, starts the fire, and skedaddles."

Francine tried to imagine Roland assaulting an unsuspecting Argentinian drifter. She couldn't even form the mental picture.

"Okay, then what?"

Bruno opened the fridge and pulled a few folders from the vegetable crisper.

"Several residents of Puerto Lobos positively identified a photo of Lischka. So we definitely have him outside of Europe." He waved a spreadsheet filled with German writing. "Lischka's name pops up on this tax credit form from a Berlin law firm in 1966. A lot of his major assets were still frozen in bureaucratic purgatory, even twenty years after the war. Lischka thought he could get some of the money from his disputed estate, and he did, but the withdrawal showed up in some end-of-year accounting."

"You found this?"

Bruno shrugged, but she could tell he was proud. "Like I said, I'm not terrible at the research part. Anyway, that blip on the radar tells us Lischka was alive in '66."

He pulled a stack of papers from the top shelf of the fridge.

"Is all this research best kept refrigerated?" Francine asked.

"A refrigerator is basically an air-conditioned filing cabinet." He slapped the chilled papers onto the table. "This is a record of testimony at Nuremberg from an SS soldier in Lischka's brigade. He says Lischka often talked about going to America, specifically 'in the west or middle' because the southern states were too black and the East Coast was too Jewish. Nice guy, huh? He said he liked the sound of the Midwest, and mentioned Indiana, Ohio, and especially Illinois by name. Apparently he had a great uncle who'd visited Chicago and liked it."

"So what's the play here? We hope he wears his uniform outside by accident?"

"You'd be surprised," Bruno said. "I mean, almost every time one of these guys get lassoed, they're holding onto something they shouldn't. A pin. A pistol. Whatever. Something they just couldn't let go of, because in their mind those were their glory days, the 'greatest' thing they'd ever do in their lives. They hold onto their past, even when it ruins them."

Well, that sounded familiar.

"What kinds of things do you guys talk about?" Bruno asked.

"Me and Roland?" Francine stalled, in no hurry to share her scatter-shot attempts at divorce therapy. "Nothing in particular. Nothing that would make me think he's anyone other than who he says he is, anyway. He did mention survival once or twice, but he also said that's the kind of stuff eighty-year-olds think about. Which makes sense to me."

Bruno studied her. "You're hoping it's not him, aren't you?"

Francine nodded. "Does that make me a bad detective?"

"No. Everyone's got their biases. I probably want it to be him just as bad as you don't."

"When I try to imagine it, I can't. I can hardly imagine him swearing, or I don't know, cheating at cards."

Bruno stood and stretched, touching the tips of his fingers to his nose. "If the Swiss thing is a ruse, it's a good one."

"Uh, what the hell are you doing?"

"Calisthenics. I sit all day, every day. Gotta keep the blood flowing. Wanna join?"

Francine rolled her eyes. "I'm good, thanks. You were saying, about the Swiss ruse?"

"He can't hide his accent entirely, so he explains it away with a European country. And even if someone realizes his accent is German, well, they speak German in Switzerland. Not the same German, but I doubt the residents of Hawthorn Woods are terribly discerning when it comes to the subtle variations." He switched to a windmill stretch. "Plus, Americans love Switzerland. Mountains. Chocolate. Cute little pocketknives. And the name Gerber might be the smartest bit of all. It's verifiably Swiss, and you can't get much farther away from mass extermination than baby food. He's done a clever job with his new identity, I'll give him that." He switched to a calf stretch. "Okay, so how about the goat?"

Francine felt a little embarrassed stacking Brownie the goat up against the Holocaust. "You really want to talk about that?"

"Hey, that was the deal," Bruno said cheerily. "When we merged agencies, we merged all our cases. And, there's always the possibility Gerber did it."

"It's possible. But if he's this Lischka guy, I can't see why he'd want to bring attention to himself."

"I'll admit I don't see an immediate connection, but it's probably hard to live like a saint for the rest of your life, even if you know what's at stake."

Francine cracked open one of Ellie and Pete's encyclopedia volumes, which she'd riddled with bookmarks. "Pagans had some weird animal sacrifice rituals and a goat has certain significance for Satanists, but the Nazis didn't do anything like that. I checked. And none of the groups used any significant triangle iconography. But here's what I got on triangles." She flipped to a tabbed page. "First, we have a constellation called Triangulum."

"Really broke a sweat naming it, didn't they?"

"Hey, I like that one. Constellations are hard to remember." She flipped to the next bookmark. "The Boy Scouts have a few triangular patches, but Eric Banderwalt doesn't strike me as the merit badge type."

"That's the bloody backpack kid?"

Francine nodded. "I know they say the guilty party is usually the person you suspect least—"

"I thought it was the person you suspect most."

"Damn, I knew I had that backwards." She flipped to the next book-mark. "'Triangles are commonly associated with the Holy Trinity of Christianity and the phases of the moon. Less specific interpretations include mind, body, spirit, and past, present, future. A triangle may also represent the Eye of Providence, the Norse Valknut, or the Greek delta of change.' So basically, it could mean anything. My only other triangle lead is Del Merlin."

"That's the guy next door to you, right?"

"Yeah. Retired Marine. He has a tattoo on one shoulder that's a sort of three-edged shield. He's also the guy who groped me yesterday."

"Wait, you were serious about that? I thought you meant it as, like, an expression or something."

"Since when is 'grabbed my tit' an expression?"

"I thought maybe it meant having a tough day. Like, 'Monday really grabbed my tit last week.'"

Francine laughed, but Bruno looked serious.

"I should say something to him. That's not right."

"I might've broken a few of his fingers, so I'm calling it even. For now."

CHAPTER 19

I am afraid of a knife or anything
very sharp or pointed.
[x] TRUE   [   ] FALSE

"A walk at dusk, I love it!" Laura Jean said as they left her driveway. "The sky is spooky-beautiful, and if I have to approve one more parade permit today I'm gonna scream. Thank you for the welcome break."

"One of my better ideas," Francine conceded.

"I read that walking is super good for you for a million reasons," Laura Jean said. "Locomotion brings blood to the brain, lets you think more clearly, stuff like that. Hell, the Greeks did it all the time, and they invented democracy, for God's sake."

"They also ate lots of green olives, so nobody's perfect."

"Okay, I gotta ask," Laura Jean said as they passed the inconspicuous mint-green house Francine had left less than an hour ago. "Where have we landed with Michael? Anything new?"

YES. Holy shit, yes.

It was hard—physically, painfully hard—for Francine not to immediately tell Laura Jean every detail of the investigation, but it wasn't her secret to tell. However, while her professional collaboration with Bruno was out of bounds, topics relating to their failed coupling were still fair game.

"We did sorta hang out today."

"Ooh, goody!" Laura Jean stuttered her feet in a little dance. "I knew you two would get together."

"We hung out as friends, I mean."

"Friends? No, no, no. That won't do. This is a romance for the ages. Trust me, I can spot these things a mile away."

"At your party he said, and I quote, 'What are friends for?' Nobody says that stupid line unless they're trying to politely tell someone, 'Hey, we're never gonna sleep together, buddy old pal.'"

"Nonsense." Laura Jean waved away a mosquito. "People say that all the time. He's probably just nervous. Or playing hard to get."

"He's not single."

"He said that?"

"It was a forced statement and kind of…waffley, but yeah, he said it."

"Well, he's not married."

"What? How do you know that?"

"Francine, please. I may not know much, but the things I know, *I know.* No wedding ring, no tan line from a hidden wedding ring, and no frequency of divorce. Yes, it's a real thing and yes, you have it. That boy has never been married."

"Maybe he has a girlfriend back in New York."

"Maybe. Or…"

"Or what?"

"Well, he could be gay, couldn't he? Did you ever think of that?"

"I thought you wanted to set us up?"

"That was before I knew he'd spurned your advances."

"One, I made no such advances. And two, if a guy's not into me, that means he's gay?"

"Honey, as my grandfather liked to say, you make a blind man see. If he's not married and he *er-um-uhs* when a heavenly vision like you asks him out—"

"I didn't ask him out."

"—then he may very well be a confirmed bachelor. I have zero problem with that, but in the case of *you*, it's his distinct loss."

"I only asked if he was single so I wouldn't confuse what we're doing."

"And what are you doing?" Playful innuendo lingered in Laura Jean's eyebrows.

Francine felt her face warm. More lies. "Spending time together. Platonically. I still have a burnt tongue from the divorce. There's no flavor in that kind of stuff for me yet. I was never that interested in him, anyway." Now she was just lying to herself. "Roland kinda steered me into it."

"Roland? I thought I was your confidante!"

Again, Francine was bursting to tell all, but couldn't.

"I can have more than one. You're my feisty Southern matron, and Roland's my ancient…Swiss oracle."

"Roland can be your big-picture, life advice guru, but he's not qualified to run your love life. That's my job. We just need to help Michael get his head, excuse me, out of his rear end. I'm gonna find you a new lipstick. I'll make my own shade if I have to. Flirty Francine Fuchsia. Naughty Neighbor Nectarine. Hey, I'm good at these! Bang Me Bruno Burgundy!"

Francine laughed. "I thought the latest prevailing theory was that Bruno didn't like women."

"I don't care if he doesn't like women, he should still like *you!*"

★　　★　　★　　★

They reached the grassy section between the Banderwalts and the Asperskis, and watched as Diana Banderwalt walked toward Lori's farm, hands cupped oddly in front of her.

"Poor thing's always pale as a sheet," Laura Jean said. "I swear, if I ever catch her brother giving her a hard time, I will bring the hellfire."

Diana unhooked a gate in Lori's fence with her elbow and went inside. The chickens flooded out of their coop and swarmed around the girl, making her laugh as she dropped a handful of corn. She spun happily in a circle, lost in the moment until she spotted Francine and Laura Jean. The spinning stopped. The smile vanished.

"Mrs. Asperski says I can be here," she said in a thin voice.

"Honey, don't mind us," Laura Jean said.

Francine approached the fence. "Do you always feed the animals?"

Diana nodded slightly. "I used to feed Brownie, too."

"It's sad that she's gone."

"Really sad," Diana agreed as the birds pecked around her untied shoes. "The chickens still like me, though. I like that they don't fight."

The side door of the Colonial flew open.

Lori Asperski shuffled her weight down the steps and rushed across the lawn with impressive speed, her eyes narrowed into slits above the rounded cheeks of her smile. "Looks like I'm hosting a party I didn't even know about."

"Hello, Lori," Laura Jean said, trading a quick look of exasperation with Francine.

Lori strode showily up to them, then lasered her attention onto Diana.

"Diana, honey, let's go ahead and agree to no more feeding the chickens, okay?"

"I can use different corn," Diana peeped, barely audible above the happy clucking of the birds.

"It's not an issue of the corn. No more feeding, okay?"

"'Cause of Brownie?" Diana whispered.

"Doesn't matter why."

"Lori," Francine interrupted. "She likes doing it. If it doesn't hurt anyone—"

"*If it doesn't hurt anyone?*" Lori repeated. "Sweetie, do I have to remind you of all the wild things that have been happening since you arrived?" The eyes inside the heavy dusting of blue eyeshadow were bloodshot, like they hadn't closed in days. The woman really did miss her goat.

"I'm sorry about Brownie," Francine said sincerely. "It's awful."

"Hollis is looking into the matter, though I think he could be looking into it a lot more. I just can't quite imagine anyone who lives here in Hawthorn Woods doing such a thing. I have to say, I think the best tourists always leave things the way they found them."

"I'm sorry," Francine said. "Do you think I—"

"Of course not!" Lori said, sounding scandalized by the thought. "As I said, it's just so hard to imagine someone here involved in such an atrocious crime. The better-known families, anyway," she added, looking over at the Banderwalts' yard.

Francine followed her gaze and saw Eric idly digging into a tree with a small knife.

"Diana," Lori said quietly. "Was your brother outside the other night when my Brownie was murdered?"

Diana shrank in on herself, looking down at the chickens who continued to peck at the last of the corn. "I don't know."

"Well was he or wasn't he?"

"Leave her alone, Lori," Francine said.

Lori turned on Francine. "I'd like to know what happened to my Brownie, is that so terrible? Do you have something to tell me instead?"

"You're scaring her."

"I assume when someone is on my property, I can treat them how I like." Lori shifted her focus hotly back to Diana. "This is my yard, these are my chickens, and if I don't want anyone feeding them, then that's that!" she ended shrilly.

Diana took a step back in fear, tripped on one of the chickens, and fell into the fence. She let out a short cry of surprise.

"Hey!" Eric Banderwalt sprinted toward them, hopping Lori's fence in one easy jump before helping his sister up. "Are you okay?"

She nodded.

Eric looked between Francine, Laura Jean, and Lori, apparently deciding where best to direct his anger. "Why are you yelling at her?"

"I wasn't *yelling*, Eric," Lori said. "I was *telling* her I don't want anyone bothering the chickens anymore, because I don't."

"She doesn't bother the chickens, she feeds them. Why can't she feed them?"

"I'm aware she feeds them. I'm the one who let her do it. I don't want her doing it anymore."

"Because of your stupid goat?"

Lori's eyes bulged like she'd just swallowed a bug.

"I was generous before, and look what happened to my Brownie. But I don't have to tell you that, do I?"

"You think I killed your goat?"

Lori flicked a finger in Diana's direction. "For all I know, it was *her*."

"She loved that goat as much as you did, you stupid bitch!"

Eric's outburst seemed to echo in the silence that followed.

"Very nice, talking that way in front of your sister," Lori scolded, but the authority in her voice was gone. "Everyone get off my property right now, before I call Chief Durham!" She stomped back up the steps, then turned. "It's no wonder she's wasting away with you scaring her half to death all the time. I hope you're enjoying killing your sister, Eric."

Eric stared with wild eyes as Lori slammed the door. Francine couldn't tell if he was going to scream or cry.

"Diana, honey," Laura Jean said. "You pay Mrs. Asperski no mind. She's just…well, that's just her way."

Hand sticky with tears and corn, Diana gently grabbed her brother's wrist, snapping him out of his trance of rage.

Eric gave Francine a look she couldn't quite classify, then walked off with his sister.

"Jeeeeez," Laura Jean whispered as they resumed their walk. "I always wondered if Eric and Lori were gonna blow up at some point. Looks like they just did."

"The worst is probably yet to come," Francine said. She should have known that a decompressing stroll was out of the question. Hawthorn Woods didn't do relaxing.

They passed the tree Eric had been jabbing with his knife. No showy initials, no four-letter words—just aimless gashes into the hard core of the trunk. This wasn't passing the time. It wasn't even vandalism. It was a buildup of bad emotion, looking for a vent.

CHAPTER 20

I like to visit places I have never been before.
[x] TRUE   [   ] FALSE

Through the window, across the roof, down the sheet, out of the yew bush.

Charlie ran beneath a flock of honking geese as they flew in a tight V across the night sky. The navy canvas was stenciled with the unmoving branches of stern oaks and a dabble of clouds in the distance.

He copied the stealthy flight of the bats he'd seen the other night, running low along the ditch with his arms out like wings, sidestepping spiky weeds. Shoes would make quick work of weeds, but wearing them before September would violate an unspoken rule of summer.

He raced past the mulberry tree where girls liked to trade colorful Perler beads, catching the faint, ashy scent of dormant burn piles in backyards, waiting for their bounty of autumn leaves. He was breathing heavily when he finally he reached Banderwalts' house, and a bedroom window that had lost its yellow-orange glow.

Just like Charlie had expected, Diana was curled up on her dirty sleeping bag, cradling a dark Glo Worm.

He pulled chunky, C-cell batteries from his pocket and set them carefully on the windowsill, feeling a little like Santa Claus as he did it. Hopefully Diana wouldn't be scared by the surprise, because it sure didn't seem like Santa visited her house the way he visited Charlie's.

Diana's bedroom didn't have much else other than the mattress, a dresser, and a rug that looked like the map of a town. There were a few glow-in-the-dark star stickers in one corner of the ceiling, but they were all a dull, weak green, robbed of whatever had once made them glow.

The breeze brought a chorus of hollow clangs from the wind chimes hanging from a tree in the backyard.

Diana's eyes opened and she saw Charlie standing at the window.

He froze, then gave a little wave.

She sat up on the mattress. "Hi."

"Hi. I didn't mean to wake you up."

"What are those?" she asked, sounding more curious than scared.

"I brought batteries. For your Glo Worm."

"Oh!" She crawled excitedly out of bed and pressed the new batteries into the Glo Worm's case. With a tight hug, the toy's fresh light lit her smile. "Thank you. Thank you so much."

She said it like Charlie had given her a thousand dollars or a flying pony.

"If you need more toys," he said, "there's a bunch of them in the firewood pile behind Mister Mystery's house."

"Those are my toys," she said.

"Really? Why don't you keep them in your room?"

"I want them to be safe."

"From what?" Charlie asked.

"Bad things."

"Like when Brownie got hurt?"

Diana kind of shrugged and shook her head. Charlie didn't know what that meant.

"Y'know, whenever I play Hide and Seek," he said. "I like to hide in window wells. You guys have covers on yours, which makes them even better. You could hide things there."

Diana nodded. "Okay."

Charlie dug his thumbnail into the windowsill. "Do you think your brother hurt Brownie?"

"No." She sounded sure, even a little angry. The smile Charlie had won with the batteries was gone. "He wouldn't hurt Brownie. He knew I loved her. Sometimes he catches animals, but then he lets them go again when I'm asleep. People think Eric's bad, but he's not."

Somewhere in the trees at the edge of the backyard, twigs snapped.

Charlie squinted at the darkness. He could just faintly make out a shape moving through the trees in the direction of the Asperski's house. Thankfully, it didn't look like Eric.

"I gotta go now," he said to Diana. "Bye."

"Bye."

Charlie darted across the backyard and followed the figure through some white-barked aspens, hanging back by the willow tree as his target walked across the Asperskis' deck, waking the chickens. As the man opened the sliding screen door and sat down in the kitchen to untie his gym shoes, Charlie finally saw the face of Mr. Asperski.

Mrs. Asperski came into the kitchen a moment later, wearing a bright orange nightgown that made her look like the sun. Her hands were curled against her hips like she was really mad about something.

"Why do you need to keep going over there so much?"

"Leave me alone," Mr. Asperski mumbled.

"What the hell did you two talk about for *three* hours?"

"Lori, I don't bother you about your hobbies, don't bother me about mine."

"I have been working my butt off getting ready for Garage Sale Day. It has to be bigger than the barbeque. You understand that, right?"

"Who cares?" Mr. Asperski pushed past her. "I'm going to bed."

But Mrs. Asperski grabbed his arm.

"We'd have to move, Dennis. If anyone found out what you do at night, we would have to move. Do you understand that? You could probably even go to jail."

"It's worth it to me," he said, pulling his arm from her grasp.

What the heck were they talking about?

Whatever it was, Charlie was certain that Mrs. Asperski was the last person he wanted to catch him snooping. He left the backyard as quick as he could, intending to go home. But the night wasn't done with him yet. A light in the upstairs bedroom of the Durhams' house signaled to him that there was still more to see. Did he want to help Aunt Francine, or not?

Charlie scrambled up the angled branches of a sycamore to peer inside the bedroom window. What he saw almost made him fall out of the tree.

Mrs. Durham was in her underwear. But it wasn't normal underwear. It was black and complicated. She was standing at the foot of the bed, where Chief Durham was reading a book.

"It was a long day. I'm tired," he said.

"You are always tired."

"Aren't I allowed to be tired?"

"You sit in your office. You have secret meetings with new girl. You have been thinking about her?"

"Maggie, you have to stop. The only one who has been thinking about her is you. Why are you so fixated on her?"

"Fixated?" Mrs. Durham shrieked a bunch of words in another language, then grabbed a flower vase off a dresser and threw it at the wall above the bed.

Chief Durham jolted from the sheets, brushing tinkles of glass from his hair. "Christ, Maggie! What the hell has gotten into you?"

She crumpled onto the carpet and began to cry.

Suddenly, Chief Durham didn't look mad anymore. He got down on the floor next to her and wrapped a big arm around her shoulders. "You know I love you. Maggie, tell me you believe that."

She continued to cry, but nodded.

"We're doing the best we can," he said as he rocked her in a hug. "We're doing the best we can."

They stayed like that for a while, sitting on the floor, hugging and rocking.

Charlie climbed down from the tree. Things were getting weird in the neighborhood. He wanted to go home and get back in bed, but there was still one more light on.

He sprinted past the willow and dove to the grass, crawling across Mr. Merlin's perfectly-cut lawn on his stomach.

The old Marine sat hunched on his couch inside, elbows on his knees, his face washed in color from his TV. Like Mrs. Banderwalt, he wasn't really watching it, just…staring. The coffee table in front of him was messy with magazines and a half-eaten TV dinner, plus the rifle he kept in his garage, taken apart next to a bunch of cleaning stuff. Eventually, Mr. Merlin turned off the TV and just sat there in the dark.

Charlie crawled across the lawn, then struggled his way back up the frog sheet and into his parents' bedroom.

When he heard Aunt Francine get up, he quickly lay on the bed with his eyes shut and his mouth open. A closed mouth was the move of a rookie fake sleeper.

"Hey, Bubba." She sat gently on the bed and wiped his forehead. "You're sweating. Did you have a bad dream?"

Charlie rolled over and looked at her, wondering if he should tell her about all the things he'd seen. But he couldn't let her know he'd been outside, not until he had something to report.

"Stranger and stranger," he whispered.

"They're just dreams," Aunt Francine said. "Things'll look better in the morning."

She kissed his head and went back into the guest room.

Charlie closed his eyes and tried to sleep for real, hoping she was right.

CHAPTER 21

It takes a lot of argument to convince
most people of the truth.
[x] TRUE   [   ] FALSE

Francine's routine for the next few days took on an enjoyable consistency: breakfast for Charlie, over to Bruno's for a morning work session, back home for lunch with Charlie, back to Bruno's for the afternoon, home for dinner and a bedtime story. Rinse, repeat.

She was definitely getting the hang of the babysitting thing. And while she and Bruno hadn't uncovered any damning connection between Lischka and Roland in Bruno's metric ton of research, she'd gotten up to speed on things quickly, and already felt like a major contributing member of the team.

Given the subject matter, it was inappropriate and weird and just plain icky to describe the work as fun, but that's what it was. The sudden surge of domestic espionage (or, if they went with Francine's name for it: *domespionage*) had brought a spark back to her soul. The fact she was doing it all with Bruno didn't hurt either, because he was the anti-Ben in almost every way. Some of those ways were not so great—Ben had been a sharp dresser and a pretty good cook, whereas Bruno had a bottomless supply of horrifying ties and seemed content to survive on Oreos alone. But the oddly likable history teacher more than made up for those shortcomings. He was interested in Francine's life. He didn't interrupt her when she spoke. His laugh was easily given, and never came at her expense.

Professional colleagues, Francine recited to herself as she crossed under the willow tree, late for their next afternoon session because Charlie had made a big deal about eating the *one* carrot she'd served with his lunch of mac and cheese. Maybe her anti-lima bean speech had been a touch too passionate.

"Hey, sorry I'm late." She joined Bruno in the kitchen. "Ew, why do you have that?"

Bruno tossed the Hardy Boys paperback he'd been reading onto a pile of textbooks about police procedure and criminal psychology. "These old mysteries have some good tricks sometimes. I think I just needed something a little less clinical for a minute. I'm starting to feel like a zombie."

"I'm not shaming the technique. You just need better taste in your lead characters. The Hardy Boys are dorks. It's all about the Drew."

"I forgot you were such a Nancy superfan."

"Damn right. My girl cracks cases with little more than a trusty flashlight and a bold initiative that, sadly, the milquetoast Hardys will never possess."

"Unfortunately, I don't think we'll be pulling a rubber Gerber mask off of Lischka, either way."

"That's Scooby Doo." Francine opened the fridge, revealing the classic bachelor staples of lunch meat, a six pack of pop, and a stack of documents marked "Euro-Argentinian immigration records."

She opened one of the pop cans, something called 50/50, and took a sip. "This stuff tastes like Windex," she said. "Though not entirely in a bad way."

"It grows on ya," Bruno said, as he began a series of callisthenic lunges. "And as far as the books go, I will say I like Nancy better too."

"Nice try, brown noser."

"It's true! Our family had a bunch of Hardy Boys books and a few Nancy Drews. I'm the youngest of five boys, so guess which books I got to read?"

"Yeah, but your brothers probably all say 'Gee' and 'Golly' now, and never get more exotic than the missionary position. You should thank them for broadening your horizons."

"And what did Nancy teach me?"

Francine slumped into a chair and kicked her feet up onto the teddy bear tablecloth. "Always look for details, trust your instincts, listen for what people say with more than their words. She and I solved mysteries all the time, even outside of the books. She was kind of my imaginary friend as a kid."

"I'm picturing lots of tea parties with stuffed animals on Friday nights."

Francine chucked a balled-up piece of paper at him. "She showed me I was good at this kind of stuff. If I'd been a shittier person, I could've been one of those psychics who charges people to talk to their dead relatives. Alas, a trace amount of morals doomed me to limit my talents to party tricks."

"Like what?"

"I'd entertain the girls at the salon by guessing what they'd done the night before, or help find my neighbor's dog. In both cases, the suspects had been breathlessly chasing the opposite sex. And one time when Ben—"

She stopped abruptly, and tried to cover her slip-up with a gulp of 50/50.

"Ben?"

"My ex-husband."

Bruno's body language tightened a little, like she'd brought up something she wasn't supposed to. If he wasn't interested, why the reaction?

She'd seen it happen a couple of times in the last few days, hints of interest that were quickly abandoned. The guy was a short-circuiting traffic light flipping from enthusiastic green to sudden red at random intervals, keeping Francine in the stressful limbo of yellow.

"Blech," she said. "I didn't mean to bring him up."

"No, it's fine. I like to know what you're thinking."

I'll take "Things Ben Never Said" for 200, Alex.

"He hangs around my thoughts now and then, which I can mostly handle. It's the dreams that get me."

Bruno nodded. "I had that, too."

"With an old flame? How'd you get rid of 'em?"

"The usual. Time, self-reflection, starting my own detective agency."

"And it's worked?"

"I'd like to up my solve-to-fail ratio on the cases, but yeah, it helped thin out the dreams to more manageable levels."

His gaze became distant, and for a moment Francine recognized in his expression loss, regret, and things she didn't have words for but understood anyway. And for the first time, she could see just how exhausted he was.

Anytime she went home to take care of Charlie, Bruno kept right on working. He almost always had a new detail or clue he'd uncovered in the kitchen's library of text by the time she returned. His enthusiasm was infectious, and she always excitedly joined in on whatever new thread he'd found. It was part of being a good partner, but her responsibility now required something a little different.

"We're taking the day off tomorrow," she announced.

"What?"

"Garage Sale Day. I think it's almost as big of a deal around here as the Fourth of July parade."

"You don't think we should keep working?"

"I think both of us could use a break from the Brigadeführer and the teddy bears."

"I guess a break would be nice, but I'm not so sure about the garage sale idea. I try to keep a low profile."

"C'mon! Fresh air, cheap junk, social opportunities. Maybe we'll have a Eureka moment while we're browsing non-functioning eight-tracks and cracked fondue pots."

"Okay. I surrender. A day off it is."

*   *   *   *

After making Bruno give a "cross-my-heart-hope-to-die" promise that he would relax for the rest of the night, which probably meant Oreos and Hardy Boys, Francine left a little earlier than usual. Charlie was still out playing and wouldn't be back for at least another hour, meaning she returned to a house that was empty and silent. Back in San Francisco, she would avoid this by regularly leaving her TV on all the time. The people were made of light and couldn't talk back, but they helped make an empty space feel just a little less empty.

She was about to head down to the family room to turn the big screen on, when something inside her volunteered the idea of grabbing the skull and crossbones tape lying in the closet upstairs. Maybe things had been going a little too well with Bruno, and some self-sabotaging part of her psyche was getting restless. Maybe it was having the power of intentionally hurting herself instead of waiting for others to do it. Whatever the reason, when she trotted down into the family room a few moments later, she did so with the tape in hand.

Ellie and Pete's family room was almost, but not quite, a basement. Walls of shiny wood met soft white carpet under the spread of low-wattage lamps, placed on either end of a pretzel-brown leather couch. A big screen TV the size of a washing machine sat between them below a row of high windows level with the ground outside. With a blanket-draped rocking chair in one corner and a fake-rock fireplace in the other, the room really gave the kitchen a run for coziest space in the house. Francine enjoyed the charm for as long as she could before slotting her cheap plastic torture device into the VHS player.

The big screen slowly warmed and brought to life the terrible harbinger of her bittersweet memories: Snuggle Bear. The stuffed animal, cursed with sentience, happily peddled a new scent of fabric softener before yielding to a glittering marquis that read: Friday Night Movie: *Pretty in Pink.*

Poor Molly Ringwald had only about twenty minutes to be bewildered by yet another romantic dilemma before the soundtrack strangled and the picture warbled to a reception hall. This marked the exact point, three years ago, when Francine had realized the horrible thing she'd done, and had screamed loud enough to wake half of metropolitan San Francisco.

Ben had run into the room with a hastily grabbed umbrella, ready to do battle with a cabal of scheming burglars. Instead, he instead found his wife cradling an ejected VHS tape and sobbing so hard it took her three tries to explain she'd irrevocably recorded over the first half of their wedding with a John Hughes rom com.

Gone were Ellie and the other bridesmaids putting on frilly tangerine dresses that made them look like loofas with legs. Gone was the cranky flower girl who threw petals at her brother until she was escorted the rest of the way by a laughing Ben. Gone was Francine's walk down the aisle, her eyes shining with more happiness than she'd previously thought possible. So many rare, treasured moments, relegated to the porous hold of memory, all because Francine had wanted to save a few bucks on a video rental.

Ben had lifted her from the floor and coaxed her into a waltz, mirroring their better-dressed doppelgängers dancing on screen. "I remember every second of you walking down the aisle," he'd said. "I don't need the tape." Then he'd used a 49ers cap and the umbrella to mime a top hat and cane, and Francine's sobs had turned into laughs. Then he had declared that dancing to the video was mandatory for every viewing, and Francine had agreed. It probably would've been a treasured tradition every anniversary, if only they'd made it to one.

Francine slid down to the carpet, resting her back against Ellie and Pete's leather couch as the punishment continued: Ben with his winning smile and sharp tuxedo; Francine in a glove-fit wedding dress, her brunette locks styled to absolute perfection. The flushed newlyweds received speeches of sentimental gold, cut it up on the dance floor, and gave a champagne toast to the gathered friends and family for helping celebrate their love.

He had been in love with her then. Hadn't he?

Francine scrambled forward and jabbed the eject button so hard it nearly broke. She yanked out the tape and drew her arm back, ready to smash the time capsule against the fireplace so she'd never fall prey to its caustic images again.

But what if Charlie came home? He didn't deserve a scene like that.

And she couldn't do it, anyway.

The tape had the same possessive grip on her as the blank quiz upstairs, and the ring on her finger. She wasn't rid of him. Not yet.

CHAPTER 22

I like to keep people guessing
what I am going to do next.
[x] TRUE   [   ] FALSE

Francine's knuckles machine-gunned on Bruno's front door the next morning. He answered in a mild panic, toothbrush still in mouth. "What's wrong?"

"C'mon!" She tied a red bandana around her head to suppress her humidity-poofed hair, then gestured to Mark and Laura Jean, who waved from the foot of the driveway. "The deals and the Cunninghams await."

"Okay. Let me throw on a tie real quick."

Francine sighed. She'd almost gotten him out of the house without one. He returned a second later, cinching a black and yellow zig-zag tie around the collar of his green shirt.

She gave it a quick tug. "Is this the Charlie Brown look?"

"Kids got me a Snoopy one, too. Where's your Charlie?"

"I gave him five bucks this morning and told him he could buy whatever he wanted as long as it didn't come from this block. Too many unknowns."

Including you, Mr. Yellow Light.

"Get a move on, you two," Laura Jean called playfully from the shadow of her huge sunhat.

Bruno and Francine reached the bottom of the driveway and Mark pulled Bruno into an enthusiastic handshake. "Michael, I propose we let these two chat while you and I discuss the Battle of Bull Run."

"Yes, do." Laura Jean shooed them away and the four of them started their stroll. "Francine, I am loving this bandana on you."

"The store was all out of white lady sombreros, so I made do."

"Excuse you, this is a sunhat! You'll be sorry when you need shade."

"Maybe I'll find one secondhand."

"You just might. Folks here in the Midwest don't really go in for storage units, so all the debris of suburban living gets crammed into garages and basements. Then comes this one magic day of the year you get the chance to buy anything you want. Provided what you want is broken, out-of-style, or the subject of a recent safety recall. Oh, Lord in heaven, would you look at this."

A banner stretched between the pillars of Lori's house proclaimed the garage sale out front as "The Event of the Summer!"

Laura Jean sighed. "I only wanted to do the parade to distract myself from the twins leaving. If I'd known I was gonna have you to bother I wouldn't even be in this competition with Lori."

"I'm sure you're going to do a great job with the parade, and you're doing as well as can be expected with me. C'mon, we *have* to check it out."

Free balloons, a boombox playing inoffensive pop music, and an umbrella-shaded kiddie pool of wine coolers accompanied a dozen tables stacked with domestic junk. The Hens roamed the aisles, assisting customers and giving change from matching orange fanny packs.

Lori stood near a makeshift Brownie memorial, accepting condolences from customers who felt obligated to give them, considering the framed picture of the goat and accompanying candles.

Laura Jean inspected a store price tag hanging from the leg of a fondue pot. "She went out and bought stuff just to make the sale bigger."

"Seven bucks for a hot cheese bowl is a good deal either way," Francine wisely noted.

She was examining a glow-in-the-dark crucifix when she saw Del Merlin one table over. Del, who had noticed her at the same time, quickly looked down, then back up again, and finally offered a sheepish wave. Three of his fingers were covered in u-bends of metal splints.

Francine nodded in his general direction and considered herself a big person for doing it.

Behind Del, Lori left her exalted position at Brownie's memorial and used her ample hips to push a woman away from a pair of zebra-print salad tongs. "Please don't touch unless you're going to buy."

Francine watched as Lori grabbed her husband's shoulder and whispered, "You're security, Dennis. Keep an eye out for light fingers." She gave him a little shove toward a table where Magdalena was examining a pair of cross-country skis she'd have a pretty difficult time smuggling out under her t-shirt. Dennis sulked over and kept watch, grinding his teeth as he did so. Francine wondered if maybe Eric wasn't the only one who needed to vent.

Francine wasn't quite ready to gift Magdalena the same nod she'd generously given to Del, but she wasn't going to start anything, either. She had bigger problems.

"Hello, Francine."

The familiar voice made her stomach drop.

She turned to find Roland Gerber seated under the big umbrella, his hands tied up in colorful string held by Diana Banderwalt.

"Hi, Roland," Francine said. "Hi, Diana."

"Hi," the girl returned bashfully.

"You'll have to forgive me for not getting up," Roland said, holding up his string-bound hands. "I find myself indisposed at the moment. We are attempting what I'm told is called a Cat's Cradle."

"You guys are doing great," Francine said.

She'd been imagining this moment for the last few days, wondering if he would look or sound any different to her. He didn't. He was same old Roland.

"Roland, I feel like I should apologize for not coming over the past few days."

He shook his head. "The fault is mine. I was too aggressive in my attempts at assisting you. Your absence speaks to a fault in my methods alone."

She'd missed his lyrical way of speaking.

"I'd like to come over again. How about dinner tomorrow?"

She said it spontaneously, not knowing if it would be a friendly get together or a chance to spy. Maybe both.

"I would adore a dinner," he replied. "Provided I secure my escape before then."

Diana giggled, the string between them more knotted than ever.

"Sounds good, see you guys later," Francine said.

She moved on to Lori's other tables, examining his-and-hers watering cans, and a bright blue sauna suit. So much crap that didn't merit a place in the house, banished to the humiliating fate of a garage sale. People always held on to something…

Francine had a sudden, Nancy Drew idea.

She snaked between the deal seekers, looking for a green shirt and Charlie Brown tie. "Lemme squeeze past ya. Ope, sorry, Carol. Bruno. Bruno!"

Bruno was examining what looked like a giant blue paperclip. "Hey. Just stocking up on, um, whatever this is."

"That's a Thighmaster. Listen, Roland's here. Over by the umbrella. He's basically handcuffed to a child."

"Okay. I don't follow."

"He's literally tied to Diana Banderwalt. His house is empty. I can run over there real quick and have a look around."

"*What?* That's a terrible idea. It's dangerous. And breaking and entering. And there's probably some other reason I can't think of yet."

"You said yourself that these guys always hold on to something. This is a rare chance to look for Gerber's something."

"And if he suddenly decides to walk home?"

Francine grabbed a referee's whistle from the table and slapped it into Bruno's hand. "Lori will make us buy it, but we can expense it to the agency."

"Francine…"

"The longer we wait, the more dangerous it gets. I can do this. Give me five minutes."

Bruno chewed his bottom lip, then gave a nonplussed nod. "Five minutes."

✱   ✱   ✱   ✱

After telling Laura Jean she was going to run home and use the bathroom, Francine eased her way out of the crowd. As she emerged through Roland's mini-forest of spruce, she saw Charlie at a garage sale directly across the street, examining a giant bag of Tootsie Pops. She probably should have been more specific in her "anywhere but our block" directive, but that could be addressed later.

She slipped into the screened-in porch, found the back double doors open, and suddenly, she was in Roland's kitchen. Standing still for a moment, she felt the uneasy excitement of being in someone else's house, uninvited. Then she got to work.

The kitchen was about the same size as Ellie's, with a much smaller table that had only two chairs. Faded paisley wallpaper was adorned with framed pictures of the Chicago skyline, a panorama of the Alps, and a crocheted doily of three silver oak leaves. A duo of hanging planters painted with hummingbirds held fragrant basil and oregano plants, which stirred gently in the breeze of a wicker ceiling fan. The cabinets held neat stacks of Pyrex dishware, a tin of dog biscuits, a Crock-Pot painted with tiny white flowers. All was as neat and quaint as could be.

She moved on to the dimly-lit living room, centered by a quilt-draped couch. Marble-topped end tables sported matching lamps, a day-of-the-week pill reminder box, an Umberto Eco hardcover clipped with gold reader glasses, and an oversized television remote. A stack of TV Guides and a stereotypical bowl of butterscotch candies dressed a dusty player piano next to a chimney. No jackboots dried by the fireplace. No Luger gleamed on the mantel. Everything fit perfectly with the Roland Gerber she knew.

The last three doors in the house waited down a short hallway. The five minutes she'd promised Bruno had to be up, but she'd come this far...

She checked the bathroom first. Tidy and unremarkable. Same for the laundry room next door. Finally, Francine stepped into the bedroom.

A bed with a patchwork quilt. An armoire of neatly folded clothes. A closet filled with suits and winter coats. No paramilitary brownshirt. No SS leather jacket. But there was something on the shelf above...

She pulled a newspaper clipping from between two shoeboxes. It was from a Chicago-based, German language newspaper. In the haze of German words, she recognized only two, "Roland Gerber," tucked into the middle of an article.

The floorboards out in the hallway creaked.

Francine's heart forgot to beat for a few seconds, then made up for lost time by going into overdrive. This had been a bad idea. Maybe deadly bad. She was about to hold the record for shortest detective career in the history of crime.

The shadow that edged into the doorway was low to the ground. Dog-like.

Francine exhaled in relief as Ajax's snout edged into the bedroom. She dropped into a crouch to keep from passing out as the dog lumbered over to lick her hand.

"Were you hiding, buddy? I scared you, huh? You scared me, too."

She pocketed the newspaper clipping, then walked back into the kitchen with Ajax. After giving him a dog biscuit from the tin in the cabinet, she left through the back door, only breathing normally once she'd cleared the line of spruce trees.

She'd done it. She was out. She—

Something was wrong at the Asperskis'. People were walking away from all the garage sales, in fact, looking scared and talking in hushed whispers. The music coming from Lori's driveway cut out abruptly.

Francine rounded the Colonial to find Mark with his arm wrapped around a crying Laura Jean, Bruno right beside them.

"Bruno, what—?" Francine began.

"I was just about to come get you."

"What the hell happened?"

He pointed down the street where there were no garage sales and fewer people. Something hung from one of the lower branches of a hickory tree. Francine squinted.

A breeze found the tree, dancing its emerald leaves and unfurling a red flag centered by a circle of white. Inside the circle were the sharp, black lines of a swastika.

She drew in her breath. "Oh my God."

Chief Durham's police cruiser screeched to a halt under the hickory. When he discovered the flag was zip tied to the branch, he simply broke the whole branch off and let it fall out of sight behind his cruiser.

"I don't get it," Bruno whispered beside her. "He never left the yard."

Francine turned to see Roland still standing under the umbrella, the string of a ruined Cat's Cradle dangling from one hand, a look of utter horror on his face.

CHAPTER 23

I have met problems so full of possibilities that I have
been unable to make up my mind about them.
[x] TRUE   [   ] FALSE

Francine pushed Charlie's dinner of liverwurst and saltines across the counter. "You, mister, will eat this."

"I, lady, won't!" Charlie declared, his face contorted into a bunny-nose of disgust.

"Liverwurst is good for you."

"It's gross! I hate it. What is it?"

"I don't know, it's like…a spiced meat paste or something. Okay, yeah, that does sound gross, but just take a bite. If you hate it, I'll leave you alone."

Despite the allure of "good-for-you spiced meat paste," Charlie didn't budge, so Francine opened the fridge for a carbonated bargaining chip.

Immediately after seeing the flag, she had grabbed Charlie and raced home. Everyone else had done likewise, and the communal excitement of Garage Sale Day had been instantly zeroed out, replaced with low-grade unease.

Charlie hadn't seen the flag, and probably wouldn't have known what it was anyway, but he seemed to absorb plenty of nebulous stress from Francine, despite her attempts to act normally. While she'd initially considered another cool-aunt popcorn-style dinner, given that Charlie had experienced yet another traumatic event, the kid couldn't live on snack food alone. Thus, the liverwurst.

"Take one bite, and you can have a pop." She displayed a can of 50/50 she'd taken from Bruno's.

Keeping one eye on the soft drink, Charlie smeared liverwurst onto a cracker, exhaled, and with unfathomable bravery took a bite.

"It's good, right?" she asked.

He kept his head low, but she could see he was grinning, unlikely to admit defeat.

"Do you understand what happened today?"

He sipped from the can and shook his head. "I just know everyone is scared or mad."

"Someone put up a flag. A flag from a long time ago that means a bad thing." Francine knifed a cracker into the liverwurst. "People are scared because they don't know who did it. Are you scared?"

Charlie shrugged. "I dunno."

"When I was little and got scared, I had a made-up friend named Nancy. She helped me anytime I was worried."

"But I don't need a made-up friend. You and me can fix things."

"I don't want you to worry about that kind of grown-up stuff, remember? Your job is to be a kid. You can do that, right?"

He nodded vigorously.

"Good." She unwrapped a Tootsie Pop from the gigantic bag Charlie had bought at a garage sale, and handed it to him. "Why don't you go find us a movie to watch and I'll be down in a sec?"

"I'll make us a fort!" he said, and galloped down into the family room with the sucker in hand.

Francine picked up the phone and dialed. "Hey, it's me."

"How are you guys doing?" Bruno asked.

"We're fine. I think he can tell I'm stressed, though."

"Yeah. Weird mood."

"You're sure Roland was at the garage sale the whole time?"

"One hundred percent. It was me, him, the Cunninghams, Lori. Everybody else was sort of coming and going."

Francine sighed. "I just don't understand what it means."

"I talked to Chief Durham while he was untying the flag and saw it up close. It was new. Some kind of synthetic nylon, so I doubt it's an antique souvenir of Gerber's. To be honest, he looked just as shocked as the rest of us when he saw it."

"What if someone wants us to think Roland's a Nazi?"

"Or they know he is, and they're threatening to expose him. 'Get Off Our Block,' remember?"

Francine switched the handset to her other shoulder. "I'm meeting with him tomorrow night."

"Francine, please. Today was scary enough."

"Exactly." She lowered her voice. "My nephew plays in this neighborhood, Bruno. I want to know what the hell is going on around here. There's nothing more to find in your history books, we've learned all we can from a safe distance. I need to talk with him face to face again. I can do it."

He sighed. "Okay. We'll prep tomorrow."

"Thanks. See ya bright and early." Francine hung up and joined Charlie down in the family room.

The boy had sandbagged all the leather couch cushions in front of the TV and stretched a bed sheet across the top in an impressive pillow fort. Seven-year-olds were natural furniture foremen.

"Hey, Bubba. Are girls allowed?"

Charlie waved her in, his focus on the big screen, where the Blues Brothers were haggling with Ray Charles about speakers.

"Ooh, I love this movie." Francine crawled in under the sheet. "Cover your ears if they say the f-word, okay?"

"How will I know until after they say it?" Charlie pointed out. "Plus, it's on TV. Nothing bad can happen on TV."

They huddled together in the safety of the pillow fort, front and back doors of the house locked, watching a movie on TV, where nothing bad could happen.

CHAPTER 24

My judgement is better than it ever was.
[   ] TRUE   [x] FALSE

Francine winced as the classical music playing on the teddy bear radio atop Bruno's fridge was drowned out by a high-pitched squeal.

"Oops. That's not it." Bruno fiddled with the dial of a radio receiver he'd set up next to the sink.

He had scoured the yellow pages and driven all morning to a spy shop in Joliet that sold some key items, including a microphone small enough to conceal in clothing, a transmitter strong enough to broadcast a couple houses away, and a receiver to record whatever was transmitted. The purchases, all advertised as amateur-friendly, were proving to be anything but for Bruno.

"How can it be both direct *and* alternating current?" He flipped through the receiver's user manual in frustration.

Francine gave him a "you can do it" pat on the back.

The newspaper clipping she'd found in Gerber's closet lay on the counter nearby. Bruno was planning to fax it to a friend in the language department of Columbia University back in New York. Below the clipping, Francine noticed a typed transcript she hadn't seen before.

"Can I read this?"

"What's mine is yours," Bruno said, still nose-deep in the user manual.

February 11, 1989. New York, NY.

Michael Bruno/Ida Nussbaum

Michael Bruno: I think...yeah, I think it's recording. Test, test. Is this light supposed to be on?

Ida Nussbaum: I've never been on a radio show before.

M.B.: This is just a recording for my records.

I.N.: I'm teasing you, Michael. Ask away.

M.B.: Oh, right. Okay, um, if it's okay with you, I'd like to know about the day the Germans came to Trnów.

I.N.: A Wednesday morning. A very nice Wednesday morning, in fact. Not a cloud in the sky when I saw the convoy of German vehicles. Once they'd arrived, the soldiers asked the men of age in our town to assemble outside the bread factory. We made incredible bread in those days. I can still smell it if I try. The Germans, always sticklers for paperwork, documented the names of all the men, then called for the rest of our village, perhaps nine hundred people in all. The Germans were polite, but clearly in charge. They told us we were being drafted into the war effort. The men were ordered to dig a trench alongside the factory. Women and children were to support the effort with food and water. What the Germans wanted with a Polish bread factory I couldn't guess. We thought perhaps they'd mount machine guns in the windows. Our men followed their orders and dug the trench. The work lasted an entire day because the Germans kept ordering the trench deeper, wider. How could soldiers fight in a trench so deep? we wondered.

M.B.: Then Lischka came.

I.N.: Yes. He arrived with his SS men the next day, once the trench was finished. The regular soldiers had acted like men doing a job, but the SS were different. You could see something in their eyes. Hatred. Excitement. Lischka most of all. I was terrified of him before he said even one word. He inspected the work thoroughly, carefully reviewing the list of names several times and climbing into the ditch himself. The soldiers from the general army left that evening, and some in our town became less afraid. I did not share their optimism.

M.B.: Did you interact with Lischka?

I.N.: Yes. My father ran the only hotel in town. We were required to put Lischka and his men up for the night. They danced with the women of our town, ate our food, drank our wine. This went on late into the night. Lischka never danced, but I brought him several glasses of wine throughout the evening. I think he might have even liked me. He was so meticulous, the only man I've ever seen wipe the bridge of his glasses every time he cleaned his lenses. His men even teased him for this. As a joke, they tried to get my father to give his own spectacles to Lischka. But my father's glasses had been a gift from me. Thin rims of gold, my initials etched upon the stems. Time after time, my father politely refused their request. In the end, it wouldn't have mattered.

M.B.: What happened the next day?

I.N.: We were all roused very early. It was dark out and very cold. All of the men in town, even the young, were asked to line up alongside the factory ditch for a new work detail. My grandfather, my father, my uncles, and my little brother. All stood next to the ditch. They were told to remove their clothes. One man refused. It was so terribly cold out. He was shot. Those who had been hopeful the day before now joined in my fear. The rest of our men quickly took off their clothes. They were instructed to put them in a pile. A pile for clothes. A pile for shoes. A pile for combs and jewelry. Neat piles. The same you may have seen in museums, but to know the owners...I will never forget the neat piles. Our men stood naked and shivering at the edge of the trench. Lischka waved his hand like he was shooing a bumblebee. His soldiers fired at them. My family, my friends, my neighbors... [Pause]

M.B.: We can finish another time.

I.N.: No. Most of the men fell into the pit, but a few who had been wounded stood yet. My brother Samuel was very young and very small. The bullets had gone over his head. My father had been shot in the stomach but was still alive. He took my brother's hand. A few soldiers held the rest of us back while the others reloaded. We screamed and cried, witnessing but not believing. Lischka approached my father, asked for his glasses. The other soldiers laughed. My father refused. Lischka pulled a pistol from his belt and held it to my brother's face. He asked again. My father gave him the glasses. Lischka tapped them down into his breast pocket, then shot my brother. [Pause] He cleared the line of fire slowly, allowing my father time to suffer the loss of his child, then he waved his hand a second time. The soldiers again fired, and the remaining survivors, including my father, fell into the ditch. [Pause] The SS put us to work immediately. Those who refused, those who fought, those who ran, were killed on the spot. Lischka proudly showed off his 'new glasses' given to him by 'the defiant Jew, now a dead Jew.' They laughed. They cheered. [Pause] Late in the day, I took a wheelbarrow past the ditch, before it was filled in. Perhaps some had survived, and I might somehow help. I was right only in my first thought. I believed it a trick of the setting sun at first, the small movements in the pile. Then I understood. Some at the bottom hadn't yet died. [Pause] I think that's enough for today, Michael.

[End of interview]

Francine put down the paper with a shaking hand, thinking she might throw up.

Bruno stopped fiddling with the receiver and pulled off his headphones.

"Are you okay?"

"I knew it was bad, but re-reading it...It's always worse than you remember," she said, her voice shaking. "I'm going to have a heart attack on Roland's welcome mat."

"We can call this off."

Francine took a few deep breaths. "It's okay. I was just...overwhelmed. How did Ida escape?"

"She and her mother ran off into the woods a day before the rest of the town was sent to the camps. Her mother died from exposure. Ida survived by herself for two weeks before she was taken in by farmers in a neighboring village. She hid there for the rest of the war. Then she came to New York."

"She's not just some random client, is she?"

"We're neighbors," Bruno admitted after a pause. "She helped me while I was going through bad times myself. She'd leave casseroles by my door, or stick a knuckle under my face and say, 'Chin up!' whenever she saw me in the lobby of our apartment building. Small kindnesses. Once I heard her story, I knew I had to try and help. I cared about my other cases, but they've all been building to this one. When I solved the last case, I thought I was finally ready to bring Ida the justice she deserves."

"Why didn't you tell me?"

"I don't know. I didn't want you to think I was too biased."

Francine looked at the glossy black-and-whites of posing Nazi battalions and officer enlistment portraits, all bizarrely held on the refrigerator door with teddy bear magnets. One of the largest photos showed a slender, bespectacled man in his late thirties wearing a high-necked uniform pinned with twin SS Bolts, a skull and crossbones on his cap. 'Oskar Lischka—Brigadeführer. Prinz-Albrecht-Straße, Berlin, 1942.' The slightly out of focus officer wore a mirthless expression that sent a chill down Francine's spine. Here was a man she hoped never to meet. Assuming, of course, that she hadn't already.

Could it really be Roland, forty-five years younger?

Francine mentally swapped her friend's soft blue blazer for a black leather jacket, the docile white husky for a snarling German Shepherd, the patience and kindness for thoughts and actions so reprehensible they were difficult to comprehend.

"On the run for almost fifty years," she tried the idea out loud.

"No. Not on the run." Bruno joined her at the fridge. "Gerber has a comfortable home and a good reputation. He has a hammock in his backyard. He hasn't been running, he's been living."

"If Roland is guilty and we turn him in, will he be executed?"

"It's possible. Depends on what country he ends up in and how the trial goes. Given his age, it's more likely he'd die in custody, awaiting trial."

The thought of Roland Gerber being hanged upset Francine's stomach all over again.

"Francine, I'll only say it one more time, but I have to say it. I owe this to Ida. You don't owe it to anybody. If Gerber is Lischka…I don't know what a mass murderer would do to keep someone from threatening the life he's built."

She looked at another picture on the fridge. A pretty young brunette with dark curls, sparkling eyes, and full, apple cheeks. Ida Nussbaum in her twenties, somewhere in New York, escaped from unthinkable oblivion and still smiling with resolve.

The least Francine could do was have dinner with her neighbor to try and shake something loose.

"Let's get that receiver working," she said.

✴   ✴   ✴   ✴

"It goes, uh, right here." Bruno handed Francine the tiny microphone and gestured to a button halfway up his shirt. "In the…breastorial region…"

"Between my boobs," she helped, enjoying his embarrassment.

"Yep." Bruno nodded. "Why don't you go ahead and do that?"

Francine clipped the microphone to her bra and ran the cord down the inside of the ghost-and-pumpkin blouse she'd borrowed from Ellie. The shirt was seasonally inappropriate and a size too small, but its busy pattern and layered folds hid the mic and wire perfectly.

Bruno began to tape the wire to her lower back.

"I got this tape from a theater place. It's the kind actors use for plays, so it won't hurt when you take it off."

Francine smiled, appreciating a little sweet in so much sour.

He clipped the transmitter to the back of Francine's jeans. The rectangle of metal and plastic was bigger than she liked and had a cord that snaked above her right love handle (also bigger than she liked), but Ellie's Halloween blouse reliably covered all.

"The guy at the spy shop asked me if we were spying on the Russians," Bruno said.

"If Magdalena keeps acting like an ass, we just might."

He sat at the receiver and slotted on his headphones. "Go ahead."

"You're listening to Francine Haddix and the Case of the Fugitive Nazi," she said to her cleavage.

Bruno nodded and slipped off the headphones. "I gotcha."

Francine gave a thumbs up, then shook out her arms, trying to scatter her gathering nerves. "Sorry. I'm just freaking out a little."

The teddy bear radio finished some terrible harpsichord sonata and transitioned to Debussy's overplayed but undeniably dreamy piano piece, *Clair de Lune.*

Bruno's face reddened a little. "Considering we're professionals, I don't know if dancing is appropriate, but I'm happy to do it if it helps."

"I think it might."

Their hands met easily and they began an improvised waltz on the empty patch of kitchen floor. Francine's free hand naturally found Bruno's shoulder, and his found her back.

"You're actually a good dancer," she observed, her nerves calming with each step they took.

"Why'd you say actually?"

"Sorry. You're just normally so…passionate in a staccato kind of way."

"That's the nicest way anyone's ever called me awkward."

"That's not what I meant!" She laughed. "It makes you more genuine. You don't sand down the corners like everyone else. I like that. I just expected the trait to come with two left feet."

Their footsteps fell into perfect sync, tracing slow circles around the kitchen as the pensive melody grew sadder and more beautiful.

"Can I admit something terrible?" she said. "History was sort of my nap period in high school."

"You'll be happy to know some of my students are keeping the tradition alive."

"What do you like about it?"

Bruno thought for a moment. "Usually, people make the same mistakes over and over again. But there are certain times when you can see the world's ready to move on. Someone does something different, something new…and everything moves forward."

Their eyes met and Francine felt the sudden urge to close the gap between them. But she didn't. She couldn't. There was no way she was going to screw over whatever third party might be involved.

Colleagues. They were work colleagues, she told herself.

Sure. Work colleagues who slow-danced to classical music, becoming ever more vulnerable as their time together grew shorter.

"I should go," she said. "I need to make dinner for Charlie, then get him washed up and tucked in before I go to Roland's."

She noticed Bruno nervously biting his lip.

"What's wrong?"

"I'm just wondering if this is the smartest idea."

"Seriously? I was hoping for a pep talk!"

"Sorry, it's just that I should be the one going in. What if I come with you? We can say I'm your cousin in town, or something. Wait, no. He already met me."

"Yes, thank you for illustrating why you won't be going in with me. You're the bumbling intelligence nerd, I'm the silky-smooth field agent." She held out her hands. "Check it out. No shake. Chalk it up to years of snipping hair around ears."

"Okay, okay. You're the woman for the job."

"I'm glad you agree. And, listen…I know it would be good for you and Ida if Roland turns out to be Lischka, but I still kinda hope it's not him. Is that shitty?"

"I know you like him, Francine. It's okay. You don't have to pretend you're emotionless."

"Thanks," she said.

"For what?"

"For that. And for letting me join the club, however this all turns out."

"You joining made it a club." Bruno tapped the top of the receiver lightly. "I'll be with you the whole time. You'll do great."

The hug she gave him didn't linger, but it wasn't an immediate squeeze and release either. In the flush of the moment, Francine could finally admit it to herself: Regardless of his relationship status, she had real feelings for Bruno. It felt good to acknowledge her growing affection, but she had to wonder why, yet again, she was gathering an abundance of warm feelings for someone who didn't want her back.

CHAPTER 25

It makes me nervous when people
ask me personal questions.
[x] TRUE   [   ] FALSE

With Charlie fed and in bed, Francine made the walk to Roland's a slow one to give herself time to think.

She was about to do one of two things: project someone's fantasy of justice onto a nice old man guilty of nothing more than good manners and a foreign birth, or give a sadistic war criminal an extended chance to catch her snooping. She'd worn extra deodorant in preparation for either outcome.

This turned out to be a good thing, because the moment she knocked on Roland's front door her fight or flight reflex peaked, threatening to send her on a hundred-yard dash in any direction away from the welcome mat under her feet. But when the door opened a moment later, social manners overruled survival instinct and she held out the dessert she'd brought instead.

"Puppy Chow. It's cereal, sugar, chocolate, and peanut butter."

Roland, wearing a white apron tied tightly around his navy blue sport coat, accepted the bowl and inhaled through a gap in the Saran Wrap. "Cooking skills as peerless as her charm."

"That could be a compliment or an insult."

"All plausible insults evaporate in your presence." He studied her Halloween blouse. "The outfit, however, is…a bold choice."

"It's Ellie's. My one dress is in the washing machine, and I didn't want to show up in a t-shirt, so this is what you get."

"I think it's splendid." He led the way to the kitchen. "I'm making *Thurgauer Käseschnitten.*"

She followed him through the living room she'd been in the day before.

"I had thurger...whatever it is for lunch, but I can have it again."

Roland laughed and set the bowl of Puppy Chow on the counter. "*Thurgauer Käseschnitten.* A fancy Swiss way of saying apples on bread. But do not despair, there is cheese as well."

Ajax nudged one of Francine's hands, which was shaking slightly, despite her earlier bragging at Bruno's.

"You hungry, too, buddy? How 'bout a treat?" She opened a cabinet door and pulled out the tin of dog treats.

"Goodness! How did you know those were there?" Roland marveled as he pulled apples from a fruit basket.

Jesus Christ, Francine.

"My mom kept our dog's treats in a similar spot when we were kids. It was either that or canine telepathy." She tried to laugh, sweating like an opium mule at baggage claim as she tossed Ajax a biscuit.

Roland washed the apples in the sink. "I wonder if I might start our evening with a confession?"

No way. No fucking *way* it was going to be this easy.

"Sure." Francine gave herself the Academy Award for Most Casual Response.

"I must admit a curiosity about your status with Mr. Bruno."

Francine's heart rabbit-twitched. He knew they were working together.

Then she remembered she'd previously mentioned an interest in Bruno. While it seemed absurd to talk about a crush, considering the task at hand, everything had to be on the level or there would be too many spinning plates. Honesty would grease the conversation.

"You were right. I got upset over what was really a misunderstanding. We didn't go the raw-advice route you and I discussed," she said tactically, knowing Bruno was hearing every word. "But we're friends."

"He's fortunate to receive whatever you deign to give, I'm sure."

"Ooh, I'll have to remember that one. I probably wouldn't have even tried to talk to him if you hadn't pushed me, so thanks for that. And for agreeing to hang out tonight."

"Please. I'm delighted. Your consideration for an old man knows no respite. You've a good heart, Francine, one that deserves to be whole, whatever efforts required of us to make it so."

"Thanks, Roland," she said, feeling a slap of guilt from his genuine concern. "Let me help you with your Thurger-whatever. And don't give me any of that crap about not wanting women to help with your labors."

Labor.

The word pinged Francine's mind back to Bruno's kitchen, to books with countless photos of ragged human beings crowded into trains or peeking out of bunkbeds stacked ten high. Barbed wire. Snarling dogs. Buildings with no exit but a chimney.

Wait. Had Roland said something to her?

"Sorry, I got distracted for a second," she said. "Heat's getting to me, I guess."

"It's been especially relentless this summer," Roland agreed. "I just said that your assistance would be welcome and appreciated. You'll find apple juice in the refrigerator and bread on the counter there. If you'd be so kind as to soak the bread in the juice."

We made incredible bread in those days. I can still smell it.

Ida's words echoed in Francine's head, summoning visions of a Polish bread factory, a deep ditch outside, a smiling SS officer beside it...

Slow your damn heartbeat, girl.

Francine grabbed the apple juice and turned to find Roland holding a long knife. She'd brought Puppy Chow to a knife fight and now she was going to die.

No. Only if Roland was Lischka, and only if she gave herself away.

So she didn't drop the apple juice, and she didn't scream. She just breezed past the blade and gave herself another Academy Award for Best Performance by an Actress at Knifepoint.

Soaking the bread while Roland cored the apples, she forced herself to relax, and her heart gradually found a more sustainable rhythm.

She stayed calm while they ate together at the little dinette, talking about innocuous, pleasant topics. Roland's apple and cheese dish was delicious and the Puppy Chow was a tasty, if unsophisticated, finish to the meal. At that point, she decided it would be weird not to mention a certain, recent event.

"Pretty wild, everything with that flag yesterday."

Roland didn't nervously pull at his collar or spit out his Puppy Chow. He just nodded, slowly. "Terrible thing. Certainly returned unwelcome memories for me."

"What do you mean?"

"I lived through the Second World War."

"Switzerland was neutral, right?" she baited.

"Of course. But some of us did what we could for the Allies, unofficially running supplies to the Belgians, and so forth."

"You did that?"

Roland nodded.

"Like a freedom fighter? That's amazing! Does anyone here know that?"

"Wartime stories don't often translate to peacetime, no matter their content."

"Do people ever ask you about the war?"

"Certainly. I came from Europe after the forties. I speak German. On occasion, those who don't know me well have wondered if I harbor Nazi sympathies."

Francine's heart iced. He'd said the word. She extended all sensory antennae to try and pick up on any change in posture or breathing. Maybe a spontaneous *Sieg Heil*.

Nothing.

"Do you ever go back to Europe?" she asked.

"I've never been back."

"Ever?"

"I love this country." Roland thumped his slipper on the floor. "A home by choice is no less a home."

Francine saw an opening for a natural conversation avenue and took it. "I'm gonna need a quick Roland Gerber biography."

"A rather dull story, I'm afraid," he said.

"All we do is talk about me. It's gonna give me an ego. Please?"

"Very well." He sighed.

$$* \quad * \quad * \quad *$$

Francine pulled out her pack of cigarettes. Roland was quick with the lighter, then leaned back in his chair.

"I expatriated from a region called Engadin. Not as popular as Zürich, but our mountain profile is featured on more chocolate wrappers. That counts for a lot in Switzerland. In any case, I found my way to America, and Illinois. With the little money I had, I bought into the barn at the front of the neighborhood, which was a dairy farm in those days. I helped build out the neighborhood, and I've never felt the need to leave since."

"Yeah, I get the feeling you kinda like it here." Francine directed her exhale of smoke up into the lazily oscillating ceiling fan.

"What is there to dislike? This is a place of spring rains and fresh-cut grass. Leaves burning in the autumn and fresh snows in winter. So many reliable treasures year after year. And yet," he dipped his head cordially toward Francine, "new wonders never cease to amaze."

She nodded gratefully back. "And you never married, never had any of your family join you here?"

"I've met some fine individuals along the way, but some lives demand more solitude than others. I've no wish to be a hermit, though I will admit I'm quite fond of the quiet days and nights I enjoy."

"I'm still surprised you've never wanted to go back to Europe. Even to visit, I mean." *Careful now.*

"Few pleasant memories await me there. My childhood was disagreeable, mostly due to my father. He was not a kind man, you understand. His loves were for the bottle and the belt. Of course, I cannot ignore those days entirely. Pain is impervious to erasure in total. As it should be, for therein lies growth. Consequently, the past should not be forgotten, but mastered. I have done so, and in time, you will too."

He gave her a reassuring smile and carried their plates to the sink.

Francine joined him with their empty glasses. "I'm doing the dishes, no arguments. You can dry."

She wrapped Roland's apron around her Halloween blouse to make sure the microphone wouldn't get wet and flipped on the faucet.

Using his long knife, Roland scraped the apple cores from the cutting board into the garbage can. "There are no conversational requirements in this house, but should you wish to speak of your marriage again, you are welcome to do so."

Francine picked at a spot of dried cheese on one of the plates as she tried to think of a way out of that particular topic. She wasn't worried about whether Roland would have worthwhile responses. She was worried about how much she wanted to hear them. But to seem natural, she had to be honest. So it was time for Francine's Divorce Radio Hour. Eat your hi-fi heart out, Bruno.

"My ex-husband, lied a lot. Little things at first. Things that didn't matter. He'd steal five bucks from my purse or buy a new shirt and then claim it was one he'd owned for years. It was almost a game between us. I'd catch him in a lie and give him shit for it. Then wedding rings went on fingers, and his lies got more...ambitious. Things that mattered. Things that hurt. After a while it wasn't much fun to play the game anymore."

Roland was silent, but attentive.

"Pretty soon, he was working late a couple nights a week. That old chestnut. I'd try to wait for him to get home so we could eat together, but eventually I started to go to bed without him, waiting for the sound of the front door hours later. And he always had an excuse that made sense, maybe because he was good at lying, or maybe because I wanted to believe him. Eventually the excuses stopped, because I stopped asking."

Roland frowned, forcefully toweling the inside of a glass. "The heart can be ruthless in its selections. You believe an indiscretion occurred more than once?"

"Eight times. At least, that's how many second chances I gave him. And the craziest part was, he's the one who ended it. He got to say 'don't go' so many times. I got to say it once, and it didn't even work. He denied everything, of course. Said I was crazy, that I was letting my imagination get the best of me. If he'd just admitted what was happening, it would've made the hell he put me in a little more bearable."

Roland cursed in German, startling Ajax. "The bastard. I knew it would not have been your fault, but hardly would I have imagined this level of baseness."

He turned off the faucet and took Francine's still-wet hands in his own, his eyes sharp and lively.

"Listen to me closely. When life is good, the bad news is, things change. When life is bad, the good news is, things change. You're due for good news, my dear. You just have to hold out until the change. And I know you will."

Francine blinked away a tear and nearly hugged him, remembering only at the last second the transmitter and microphone attached to her body. She course-corrected and pecked his cheek instead. "Thank you, Roland. I appreciate it."

Roland nodded and took off his foggy tortoiseshell spectacles, wiping the lenses, then the bridge in between.

CHAPTER 26

I have never been in trouble because
of my sexual behavior.
[   ] TRUE   [x] FALSE

F rancine was so numb with excitement, she practically floated home. She couldn't wait to share the news with Bruno.

Yes, the glasses polishing was a notch against her Roland-is-innocent campaign, and they hadn't gotten it on tape, but a piece of Bruno's research had worked in concert with her field observations. They'd *detected* something, and holy shit had she missed the feeling of exhilaration that registered somewhere between first kiss and second dessert.

Breezing into Ellie and Pete's kitchen, she took off the microphone and transmitter, and was about to pick up the phone when she saw a moving cloud of cigarette smoke on the cement patio out back.

"Bruno?" Francine opened the screen door and he stopped pacing, newly-bought headphones still around his neck. "Are you okay? I thought we said I should call afterward?"

He looked at her uncertainly.

"I...I didn't know you went through all that with your ex-husband."

"Oh."

"Hearing you talk about it made me...I've been trying not to feel..."

He stepped forward and kissed her.

Francine softened, melting for an instant before her rational mind yanked her out of the kiss. She slapped Bruno across the face.

He staggered a half-step, then straightened up like he'd just come out of hypnosis.

"I'm sorry," he said. "I don't know why I did that."

"You listen to me tell Roland my ex-husband cheated on me and your response is to try and do the same thing to your…whoever?"

"Francine."

"Get out of here, Bruno."

"Please—"

"Go."

Bruno hesitated a moment longer, then did what she asked.

Back inside the kitchen, Francine wore a new path into the linoleum as she tried to work off the rage boiling inside of her. There was no uncertainty about it: Bruno was *certifiably* an asshole. She could still taste his kiss as evidence. Ben had blindsided her so badly she'd thought it would've been impossible to entertain affection for someone that cruel ever again. How could she have been so stupid?

But what had just happened on the patio didn't make sense. Something about Bruno was different than everyone else, something important. He'd gotten through to her in ways no one else ever had, and maybe she'd started to reach something inside of him too. This wasn't just a crush— the two of them shared a frequency no one else was on. It was time to figure out what that meant.

Clover flattened under Francine's shoes as she passed under the willow and marched up to Bruno's front door. When he didn't answer her knock, she let herself in. "Hello?"

There was no one in the kitchen, or the dining room, or the bedroom.

Francine padded down the basement stairs and found him with his head laid on the bar, one hand around the Cutty Sark.

"Bruno?"

He straightened up in surprise, one cheek still red from her slap. "Hey. I didn't hear you come in."

Something was on his mind, something beyond what had just happened on the patio. He looked raw and vulnerable, like a hermit crab without its shell. A hermit crab making its way through a glass of scotch with frightening speed.

"I'm sorry I hit you," she said. "That was wrong."

"It's okay." Bruno took a too-big swallow of booze and coughed.

When he moved to pour more, Francine intercepted, threading the cap back on the bottle. "Why don't we talk instead?"

He wandered to the edge of the pool table and sat down, his mania settling into a thoughtful daze.

"There's something I haven't told you. I wasn't trying to lie, I just didn't know how to say it. Years ago in New York, I had a girlfriend. And she was killed."

Francine's mouth dried.

"We had a little apartment in Queens. It was pretty shitty, to be honest, but there was a nice park within walking distance and the rent wasn't too bad. We liked our shitty little apartment. One day while I was still at work, she came home from a waitressing shift and walked in on someone in our apartment, stealing our mismatched silverware. The cops said whoever was there probably hadn't come with the intent to kill her. It was just…bad timing."

He braced his hands on the pool table, chin sinking to his chest. "Everyone just moved on after a while, but I kept trying to find out what had happened, and how I could fix it. When I'm around other people, it's like they all know something I don't, or maybe I know something they don't. The things you said tonight, about your marriage. I recognized something in your voice. Like you knew the same feeling. Does that make any sense?"

Bruno's eyes met Francine's, sending an invisible knuckle raking up her spine.

"Yes," she said.

Nothing about the night had been romantic, but somehow their hearts chose this moment. The world went into soft focus, and they both leaned forward for a kiss. A tickle of desire improved Francine's posture from hips to head in a welcome sensation she'd forgotten existed. She stepped into Bruno, kissing him again as they climbed up onto the pool table together.

The next kiss was the last distinguishable as desire crested, and clothes couldn't come off fast enough. She leaned deeper into him, fingers forking through tangles of jet-black hair as the tension in her body soon found release.

CHAPTER 27

Everything tastes the same.
[   ] TRUE   [x] FALSE

They lay flat on the pool table, watching smoke from their shared cigarette pool in the billiard lamp above.

"I think maybe we should re-felt the table," Bruno said. "You know, as a courtesy for the people moving in?"

Francine tapped the cigarette ash into a highball glass. "They'll have their hands full with the teddy bear wallpaper. So. From the minute you met me?"

Bruno nodded. "I thought you were funny and, I don't know, mysterious. And when you wore that red bandana…" His voice trailed off and he grinned in embarrassment.

"What?"

"It gave you a kind of Rosie the Riveter vibe. Apparently, Allied propaganda really does it for me."

Francine laughed and flexed her bicep. "Sure, I'll take a Rosie comparison. Oh, holy shit!" She jolted up, accidentally dropping the cigarette onto Bruno.

He swatted the embers out of his chest hair. "What's wrong?"

"I forgot to tell you about Roland's glasses! He cleaned them at dinner." She mimed Roland's routine. "First lens, second lens, *bridge*."

"Holy shit," Bruno repeated their company motto. "Lischka did that."

"Yep."

"Francine. Nice work. This could really be something."

174

They both lay back down, enjoying their small victory as they silently watched the smoke swirl languidly overhead.

"You started this kind of work because of your girlfriend, didn't you?" Francine asked, after a while. "That's the thing Ida helped you through."

Bruno nodded. "I figured if I couldn't get answers for myself, maybe I could get them for other people. It'd be nice to get an answer for Ida. She deserves to know if Lischka's still walking the earth, unpunished."

"You're a great, dinged-up train, Bruno."

"A what?"

"Nothing."

She skied her fingers around his chest, playing with the thin gold necklace that dipped into the scoops of his clavicle.

"I didn't take you for the jewelry type."

"Ida made it for me. I promised to wear it as a talisman for the duration of the investigation. I wouldn't be surprised if you got something too."

"You told her about me?"

"Of course."

Francine put the cigarette out in the highball glass, and as she did so, her wedding ring clinked lightly against the edge. It might have just been the summer heat swelling her finger, but the piece of metal had begun to feel more uncomfortable and less necessary than ever before.

She looked over at Bruno, who'd started to fall asleep.

"Bruno?"

"Mmhmm?"

"Do you still think about her?"

"Ida?"

"No."

"Oh. Yes."

"Every day?"

He nodded. "She may not be mine anymore, but I'm hers. In some ways."

"Doesn't that scare you?"

"I used to worry I was getting smaller and smaller. Losing pieces of myself I'd never get back. I thought one day I might just wink right out of existence. But I didn't. I'm still here. And so are you."

Francine gently laid her head on his chest and drifted off to sleep, listening to the deeply-missed sound of another person's heartbeat.

CHAPTER 28

"*On the pool table?*" Laura Jean squirmed with excitement on a bar stool in Ellie and Pete's garage. "Thank God the previous owners hated foosball. I *knew* I liked Michael. How was it?"

"Sit still, or you're going to have a bald spot, and where we did it is not the important part." Francine's scissors flew expertly around Laura Jean's waterfall of blond, dropping snippets of hair onto the smooth concrete below. "No matter what happens, there's an expiration date."

"Summer flings are okay too."

"I don't think it's a summer fling. Not for me, anyway. I'm sure it would freak Bruno out to know I'm thinking about the future already, but it's not like we have months to court and see what's what." Francine eyed one of the ice-cubed glasses of white wine dribbling condensation onto the trunk of Pete's Volvo. She risked a quick sip.

"Hey, no fair! I'm trapped under this cape of sobriety."

"All right, settle down." Francine lifted the other glass to Laura Jean's lips. "There's something about him that I never had with Ben, even at our best. Bruno's just…I get him, and weirdly enough I think he gets me. It's a fit."

"Why don't you guys stay in Hawthorn Woods? I could get used to the free haircuts."

"He has to go back to New York to prep for the school year, and I have to go back to California."

"Okay, but it sounds like San Francisco is scorched earth for you. Women have hair on the East Coast too."

"You think I should go to New York with him?"

"I don't know how much it matters who goes where. All I'm saying is if the two of you are vat-dipped in affection, which you clearly are, it might be worth considering. You don't need anyone's permission. Except mine. Which I freely give."

Laura Jean poked a wrist out and checked her watch.

"Ooh boy, I gotta get going. Candy for the parade is getting delivered to the barn in half an hour. I might have to ready a fire hose in case any kids get wind of the delivery."

Francine laughed. "Two seconds. You're almost done." She did a final pass with her scissors and handed Laura Jean a mirror. "What do you think, Parade Marshal?"

"With a cut this good I think I could run the Macy's Thanksgiving Day gig. I love it, thank you." She kissed Francine on the cheek and started home with the empty wine glasses. "Give the relocation idea a think or two. And I want to hear about any more billiards sessions!"

Francine laughed and waved goodbye.

The idea definitely was worth a think or two. There was little keeping her in San Francisco, other than the inertia of already living there. What if she and Bruno stayed in Hawthorn Woods, or tried New York together?

She brushed off the stool and carried it toward the back corner of the garage, failing to notice what was hiding there until she was practically on top of it.

She dropped the stool and screamed.

$$* \quad * \quad * \quad *$$

Francine stumbled out of the garage, trying to catch her breath, and nearly ran into Eric Banderwalt, who had raced up the driveway.

"I heard you scream," he said.

"There's an animal." Francine pointed to the corner of the garage.

"Oh. Want me to get it out for you?"

"Yeah, sure. Please, I mean." She grabbed a pair of yellow work gloves and handed them to Eric. "Don't get rabies or anything."

He unslung his BB gun from one shoulder and leaned it against Pete's Volvo. With casual confidence, he pushed a cardboard box out of the corner. "It's just a chipmunk. They're easy."

The chipmunk chattered wildly as Eric closed in with the gloves.

"It sounds pissed," Francine worried.

"That's just 'cause he's cornered. Cornered things get scared." He snatched the animal up, and it immediately sank its tiny teeth into the rough work glove. "Then they get mean."

He walked to the edge of the garage, hesitated, then set the chipmunk onto the lawn. The frightened animal sped across the grass and disappeared under a clump of bushes.

"Thank you," Francine said.

This could be a golden opportunity to wring some information out of your cagiest suspect, the detective part of her mind piped. *It could also just be a chance to show kindness to a wayward kid,* a better part added.

Francine decided to split the difference. "You want something to drink?"

"Yeah. Do you have Old Style?"

"Nice try." She grabbed two cans of root beer out of the small garage fridge and sat on the Volvo's bumper.

Eric took a sip of his root beer, then turned the tab on top, halving the opening.

"Why do you do that?"

"Bees like the sugar," he said. "Got one in my mouth once. It wasn't fun."

An awkward pause lengthened. Francine examined the BB rifle propped up against the bumper, and was surprised to see the shoulder stock covered in drawings of flowers and butterflies.

"My sister," Eric explained.

He leaned against the rail of the garage door. His long, bony frame looked like the product of a recent growth spurt, one that had left him a kid at the controls of something bigger than himself. He produced his lime green pocket knife and began to flick it open and closed.

Francine tried not to think of the tree trunk she'd last seen him use the blade on to great effect. "Your dirt bike's the same green, right? Is that your favorite color?"

He smiled like she'd told a joke.

"What?" she asked.

"Nobody's ever asked me that before." He snapped the knife shut. "Yeah, it's my favorite color."

"Yellow's mine. But it has to be, like, the right yellow, you know? I'm talking sunshine or lemon, none of that mustard bullshit."

Eric couldn't hide a grin. "Maybe you're not as bad as Mrs. Asperski after all."

"Jesus, I hope not. I bet I'm as scared of her as you are."

"I'm not scared of her," Eric said forcefully, snapping the knife open. "Her husband probably is, though. She gave him a hell of a shiner."

"Dennis?"

Eric nodded. "Black eye for sure. Must've pissed her off. Not that they always need a reason."

The subtext on his face was obvious to Francine. "Your dad was a piece of work, wasn't he?"

"He's a piece of shit." Eric said reflexively, his voice unsteady. He stared down at his sneakers, looking embarrassed at having shown so much emotion. "He wants to take my sister."

"Eric, if something's wrong at home, we can talk to the Chief—"

"No," he said. "That always just makes things worse."

Francine searched for the right words. "I was lucky with my dad. But I've definitely known my share of bad people. It's never easy."

His eyes, looking much too old for someone his age, found hers for the first time. "Is it always this bad?"

This was a situation where you lied to the kid. All parts of Francine's brain knew that. But she couldn't do it.

"You can't always go around the bad parts. Sometimes you just have to go straight through."

Her words sounded so trivial and weak. She tried again.

"But if you go through enough of them, you learn to weather the others better. It's like the one superpower of being an adult."

They watched the breeze carry gold hyphens of hair down to the street where a few boys rode their bikes under a plum dusk sky. They were a bit younger than Eric, but Francine got the feeling he would never have fit in anyway. How could they understand his life? How could she?

"I, uh," he began. "I didn't mean to scare you off that one night. You just surprised me, is all. I wasn't mad or anything."

"When Lori yelled at Diana? I think you had every right to be mad."

"No, I mean before that."

The line of boys on bikes suddenly divided in half, as they moved out of the way of a pale blue pickup that sped down the road.

"That's my dad," Eric said, half in disbelief. Then he grabbed his BB gun and took off across the lawn.

"I can help!" Francine called out.

"No!" Eric yelled back. "You'll make it worse."

Watching him go, she buzzed with anxiety and helplessness. How could she stay out of it? But he had been adamant. Pleading, almost. She tossed the cans of root beer in the trash and went inside, where Charlie was waiting for her.

"Was that Eric Banderwalt?" he asked, sounding mildly horrified.

"You should be getting into your pajamas, Bubba."

"Geez, do you play checkers with Darth Vader too? Why were you talking to Eric?"

"He's not such a bad kid. I don't want you giving him or his sister a hard time." Francine went into the kitchen and picked up the phone. Charlie followed her.

"Me give *him* a hard time? He's the scary one. And I'm friends with Diana. I even gave her some of our batteries for her toy."

"That's great. Pajamas. Pronto."

"9-1-1 emergency," the dispatcher on the phone said, with a voice that sounded oddly familiar.

"This is Francine Haddix. I'm staying at my sister's place on Lynn Drive."

"Hello, Francine." The tone was arsenic with a saccharine glaze.

Francine sighed. "Hi, Lori. Um, I was just talking to Eric Banderwalt, and his dad drove by. Going pretty fast."

"Yes?" Lori said, with far less urgency than Francine would have liked.

"I thought I should give a heads up. Eric seemed pretty upset."

"He did, did he?" Lori's response still had all the urgency of a sloth on Quaaludes.

"Can you please just tell Chief Durham that Mr. Banderwalt is in the neighborhood, Lori? I'm pretty sure he's not supposed to be at that house. Right?"

"Hollis is already in the area. I'm sure he'll see any disturbance. I'm head of the neighborhood watch, by the way. If you're interested in re-porting a crime, you can join and I'll be happy to relay any concerns."

"That's what I'm doing right now."

"Yes, but it would be through a more proper channel if you're in the watch."

"Great, thanks, Lori." Francine slammed the phone down, then called up the stairs. "Charlie? I gotta go out for a sec. Brush your teeth and I'll tell you a bedtime story when I get back, okay?"

"'Kay."

She banged out the back door for a casual walk n' smoke across the block. If she just so happened to find trouble on the other side, she'd find it by pure coincidence, and nobody could say boo.

CHAPTER 29

People have often misunderstood my intentions
when I was trying to be helpful.
[x] TRUE   [   ] FALSE

Cigarette puffing like a locomotive stack, Francine power-walked under the willow, slowing her pace only when she saw Chief Durham's brown and white cruiser parked alongside the pickup in the Banderwalts' driveway.

Eric stood at the top of the concrete ramp that led to the front door, his arms outstretched across the teal railings to shield his mother behind him. On the lawn before them, a bald, red-faced man paced the grass. Chief Durham stood between him and the house, his hands up, appealing for calm.

"Mr. Banderwalt, let's just relax," he said.

"I can't visit my own family? I can't see my children?"

Mr. Banderwalt bristled with muscles that looked to have accumulated in slow, patient layers, perhaps over a lifetime of manual labor. To Francine, his brawn looked much more lethal than the Chief's, which although impressive, had clearly been earned in a gym.

The bald man neared the ramp and poked his son in the chest. "Who called the cops? Was it you, Eric?"

Chief Durham stepped between them. "There's no need for that. Nobody called me, I was driving by and—"

"I called," Francine shouted, wanting to take some of the pressure away from Eric. Her adrenaline was fully running the show as she strode across the lawn.

"Who the hell are you?" Mr. Banderwalt shouted, stepping towards Francine.

But Chief Durham moved quicker, twisting one of the man's hands behind his back and holding it there.

"Mr. Banderwalt, I asked you to calm down. You're not welcome on this property. I'd like you to get back in your truck and go home. If you wish to speak to your wife, you can do so over the phone."

Mr. Banderwalt tried to yank out of Chief Durham's grip, without success. Then he gave Francine a quick sneer, as if he were marking her.

"Okay. I'll go." He relaxed, and Chief Durham let him out of the hold. He pointed a finger at Eric and Mrs. Banderwalt as he walked away. "Next time, your nosy neighbor bitch and dandy-haired cop won't be here to interfere."

He slammed the door of his truck and roared out of the driveway, headlights knifing erratically around the end of the block as he sped off.

"Where's your daughter?" Chief Durham asked Mrs. Banderwalt.

"My daughter?" Mrs. Banderwalt said, with a note of confusion. "I-I don't know."

Eric looked at her with panic. "I thought she was in her room."

"She ran out when she heard the truck."

"Is that her?" Francine pointed to the side of the house, where one of the window-well covers radiated a pale, yellow-orange light.

Eric rushed over and pulled off the cover. His body visibly relaxed as he knelt down and carefully lifted his sister and her glowing stuffed animal out of the well.

"That's a good spot," he said to her.

Diana looked bashfully at Francine. "Somebody told me about it."

"Come inside, baby," Mrs. Banderwalt said. Diana gave one last glance at Francine, then ran to her mother.

Chief Durham pulled a card from the breast pocket of his uniform and handed it to Eric. "He comes back, you call 9-1-1 right away. This also has my pager and home number in case you have any trouble getting through. All right?"

Eric nodded.

The Chief clapped him reassuringly on the shoulder, then turned to Francine. "Ms. Haddix, I'll bring you home."

They got into the squad car and rode in silence for a moment before Chief Durham spoke.

"Did you really call it in?"

Francine nodded. "How long has Lori been a dispatcher?"

"When we didn't arrest anyone for Brownie, she decided the police force could use her talents, and since we were a little understaffed anyway, it seemed like the least disruptive option. She's been running in extra-high gear ever since she lost the Fourth of July parade job. It's a pretty big deal around here."

"So I've heard. Well, in any case, thanks for grabbing Mr. Banderwalt. I'm glad you keep your gym memberships longer than I do."

"Not a big deal, working out comes naturally to me. I can thank my father for that."

"Was he a fitness nut?"

"He had some strong beliefs on what it meant to be a man. I couldn't measure up in every category, but weightlifting was something I could always do. Now I'm a certified gym rat."

"Is that where you met Magdalena?" Francine fished.

Chief Durham gave her a sidelong glance. "No doubt you've heard other theories. Perhaps involving the words 'mail' and 'order?'"

"People say things," Francine said noncommittally. "I'm not trying to be nosy, I'm just a sucker for how-we-met's."

"Maggie comes from a tough area in Russia where there isn't much in terms of future prospects. Her brother came to Indiana a few years ago for work, and he met and married my sister. When I heard about Maggie and her situation, I thought she might fit into mine. Win for everyone."

"That's amazing," Francine said, though it wasn't the most romantic story she'd ever heard. "I have to admit, I'm still trying to figure out how I could've made her so mad that first night."

"Oh, you haven't seen her mad. Trust me on that. I'd take on Mr. Banderwalt with one hand tied behind my back before I'd tussle with her. She's tougher than anyone I've ever met."

"I haven't seen her around much lately."

"She's been staying inside a bit, with all the strange things happening."

They pulled into Ellie and Pete's driveway.

"Staying inside might be a good course of action for everyone," the Chief said. "You included."

"What do you mean?"

He threw the cruiser in park. "When you came into my office, I may have encouraged your interest in looking into things around here. But now I'd like you to stop."

"Why?"

"You saw how upset Mr. Banderwalt got? It's always like that. When people get involved in things that don't concern them, fingers start getting pointed, and everyone gets riled up."

"Those kids are terrified of their father, and their mother won't or can't do anything about it. I don't think it should fall to a teenager to fix things. It should be on the police. On you."

"Do you have something to say about how I do my job?"

Francine sighed. "I didn't mean it like that. It's just…sometimes when things get left alone, they get worse."

"Until I have evidence of Mr. Banderwalt breaking the law, he has the same rights you do. Lori wanted me to lock you up the night her goat died. Had her little followers calling in, one after another. 'She seems suspicious.' 'She came from somewhere else.' On and on. I told them the same thing I'm telling you now. I can't arrest people for no reason, not without cause or proof. Sometimes in law enforcement we have to wait for something bad to happen before we can act."

"That's reassuring."

"That's the law, Ms. Haddix. You're on your way home soon, and until that time, I advise you to stay uninvolved in local affairs. That way you can enjoy your vacation and stay safe. Sometimes things just work themselves out on their own."

Francine got out of the cruiser. "And sometimes an innocent animal gets its throat cut instead. Thanks for the ride, Hollis."

CHAPTER 30

The future is too uncertain for a
person to make serious plans.
[x] TRUE   [   ] FALSE

F rancine and Bruno weren't quite finishing each other's sentences,
but they continued what they'd started, dancing to classical music,
playing more games of 'billiards,' and delving more deeply into
one another's lives. Heart strings were definitely intertwining, which for
Francine was simultaneously thrilling and terrifying.

She had visited Roland two more times, always in a flowy blouse of
Ellie's to conceal the microphone and transmitter. A transmitter with
which she'd recorded no contradictions, no inconsistencies, not so much
as a single stutter.

And suddenly it was July second. The runway for interrogating Roland, and for whatever was going on between her and Bruno, was short.

She walked through the agency's front door, ready to dive into their
usual pre-Roland meeting prep, and found Bruno waiting with a duffel
bag and a big smile. "Hi."

"Well, hello. What's in the duffel bag?"

"Ah, but this is no duffel bag. It's a picnic basket. I thought we could
have a quick dinner before you go. To Roland's, I mean."

They walked to the front of the neighborhood, and Bruno laid out the
teddy bear tablecloth next to what Charlie had called Haunted Pond. He
showily presented Francine with a mini bouquet of mature dandelions,

their fluffy white seed heads shivering in the breeze. Both of them blew into the flowers at the same time, filling the air with a swirl of seeds.

"Good to see we have the same maturity level," Francine said, laughing.

Bruno began pulling things from the duffel bag, starting with two cans of 50/50. "*Voilà.* Soda, since we need you good and sober for your date tonight. Um, a pack of cigarettes, I thought these might be good for the mosquitos. Don't worry, they're your brand. Oh, and while I think your burgundy nails are great, I remember you had yellow ones when I first met you. I don't know if this is the exact same shade, but it think it's close. Sunshine Yellow, it's called. Ah! Finally, the *pièce de résistance.* Olive-shaped pancakes. I know you hate olives, but totally giving up on a food limits your world view, so I thought maybe if I made your favorite food in the shape of your least favorite, it could be a baby step forward."

When Francine didn't have an immediate, witty response, Bruno looked self-consciously down at the spread.

"I know it's not the fanciest picnic. And I might have used too many eggs in the pancake batter. I just thought it might be fun—"

"It's perfect." She leaned forward and kissed him, fighting back tears. "I love it, thank you, Bruno."

It was the sweetest thing someone had done for her in ages, and for the first time she was touched in a way that didn't relate to something Ben had or hadn't done. It was just Bruno.

She opened the pops, swiveled the tabs, and handed one over. They talked over cigarettes and pancakes while a late afternoon breeze stirred the cattails in the pond. Bruno told her about his first day as a teacher, when he'd been so nervous he mixed up Austria and Australia. Francine recounted the depths of her elementary school gym class, like the plastic hockey sticks that had bruised the hell out of her shins and the nightmare of square dancing with pre-pubescent boys. It was nice to just talk like normal people, the topics naturally disorganized and wandering.

"Okay, but there were gym class heights too," she said, biting into a pancake olive. "Like the Presidential Fitness Test."

"I don't think we had that."

"It was great, you got tested on the v-sit and pull-ups and running a mile, I think. But the best part was the rope climb. We got a little paper monkey by our name every time we reached the top. I'm a natural-born climber, so I always had a troop of monkeys."

"We're all good at something."

He took an extra long drag on a cigarette and watched the water bugs that dented the surface of Haunted Pond.

"So listen," he said. "I don't want to freak you out. But I've been thinking a little about…what's next."

"With Roland?"

"With us."

"Oh." The conversation that Francine had been both dreading and looking forward to. One thing was for certain, she definitely didn't want to go first. "What'd you have in mind?"

"Well, I know it's fast, but I was thinking…What if one of us moved? I mean, you could probably find a salon in New York, or I could find a school in San Francisco. Not that it would be easy either way. I just thought we should talk about it, since our time's almost up here."

Laura Jean had suggested it, and Francine had definitely thought about it, but now that the option was actually being discussed, she panicked. It was almost like whatever answer she gave would be the wrong one, and she'd ruin this fragile new thing in her life. She took the cigarette from Bruno.

"I've been thinking about it too. I just…I don't know if I trust myself enough to make a decision like that quite yet. And I don't know if I could justify asking you to move three thousand miles on a 'maybe.'"

"A maybe is the only way anyone ever can justify moving three thousand miles. There are no guarantees on the big stuff."

He smiled, and for a brief second the future seemed a little less scary.

"Excuse me!"

A minivan had pulled over on the side of the road. Leaning out the driver's side window was Lori Asperski. "I'm sorry, but you need a permit to eat by the ponds."

Francine thought she was joking. "Right. Thanks, Lori."

"I'm afraid I'm serious. As a member of the law enforcement community and the neighborhood watch, I can't ignore a violation like this."

Francine stood up. "Is it kind of like that rule that you can't keep farm animals in your yard?"

Lori put the van in park. "You know, when I go somewhere new, I cop to that place's way of doing things. If I went to Mexico, I'd try to speak Mexican. Understand?"

"We speak English," Bruno said.

"When my Brownie passed away, I think you two should've made it clear you had nothing to do with it."

"We didn't have anything to do with it," Francine said.

"I'm saying, you should have made that extremely clear!" Lori's voice wavered with anger before she hogtied it back into condescension. "I think I've been more than polite these last few weeks, but I have to say I'm looking forward to your departure. The both of you. I'm sure all these little oddities will stop after you leave, and everything will go back to normal." She glanced up at some gathering rain clouds. "Hmm. Looks like your illegal picnic is about to get rained out anyway. I'd give you a lift back, but I'm late for duty. Don't forget your garbage."

She shifted back into drive and puttered off toward the barn.

"Good God, I hate that woman," Francine muttered.

"Lori works at the police station?"

"As a dispatcher. Next thing you know, she'll have a star on her chest. Hey, that could be something."

"What?"

"Chief Durham's badge. It's a six-pointed star. What if the triangle on Brownie was a half-finished star?"

"Best triangle theory so far." Bruno looked up at the darkening sky. "Maybe we should discuss it on the go. We still have to get you wired."

They packed up the picnic in silence, neither wanting to finish the conversation about what came next.

CHAPTER 31

In everything I do lately, I feel
that I am being tested.
[x] TRUE   [   ] FALSE

Ellie's wardrobe came through as usual, this time with a light cardigan embossed with a wonderfully obscuring polar bear. Francine brushed mac and cheese dust from Charlie's dinner off the arctic predator's nose as she left for Roland's house.

The growing number of undercover meetings she'd had with Roland had given her an added confidence in her work. And since they'd found absolutely zero evidence that indicated Roland was anyone other than who he claimed to be, aside from the lone spike of the glasses polish, she was basically preparing for a relaxing evening with a friend.

Her confidence was doused by the light rain that began to fall when she was halfway to Roland's. Despite running the rest of the way, she was partially soaked by the time she cleared the line of spruce trees and rushed into the screened porch.

"My goodness!" Roland said. "I have towels and clothing if you wish to change."

"No, no. I'm fine. It's actually kind of refreshing." Francine used a few napkins to dab off the rain and plopped down onto her loveseat, admiring the usual refreshments on the coffee table. Tonight the tea and cookies were accompanied by a large bottle of green liquid. "What do we have here?"

"Absinthe. As our time together nears a close, I thought we could risk hangovers one last time."

"I don't think I've ever had absinthe."

"It is not entirely legal in this country. I am trusting you not to notify the police." He winked. "Perhaps your silence can be bought with cookies. I hope chocolate chip will suffice."

"Chocolate chip will always suffice. You can put that on my headstone." Francine downed a cookie, still hungry from the interrupted picnic.

Roland poured some absinthe. "You may drink it plain if you wish, but I myself prefer the sweeter approach to life."

He placed a sugar cube on a slotted spoon above the glass of absinthe, then poured water over the spoon, dissolving the sugar into the alcohol below.

Francine followed his example and they drank together.

"Good, yes?" Roland asked.

"Tastes like those cookies." Francine coughed. "Asinine? Arsenic?"

Roland chuckled. "Aniskrabeli."

"But somehow the liquor burn makes it tolerable." Francine smacked her lips. "I like it."

Roland clapped his hands. "*Wunderbar!*"

The intermittent drizzle outside had dropped the temperature and brought a wonderfully fresh breeze. Rain-riled mosquitoes bumped against the porch's screen walls while Ajax nibbled at some cookie crumbs around Francine's shoes.

Roland gently shooed the dog away. "He's quite taken with you."

"I suspect it may be cookie crumb-related, but I'll take it."

"Nonsense, you're his favorite guest."

Denied his crumbs, Ajax grunted in frustration and lay down in the corner next to an empty six-pack of beer bottles. The trash struck Francine as strange, since Roland didn't drink beer.

She took another sip of her absinthe. "Do they drink this stuff back in Switzerland?"

"Often. Or rather, we used to. I am not current on European trends."

"You really don't look back, do you? I'm jealous."

Roland took a bite of cookie. "When I found a new beginning here, there was no need to return, in person or in thought. The whole continent had been scourged by war. When what is done is done, reflection has value, but only to a point."

"Hey, you're getting started early tonight. And nice try, but love and war are vastly different things, despite the 'all's fair' bullshit."

"Life's truest wisdoms are often the most common, applicable to maladies of every scale."

"Roland, as much as I hated my divorce, it didn't kill millions of people."

"You have felt tremendous pain. Why should another's suffering disqualify your own?"

Francine drew in a sudden breath as a quick pain, much more present than the kind they were discussing, spiked into her back.

The transmitter. It must have gotten wet and shorted out. Another mild shock made her jump.

"Are you all right?" Roland asked.

"Oh, sure. Can I use your restroom?"

"Too much too fast," he chided jokingly.

She nodded and walked quickly through the double doors.

"Down the hallway, last door on the left," he called after her.

"Left?" She feigned looking for the bathroom. "Ah, got it."

Another small bite of electricity found her lower back as she shut the door. She ripped the transmitter off and pulled the microphone out from under the cardigan.

"Bruno, if you can still hear me, I'm fine," she whispered into the mic. "The transmitter's screwed up from the rain. I'm going to dump it, but everything's okay."

She shoved open the bathroom's tiny window and peeked outside. The uncovered window well below was a soup of leaves and rainwater. Francine dangled the mic and transmitter out the window and dropped them, watching with relief as they sank into the leafy sludge below.

She ran the faucet on high for appearances and strolled back to the porch.

"Now then, where were we?" She dropped onto her seat, feeling oddly more relaxed without the wire, even though she no longer had her mop-haired guardian angel listening in.

Roland held up refilled glasses.

"I need to pace myself," Francine said.

"Nonsense. You'll ruin my plan."

"What's…your plan?"

"To remove inhibition so as to better access the truth."

✶   ✶   ✶   ✶

He meant inhibition about discussing her divorce. Didn't he? "I'm loathe to admit it," Roland said, "but as I said before, our time together grows short. What would you say to some accelerated therapy techniques?"

"What would these techniques entail?"

197

"I ask you a question, and you give me your first reaction. Not your first thought, you understand, just your reaction. Understood?"

Well, this couldn't possibly be super fucking dangerous. But before she could think of a reasonable excuse, the test had begun.

"When did the trouble begin in your relationship?"

"Well, I mean, it was probably all there from the beginning. I thought we were compatible at first, but less so later on."

"That was a thoughtful response. React, Francine. Did you love your husband?"

"Yes."

"Did he love you?"

"I…Yes."

"Did he love you?"

"I don't know. I think so."

"When did he stop?"

"How could I know that?"

"When did he stop?"

"When I had a breakdown."

Roland leaned back in his seat. "Would you like to talk about that?"

"I might have to think a little to do it. Is that allowed?"

He nodded.

Francine took a drink. She wouldn't have told Laura Jean about the breakdown. Even Ellie knew only bits and pieces. She definitely wasn't ready to tell Bruno yet, and for once, he wouldn't overhear it by accident. This was one of her last opportunities to get Roland's sharp perspective on her problems.

"I get confused every once in a while. Like, I was really into Nancy Drew as a kid. She's the teenager that solves mysteries, you know? Eventually she became my imaginary friend, and probably hung around a little longer than she should have. I didn't actually think I was Nancy Drew, but I'd sometimes introduce myself as 'Nancy' for fun at parties, or her words would bleed into mine. That kind of stuff. Never anything too exciting, just a mild episode here and there. When I was married to Ben, if I got really stressed out, I'd briefly have trouble understanding what was real and what wasn't."

The rarely voiced words sounded heavy and clumsy coming out of her mouth, but Roland remained patiently silent.

"I was gonna get help, but Ben didn't want me to. He said it would look bad for both of us. That sounds horrendous hearing it now, but at the time he made it seem reasonable. He was good at that. I was embarrassed, so I tried to keep everything together on my own. When I found out Ben was cheating, I tried everything I could think of to fix the situation. I kicked him out, took him back, begged him to stop. Nothing worked. And when he wouldn't change, something inside me that I'd been holding together came loose. I became someone else for a night, someone with a different name and a different life. Someone without a husband who couldn't stop lying and cheating. I went out to a bar, found a guy, and slept with him. I was someone else while I did it, but I did it."

"You were not responsible," Roland objected. "It was an episode—"

"No. I'm telling you all this to explain how I felt, not to use it as an excuse. Someone else was at the wheel that night, but I kinda let them drive, you know? I was unfaithful to the marriage just like Ben was."

"And he knew something had occurred?"

"Yes."

"Because you told him."

"I couldn't lie like he could."

Roland shook his head. "It was a single offense versus an instigating action performed countless times."

"I don't think Ben liked the single offense, but when I told him *how* it had happened, the distance I'd felt from myself, he didn't want to deal with that. He liked me better when I was an easy read."

The absinthe was packing the wrinkles in Francine's overclocked brain with warm licorice lint, fresh out of the dryer. She was putty.

"I want you to listen to me closely," Roland said. "You were mistaken in your choice of partner, and you believe that choice took a part of you away without permission. That isn't true. As you were then, so you are today. Whole, and deserving of love."

"Thank you, Roland."

Francine's mind made itself up all on its own. The man before her was not Oskar Lischka. In the relief that ensued from this knowledge, she relaxed, and they drank, adding more sugar to their drinks to match the sweeter conversation.

Francine brought up less dramatic memories of San Francisco, like the Embarcadero movie house that showed bad King Kong sequels. She always loved to watch monsters fight monsters.

More sugar. More water. More absinthe.

Roland talked about Ajax being too kind for his own good. The husky who wouldn't hurt a fly, let alone a squirrel, which there were definitely less and less of around the neighborhood these days.

Sugar, water, absinthe.

Francine said August was a tacky month to get married, let alone re-married. Roland agreed.

Sugarwaterabsinthe.

Roland said Hawthorn Woods was a special place, even if it occasionally suffered misfortunes like Magdalena Durham. Francine agreed wholeheartedly.

Soon—or had it been a while?—the bottle was empty, and Ajax was nudging impatiently at the back door.

Roland clapped his hands. "Our canine compatriot is either weary of our ramblings, or desperately needs to relieve himself."

The three of them went out into the backyard. Ajax sniffed around the grass, then cocked his head at a high, whining sound: Eric Banderwalt's dirt bike, screaming through some other part of the neighborhood.

"Menace," Roland grumbled.

"That's what I used to think," Francine said.

"It is not so?"

"I dunno for sure, but his father is not a nice man."

"I couldn't wait to get away from my father. Perhaps this boy has a fantasy of escaping on his bike, though I wish that fantasy were just a bit quieter. Ajax is drawn to engine noises. I worry about him running into the street."

The husky inadvertently startled a pair of brown rabbits feeding on the grass near a slab of stone leaned against a tree trunk.

Looking closer, Francine saw it was an unused tombstone. With some drunken difficulty, she read the poem etched across its face. "'Warm summer sun, shine kindly here. Warm southern wind, blow softly here. Green sod above, lie light, lie light. Good night, dear heart, good night, good night.' That's beautiful."

"I found it in a book of poetry and thought it fitting for my grave marker. It narrowly won out over 'Chocolate chip will always suffice.'"

"Oh, shut up." Francine smirked. "Kinda morbid to have your own tombstone waiting in the backyard, isn't it?"

"At my age, it is a mere practicality. I have no next of kin, and rest a touch easier knowing the words I'll lie forever below are as sublime as these. Death for me now is less about the when, and more the how and where. There's a small graveyard deeper in the neighborhood where I have a plot reserved. I think Hawthorn Woods will make a fine point of departure."

"You deserve a fine point of departure," Francine said, seeing Roland as a child of abuse who'd forged a better life halfway across the globe, and aspired only to have kind words on his grave.

The single headlight of Eric's dirt bike knifed down the street. Ajax darted through the spruce trees, running toward the engine noise.

"Ajax!" Roland called, but the dog was already in the street.

Just as husky and bike were about to meet, Eric steered expertly around the dog and skidded to a halt on the side of the road, where he killed the earsplitting engine.

With surprising speed, Roland was in Eric's face, poking him so hard in the chest he knocked him off the bike. "What's in your head, boy, driving so fast? You nearly hit my dog!"

"I didn't know he was gonna run into the street," Eric said, getting to his feet.

"You shouldn't be driving so fast!"

Eric's eyes went to Francine. Did he expect her to say something? To stick up for him?

"Eric, that's too fast for around here," she said. "You could've hurt someone."

He looked at her a moment longer, then picked up his bike and spit on the road. "Maybe try leashing your dog next time. He's no good as roadkill." He drove his foot down on the kickstart and cranked one handle, kicking up a spray of gravel as he took off.

They watched him speed away through a thin cloud of exhaust.

"And just like that, he's my number one all over again." Francine slurred.

"Number one?" Roland asked.

"For Brownie. I'm going to find out who killed her, no matter what. Eric and his little green knife seem to fit quite nicely."

Roland's gaze remained on the bike's diminishing tail light as he patted Ajax's head. "A sound bet, indeed."

CHAPTER 32

At times I have enjoyed being
hurt by someone I loved.
[   ] TRUE   [x] FALSE

Francine stumbled home to find Bruno sitting on the back of Pete's Volvo.

"Hey!" he greeted her in a hushed voice. "Everything okay?"

"Yeah," she said, much more loudly, still riding the wave of absinthe. "I mean, I'm a little disappointed you didn't kick Roland's door down when the mic went out, but that's okay."

"I thought about it. I tried to come over to keep an eye on things but I got stopped by Chief Durham. By the time I got to Gerber's, you guys were outside and I didn't want to be seen. So I came here to wait."

"What did the Chief stop you for?"

"Curfew," Bruno said, after a pause.

"You're a shit liar, Bruno. C'mon, what was it?"

"He...um, well, he hit on me."

"What do you mean?"

"As in, he prefers men to women."

"*What?* No shit?"

"I think he might have mistaken my intense interest in the flag the other day as interest in him."

"Oh my God. That's it!"

"What?"

"That's Magdalena's problem with me! I mean, if the Chief is gay, it's probably not nightly fireworks in their bedroom. Then I roll into town, and yeah, I didn't wear a bra once or twice, and I talked to her husband once or twice, though technically one time was an interrogation, and boom, she's threatened. Bruno, I don't think she knows. He's gaslighting her. Guys. Always with the fucking gaslighting."

Bruno grinned at her. "You're feeling no pain right now, aren't you?"

"I'm not not drunk, I'll say that much."

"Oh, listen to this. I heard back from the translator about your newspaper clipping. The article is from an Oktoberfest in Chicago a couple years ago. Gerber went for fun, and just happened to get interviewed. Man on the street kind of thing. As you and I talked about, people in Switzerland speak Swiss-German, which has lingual variations from Standard German. The translator said Gerber's responses were a weird mix of both, leaning more towards Standard German. I think he might've had a drink or two and gotten a little careless."

Francine's enthusiasm dissipated. She wasn't looking forward to telling Bruno her settled opinion on Roland.

"It may not be a nail in the coffin," Bruno said, "but definitely another vote in the guilty column. Not that we need too many more."

"What do you mean?"

Bruno looked at her quizzically. "I think we have enough already."

"Bruno." Francine joined him on the trunk of the car. "What if we're wrong?"

"We're not wrong. That's why we've been building our evidence."

"But we haven't really built that much."

"Sure we have. All of Lischka's suspected travels and known locations line up neatly with Gerber's history. We have the whole thing with the flag on Garage Sale Day. I mean, I know it wasn't him directly, but he's got to be connected somehow. He matches the description from Ida's story, and he has nothing to verify his life in Switzerland that couldn't have been bought at a gift shop. And now this article you swiped shows him speaking Standard German."

"Okay, but what if he lived on the border or something? I mean, all our evidence is circumstantial."

"What about the way he wiped his glasses?"

"Definitely strange. I'll give you that. But is it enough?"

Bruno stood up from the bumper. "We might not have a fire, but there's plenty of smoke. He's hidden any direct links so far, but he can't obscure everything forever. That's why we report him to the proper authorities and start the downfall."

"But it's never been some shaky story. He's said it all so easily. Everything, since the moment I met him."

"I admit he's good at it—"

"Or maybe it's just *him*, Bruno. You looked into his past. I've talked to him face to face. When will it be enough?"

Bruno looked confused, then a little annoyed.

"The guy has been telling the same lie for almost fifty years. Rehearse a speech for that long and see how many mistakes you make. Nothing about who he 'is' will sound improvised, because it isn't. He's lived in the Roland Gerber costume for so long it's hard to see the seams, but it's still a costume."

Francine didn't like how judgmental Bruno was starting to sound, so she raised her voice to meet his. "Even if Lischka went to Argentina, who's to say his body wasn't the one in the fire? And even if he escaped Argentina, who's to say he ended up here?"

"I showed you my work—"

"I know. Nothing disqualifies Roland from being Lischka, but nothing confirms it either. These guys always hold on to something, right? That's what you said." She held up empty hands. "So where's that something?"

Bruno shook his head. "You make it sound like I'm trying to rough up an innocent senior citizen for the fun of it. Some of these old Nazis are white-haired and brain dead, drooling as they're loaded onto an extradition flight, facing charges of war crimes from a decade they hardly remember. That's not Lischka."

"Don't call him Lischka."

"Fine. *Gerber's* as sharp as ever. He's an expert liar who's been successfully hiding from international law enforcement for half a century. You don't think he can resist the great penetrating eye of a history teacher and a hairdresser on vacation?"

"Hey!" Francine jumped to her feet. "It's not easy to do what I've been doing! I'm one-on-one with him, okay? It's hard enough to do that without having to defend myself to you. We're supposed to be on the same side."

"We are on the same side. Look, I know he's chock full of bite-size advice and has an incredibly sympathetic ear to anything you want to talk about, like saying how much of a dirtbag your ex-husband is and—"

"My ex-husband *is* a dirtbag."

Her words echoed in the garage as the gutters rhythmically dripped rain onto the driveway.

"Maybe we should go inside, have a glass of water," Bruno said.

"I told you I don't want Charlie mixed up in this."

"I thought you said Gerber was innocent."

"Maybe I don't want to confuse the kid with an Uncle Mike a few days before Uncle Mike goes back to New York."

"Is that what this is about?"

"*No*. But it doesn't fucking help."

"I said I'd go with you to San Francisco."

She didn't have a good answer to that.

Bruno's voice became forcibly measured. "Look, Gerber tells you what you want to hear, things that just so happen to support his own outlook on life. Forgiveness is power. Leave the past behind where it belongs. Who might want to push that kind of narrative?"

"Well, it's true, isn't it? The past should be left behind."

"Yes. When it comes to divorce. Not genocide." Bruno held his hands up in exasperation. "I'm glad this investigation is helping you be less sad about your ex, but to me and Ida and a lot of other people, it means a lot more than that."

"You're saying I can't care because of my past? You started all of this to get over something too. Don't act like you don't want him to be guilty as much as I want him to be innocent."

"We have to be impartial. If we're not objective—"

"How the fuck are you objective, Bruno? Only one case solved, and now the one most important to you has stalled. I wonder if that could possibly push you toward considering him guilty? Even if Roland is Lischka, it won't bring your girlfriend justice. Having a murdered girlfriend doesn't—"

She stopped herself.

"Oh God, I'm sorry."

"Finish it," he said.

"Bruno."

"Finish it."

Francine couldn't look him in the eyes.

"I just mean…our own life experiences don't have anything to do with whether Roland is guilty or not. It's easy for both of us to forget that sometimes. But if we're wrong, we'll destroy what's left of an innocent man's life."

Bruno stared at her. Was he going to cry? Hit her?

"Maybe you've watched too many Saturday morning cartoons and adventure movies where we laugh at the Nazis and rest easy, knowing they'll be outfoxed by the time the credits roll." His words were slow and careful. "But there's a reality most people seem to have forgotten. This was a very specific ideology that perpetrated very specific crimes on the people of this world. People who were skinned alive, dumped in ammonia, thrown away like garbage into mass graves—"

"Stop," she said quietly.

"That was the work of people like Lischka, and he's never answered for it. I may be a discount detective, but you're letting him numb your conscience with tea and cookies and sycophantic bullshit. He moves gingerly. He has a nice dog. He's polite. So what? Good table manners don't exonerate someone from evil actions. It's an act, Francine. You're being manipulated. Again."

"Please stop." A tear rolled down her cheek.

Bruno looked like he wanted to say something else, but just shook his head. And when he walked away, she didn't try to stop him.

What had she expected? Bruno was just like her, stumbling around in the dark, grabbing for anything that hurt less than what had come before. What if they'd both grabbed onto the wrong thing?

A figure moved sheepishly up the driveway.

"Hey," Laura Jean said tentatively. "Are you all right?"

"I'm fine." Francine wasn't in the mood to talk, not even to Laura Jean.

"I'm not trying to be nosy, but you could hear it up and down the street. I didn't hear what you were arguing about," she added quickly. "I just wanted to see if you were okay."

"I'm fine."

"Sometimes—"

"I said I'm fine, Laura Jean!" Francine snapped. "You don't have to mother me right now. I can screw this up all on my own."

"Okay," Laura Jean said softly. "Just let me know if you need anything."

She retreated back down the driveway, and Francine felt like she'd kicked a puppy. But she didn't feel much like apologizing to anyone at the moment.

Why? *Why* had she gotten involved with Bruno and his clusterfuck of a case during this last chance at turning her life around? Now she'd be going back to San Francisco with her heart and mind worse than ever. What would her life look like six months from now? Six years? She couldn't even bear to think about it.

Inside, she found Charlie asleep on the family room couch with his mouth hanging open, an old horror movie playing on the TV. She sat down next to her nephew and watched his untroubled dreaming. What had she told him? Things always looked better in the morning?

She was going to let him believe the lie as long as she could.

CHAPTER 33

I am afraid to be alone in the dark.
[x] TRUE   [   ] FALSE

Charlie counted one hundred Mississippi and cracked an eye open to see Aunt Francine sleeping on the couch next to him.

She'd been yelling at Mister Mystery in the garage like Charlie had never heard her yell before. Whatever was wrong in Hawthorn Woods was getting to her. She needed his help now more than ever.

He crept carefully across the carpet, up the stairs, and out the front door, not stopping until his feet reached the spot where the driveway's blacktop met the asphalt of the street. There was safety in the driveway, like keeping all your toes under a blanket at night. But there was nothing to be discovered in safety.

He took off into a night that felt extra dark. No parties, no kids on bikes, no Kick the Can. Just a gentle hook of moon, and the scant light it provided.

He could hear the voices arguing before he even got to the Banderwalts' house.

"Two more hang ups today," Eric said. "He's gonna come back. You know he will."

Mrs. Banderwalt, her wheelchair in front of the TV like always, didn't respond.

"Mom!"

"What, Eric?" she said tiredly, like he was bothering her.

"He'll do anything to get to her."

"That's why we moved," Mrs. Banderwalt said. Her voice was soft and thin, as if it were coming from somewhere very far away.

"Why do you talk to him at all?"

"He won't send child support if I don't. There's nothing else I can do." Her voice fluttered, like she was going to cry. It was the most emotion Charlie had ever heard from her.

"He barely even sends anything anyway. And we don't need his money. I'm taking care of us. I do the cooking and the cleaning, and I'm fine doing it, but he can't come back."

"I told him not to."

"Did you forget why you're in that wheelchair? Why Diana can't sleep at night? He's going to try and take her."

But Mrs. Banderwalt was gone again, far from whatever feeling she'd been close to reaching. "I don't know what you expect me to do, Eric."

"Just stay out of my way if he comes back."

He banged out the front door and stormed over to the shed. The dirty lightbulb inside blazed to life, drawing a hurricane of soft-winged moths that made the light jump and dance.

Charlie scampered over to the shed, his fingers feeling along the wavy sheet metal until he reached the door hinge and peeked inside.

Eric had set a new piece of plywood across the two construction horses, and this time there was actually something on the table to be chopped. Down came the cleaver.

Thwack.

The sound was meaty and wet.

Thwack.

The smell coming from the table made Charlie sick.

Thwack.

For a horrible moment, the moths cleared away from the lightbulb, and Charlie saw, with perfect clarity, the pile along the back wall.

THUNK.

The knife buried into the plywood as an opossum's head rolled off the table.

Charlie didn't cry out or scream. He walked slowly and carefully away from the shed to the safety of the willow tree's umbrella and sat against the huge trunk, not knowing what to feel.

Through the shifting curtain of leaves, he watched a police car roll down the street. They'd probably want to know about what was inside Eric's shed, but it was past curfew. If he talked to them, he'd be in trouble.

He stayed put, nuzzling into the willow roots. Crickets buzzed. An owl hooted as fireflies drifted around the tree like wandering fairies. Charlie's eyelids grew heavy…

The pained yelp of an animal filled the still night air.

Charlie jumped to his feet and ran, no longer caring what was wrong in the neighborhood as long as he could get home.

"Charlie!" Aunt Francine clacked the phone back into its cradle as he came through the back door. "I was just about to call Chief Durham! Where were you?"

He fell into her arms. "Something's hurt!"

"What? Are you okay? What's wrong?"

She held him out, looking for an injury, but he pushed her hands away.

"Not me! Somebody hurt an animal! Over by Eric's house!"

"Charlie, calm down. I don't know what you—"

"He has bones in his shed!" Charlie yelled. "And I think he just hurt something new!"

CHAPTER 34

It does not bother me particularly
to see animals suffer.
[   ] TRUE   [x] FALSE

Francine's yellow flashlight stuttered as she walked down the driveway. Since Charlie had given their spare batteries to Diana, it seemed like this was the best she was going to get.

Her head wasn't in the best shape either, pounding from the bucket of absinthe and a horror-movie infused nap. Waking to an empty house and then hearing her nephew scream about hurt animals hadn't helped things much.

She'd given Charlie a glass of warm milk, told him a quick bedtime story, and promised to go see what happened. His story hadn't changed. A shed of bones and a whimpering animal. Francine was ninety-nine percent sure the boy had been confused by the horror movie on TV, but a promise was a promise, so out she went.

A simple call to the police station would've been nice, but she didn't want to get Lori, considering this "emergency" was even flimsier than the last one. "Oh, your nephew got scared wandering around at night while you were supposed to be watching him? And you were what? Drunk and fighting with your boyfriend? I hope you know I'm obligated to tell Ellie all about this when she gets back." Francine would run a marathon to avoid a lecture from Lori. A quick loop of the block was an easy compromise.

She slapped her palm against the plastic casing of the flashlight, but the output didn't improve. A sharp hoot brought her beam to the top of a gnarled elm, where it lit the huge eyes of an owl.

The damp chill left by the rain seemed to find Francine all at once, and she pulled the polar bear sweater tighter around her body, walking faster as she did so. The pathetic flashlight revealed only a few feet of road at a time. If she found something on the way to Eric's house, she was going to find it suddenly.

A small animal scampered frantically across her spill of light.

"Son of a bitch!"

The flashlight's bulb died, then came back to life, showing a mouse in the streetside gravel. That wasn't so bad.

A soft whooshing compelled Francine to look skyward just in time to see two outstretched talons bearing down. She screamed and shielded her face. The owl banked around her and collapsed onto the rodent. The light went out again. She heard the briefest of strangled squeaks and a piston of wings before the flashlight sputtered back to life, revealing a still-blinking mouse head in the gravel.

Annnd that was enough exploring in dead of night.

Francine was about to head straight home when she heard it. Not the scream and sudden silence of something being killed, but the moaning cry of an animal, badly hurt.

She closed her eyes and listened. Between the lazy clang of windchimes and the five-note call of a mourning dove, the whimper came again from somewhere up ahead. She walked forward into the vacant dark, pulled by the same terrible lure that had drawn her toward Brownie.

Then the flashlight found another surprise: a thin ribbon of blood running jaggedly from the Banderwalts' yard, out into the street, and back into the Asperskis' yard, where it disappeared into a ribbed metal pipe that ran underneath the driveway.

Cold rainwater squished under Francine's knees as she knelt in the ditch at the edge of the pipe, the inside of which was about a foot and a half wide, and completely dark. She held up the flashlight to reveal narrowed eyes and sharp teeth that gnashed at her before backing deeper into the pipe.

"Jesus!"

She fell back in surprise, fully soaking her clothes in ditch water. Her heart was racing, but she slapped her flashlight back to life and crawled toward the pipe edge again. The eyes inside gave another phantasmal glare in the light, but the bared teeth disappeared as the husky licked blood off its front paws.

"Ajax?"

Francine covered her hand with her mouth. She'd been worried about finding an injured raccoon or groundhog. The sight of Roland's harmless dog, bleeding in a pipe, broke her heart.

She staggered out of the ditch and sprinted to a nearby front door.

Chief Durham answered her furious knocking, dressed in plaid pajama bottoms and an undershirt.

"Ms. Haddix?"

"Ajax is hurt. He's stuck in a pipe!"

"Gerber's dog?"

"He's bleeding under the Asperskis' driveway. I don't know how to get him out."

"Okay. Wait here."

Chief Durham hustled up the stairs, past Magdalena, who didn't seem overwhelmed with joy that Francine had shown up at her house in the middle of the night. Hearing of the Chief's flirting with Bruno had certainly softened Francine's animosity toward the woman, but she didn't have time for a heart to heart right now.

Chief Durham returned mercifully quick with his duty belt slung around his pajama pants. "Hon, lock the door behind me. Love ya."

Moments later, the Chief's infinitely superior flashlight clearly illuminated Ajax, shivering and baring his teeth in periodic growls from the middle of the pipe.

"He's really in there," the Chief said. "Can you go get Roland for me?"

Francine nodded and took off.

"And bring back some meat if you can!" he called after her.

She sprinted all the way to Roland's welcome mat, then rang the doorbell and knocked as loudly as she could.

"Roland? Roland!"

Nothing. The house was dark and silent.

Then she saw a light on over at Del Merlin's.

She sprinted again and found Roland, chatting with Del on the couch. She wrenched the back door open without knocking, startling both men.

"Roland, Ajax is hurt."

"What? Are you all right?"

"I'm fine. Ajax is stuck in a pipe. He's bleeding."

Panic flooded Roland's face.

"Chief Durham's already there," she said. "He told me to bring back meat."

Del disappeared into the kitchen and reemerged a few seconds later with a Styrofoam dish of raw hamburger. "Let's go."

The three of them ran across the block and found Chief Durham's broad shoulders huddled by the pipe, a steady, vibrating growl coming from the animal inside. Del poked his fingers through the plastic covering the hamburger and handed over some meat. The Chief held it patiently in front of the pipe for a few seconds, then shined his light down the hole. Ajax hadn't budged.

"Move." Francine took the hamburger from Chief Durham and pushed close to the pipe opening, until her entire arm was inside. Against all instinct, she reached out and waited, trying not to imagine a frightened animal with sharp teeth crawling toward her hand.

Just as she was about to pull back, a cold dog nose gently nudged her fingers. Ajax sniffed, then began to lick the hamburger.

Francine edged slowly back, drawing Ajax forward until his snout gingerly emerged into the circle of Chief Durham's flashlight.

"C'mon, boy. That's it," she cooed.

His tail had just cleared the pipe when Del dropped down from the driveway above and clamped his hands around the dog's muzzle. Ajax wriggled furiously, but was no match for the Marine's toned arms.

"What are you doing?" Francine said.

"Wrap him, Roland!" Del commanded.

Roland wound his belt around Ajax's snout and cinched it tight.

"He'll bleed out before we can get him to a vet," Del said. "I should have what we need at home."

With Ajax writhing in his arms, Del led the way back to his house and into his kitchen, where he laid the thrashing dog on the table.

"He's going to hurt himself even worse," Chief Durham said. "We need to calm him down."

"I might have sleeping pills." Del said.

He hurried down the hall, leaving Chief Durham and Roland to re-strain Ajax while Francine threw open one cabinet door after another until she found a jar of peanut butter. She spread a spoonful on a plate just as Del returned with pills and an electric razor.

"I only have Benadryl, but it might do the trick." He crushed up some of the pills and Francine mixed the pink powder into her peanut butter.

"He's getting loose," Chief Durham warned.

Francine slid the plate under Ajax's belt-muzzled snout. The second the dog got a whiff of the peanut butter, his thrashing slowed.

"Loosen the belt," Francine said.

Roland did, and Ajax took to the peanut butter with reliable dog gusto, licking himself into a languid stupor that eventually ended in sleep.

Using the clippers Del had brought, Francine took off the top layer of blood-matted fur on the dog's chest, just below the neck. She let out a gasp of horror as a second, more delicate pass revealed a long gash in the skin.

"My God," Roland mumbled.

The wound was erratic and uneven, nothing like the one they'd found on Brownie. Fortunately, there was no geometric carving in the white fur of the dog's stomach.

Del pinched on a pair of reader glasses and sterilized a sewing needle with a lighter. Then he began to methodically stitch the wound while Francine used a dish rag to wipe away trickles of blood.

Once the work was finished, a pile of bath towels were nested into a makeshift dog bed under the table and Ajax was left to rest, his breathing shallow but even.

Del took off his glasses and looked at the rest of them. "Now we wait."

CHAPTER 35

In walking, I am very careful to
step over sidewalk cracks.
[　] TRUE [x] FALSE

They sat in the living room, wiping dried blood from their hands and clothes as the first bits of sunrise colored the front window.

"What happened to the hand, Del?" Chief Durham asked as the Marine passed around cups of instant coffee.

Del caressed his metal-splinted fingers and gave a sheepish glance in Francine's direction. "Hood came down on me. Never too old to make stupid mistakes."

Francine wasn't concerned with Del Merlin's feelings at the moment. "Could an animal have done that to Ajax?" she asked him.

"Definitely a knife wound," he said. "Lucky it didn't nick an artery, or he'd be done for. The angle moves upward. I think someone was standing over him. Kind of looks like they were trying to cut his throat, but he moved at the last second."

"Can you tell the size of the knife?"

Del shook his head.

"Where does the dog sleep, Roland?" the Chief asked.

"Out on the porch, where the air is cooler. There are no locks on the doors, but they're latched, so he can't push them open. Someone came into my porch. It had to be that Banderwalt boy. I had words with him when he nearly ran Ajax over. Francine was there."

She nodded.

Chief Durham put a hand on Roland's shoulder. "Just stay calm for me, okay? Del, is it all right if the dog rests here a bit?"

"Of course."

"I'll look into it, Roland," Chief Durham promised, and left.

Roland walked back into the kitchen and slowly got down onto the floor next to the still-asleep Ajax to stroke his fur.

Francine moved to follow Chief Durham.

"Francine, wait."

She turned to face a bashful Del.

"I've been trying to leave you alone. I thought that would be the best thing I could do after I acted like…"

"A shithead?" she finished helpfully.

"Yes. There's no excuse for what I did. I don't regret getting called on it, I regret having done it in the first place."

"Del, I've known lots of men like you. Most women have."

"No," he said firmly. "That isn't who I am. You don't have to forgive me. But I want you to know that's not who I am."

Given the chaos of everything else in her life, Francine had mostly forgotten about the grabbing incident. But Del clearly hadn't, and she couldn't help but feel a smidge of sympathy for the lonely widower. If Eric's little green knife ever went after something other than a defenseless dog, it might be nice to have a Marine and his rifle on her side.

"You ever pinch my butt, I'll put you in traction. Understand?"

Del nodded. "You sound like that guy, Bruno."

"Bruno?"

"He came over the other day. Said if I gave you any more trouble, he'd relieve me of a few teeth."

"I didn't ask him to do that."

"I deserved it. The guy's a toothpick, but I could tell he meant it. You've chosen well."

"Yeah, okay." She moved for the door, but Del spoke up again.

"I think you should stay out of this, Francine. Just go home, then go all the way home to California. Whatever's happening here isn't worth getting hurt over."

"Who says I'm going to get hurt?"

"I've seen you snooping around at night. I don't know if you're still trying to figure out the goat thing or what, but you should leave it be. Whatever is happening with the Banderwalt kid—"

"I stood up for him. I defended him last night and look where we are now." Francine opened the front door. "Thanks for stitching up Ajax. You and me are good."

And off she went, walking in the direction of a punk kid who liked to brandish his knife and BB gun, and antagonize the neighborhood with his nuisance of a dirt bike.

Eric Banderwalt seemed to hate just about everyone in Hawthorn Woods, and Francine was starting to hate him right back.

$$\ast \quad \ast \quad \ast \quad \ast$$

Francine found Chief Durham talking to Mrs. Banderwalt on her front stoop. Eric stood in the doorway behind her, doing a great job of looking sleepy and confused.

"Why do you think my boy did it?" Mrs. Banderwalt asked.

The Chief shook his head. "I didn't say he did. The dog was found in a culvert next door and there's blood in your yard. I'm just trying to get a picture of where everyone was a few hours ago."

"I was asleep," Eric said.

The little liar.

Francine stormed up the lawn in a rage. "First he killed the goat, and now he's moved on to dogs!"

"Francine, please," Chief Durham said. "Go home and—"

"He's got bones in the shed!" she shouted.

Eric's drowsy façade fell away. For a moment, no one spoke.

The Chief looked at Eric. "Is that true?"

"Of course not," Mrs. Banderwalt said.

But Eric, staring down at the dirty carpet between his toes, said nothing.

"Will you open the shed for me?" Chief Durham asked.

"Do I have to?"

"No. But I'm asking if you will."

Eric pushed roughly through them and stomped down the ramp. Using the key he wore around his neck, he opened the bike lock on the shed and stepped back, giving Francine a look of pure loathing as the lock fell away.

Chief Durham eased the door open.

They first saw a workbench, covered in a spectrum of red stains. A meat cleaver with bits of fur stuck its blade hung on the wall. Chief Durham pulled the door all the way open, spilling light into the back of the shed. That's when they saw them.

Skeletons from dozens, maybe hundreds, of animals. Skulls with hollow eye cavities and rows of sharp teeth in a nightmare pile of ribcages and broken limbs stacked from floor to ceiling.

It was over. Charlie had told the truth. Eric had killed Brownie and now he'd tried to kill Ajax. But he hadn't counted on Francine. She waited for the cuffs to come out, but Chief Durham hadn't moved.

"What am I looking at, Eric?" he asked.

Eric's chin was glued to his chest, his face flushed red. "Sometimes I hunt squirrels. Pick up roadkill. We don't always have enough. I didn't know how to get rid of the bones…"

"It's all right," Chief Durham said softly. "You can lock this back up."

Mrs. Banderwalt stared in disbelief at the bones. "Eric. What have you been doing?"

Eric fumbled with the bike lock, then gave up and fled back into the house.

"I don't understand." Mrs. Banderwalt sounded dazed. "I…I didn't realize where he'd gotten all the meat from."

Chief Durham shut the shed door and secured the u-bar. "Mrs. Banderwalt, I think you should go inside and be with your children."

She looked at him blankly, then nodded and slowly rolled her way back up the ramp.

"Everything all right, Hollis?" a voice called from the street. Lori and the Hens walked in place, craning their necks to try and glean more information. "Need our help?"

"Everything's fine, Lori." Chief Durham waved. He waited for the group to reluctantly resume their speedwalk, then took Francine gently by the arm. "I'm escorting you home. Again."

She shook him off. "You're mad at *me*? There's a fucking catacomb in that kid's shed!"

"Ms. Haddix, you need to stop this. It's my job to figure out what's happening here. Not yours."

"Then you need to do your job better."

"Thank you for your input."

"How in the hell do you explain what we just saw?"

The Chief looked at the windows of the Banderwalts' house and lowered his voice. "For some folks, a dead animal on the side of the road is an opportunity to eat a little better that night. The Banderwalts barely get by. Do you understand? Do you think Eric is proud of what he has to do? You just humiliated him."

"Okay. I'm not going to freak out over a few squirrels or some roadkill, but the neighbor's dog?"

"I don't know if Eric had anything to do with Ajax, and neither do you. I don't think he'd feed the neighbor's dog to his mother and sister. I also don't know if he had anything to do with Brownie, and again, neither do you. I want you to leave the Banderwalts alone. I want you to leave Magdalena alone. Your time here is almost over. Please." He sounded deeply exhausted.

Well, Francine felt just as exhausted. And pissed off that the sweetest dog on the planet had been attacked and nobody was doing a damn thing about it.

"My ex-husband cheated on me, Hollis. And the thing that hurt most was that he felt he couldn't be honest with me. I knew something was wrong, and he denied it. Again and again and again."

Chief Durham looked unnerved. "What's your point?"

"My point is, maybe Magdalena's not bent out of shape because of me. Maybe someone's gaslighting her, doing one thing and saying another. Chalking it up to her wild imagination. Maybe most of all, she resents being brought halfway around the world for a lie."

She left the Chief standing in the driveway and headed home, already feeling bad about what she'd said, or at least how she'd said it.

CHAPTER 36

I like adventure stories better
than romantic stories.
[x] TRUE   [   ] FALSE

After a shower to get the rest of Ajax's blood off, Francine fell onto her butterfly sheets in a forest of clocks.

The fight with Bruno. Ajax getting hurt. The Chief's unwillingness to hold Eric responsible. So many awful things had happened in the last few hours that they congealed into a general mood of despair too wide-reaching to process.

The pillow under Francine's head was heaven, begging her to cozy up and rest her eyes, but someone deserved her attention more. She somehow found the energy to get up again, and head into the master bedroom where she sat on the edge of the bed.

"Morning, Bubba."

Charlie slowly stirred. "Morning, Aunt Francine. What happened last night?"

"Somebody hurt Ajax, but he's okay now. You helped keep him safe."

"Was it Eric?"

"I don't know who did it. And we're gonna have another talk about you sneaking out at night," she pinched one of his toes, "but that's not what matters most to me right now. It's been so crazy around here, I feel like I haven't even seen you much lately. What do you say we spend a special day together, just you and me? We'll do whatever you want."

Charlie thought hard. "Can we have cookies for breakfast?"

If the last few days had been intense for Francine, and they definitely had, she could only imagine how Charlie felt. She hated to think about how many horrible things he'd been introduced to for the first time during her stay. She owed him some pleasant memories too, and that's exactly what he was going to get.

From her helm at the mixing bowl, she called for ingredients and watched as Charlie darted from the fridge to the cabinet and back to get them. When he dropped an egg on one of his trips, she let him squish the yolk between his toes, eliciting a scream of grossed-out laughter from both of them. They covered the kitchen table in a snow of flour and dumped out the chocolate-chip batter, using a rolling pin and some cookie cutters to make as many constellations as they could dream up. Then they sat on the oven-warmed linoleum and pointed through the glass at their rising creations, choosing which ones they were going to eat first. When the timer dinged, Francine set the hot tray of cookies on some potholders while Charlie poured two big glasses of milk. They sat beneath the Tiffany lamp and counted to one hundred Mississippi, only making it to twenty before they started to eat.

She asked him why kids hated baths. "'Cause they aren't fun." He asked her why grownups ate so much broccoli. "Beats me." They both picked the superpower of flight over invisibility and agreed that smooth peanut butter had nothing on chunky.

Then it was time for a Godzilla movie with the sound so loud it rattled the Precious Moments figurines on top of the big screen. To battle the monster, the Japanese military used a futuristic flying ship called the Super-X, so Francine and Charlie quickly covered a laundry basket and bike helmet in tin foil. Then she dragged him around the carpet, shaking the basket as it took damage from an invisible, atomic lizard.

When she drew Charlie a long-overdue bath upstairs, he got in without protest. She sat outside the curtain and read aloud from Pete's dog-eared copy of *The Hobbit*, skipping to the dragon fight at the end so Charlie could act out the action in the tub, using measuring spoons for the dwarves and a black spatula for the fire-breathing Smaug.

Afterwards, Francine made fried baloney sandwiches for lunch, letting Charlie poke holes in the meat as it ballooned in the pan. They took bites of each other's sandwiches out on the back patio, tossing bread crusts to birds and a chipmunk who may or may not have been the garage intruder from days before. And after root beer floats, they laid on the dining room carpet in front of the air conditioner and made up poems about the wonderful months of summer, and Godzilla, and a girl named Nancy Drew. Before long, Charlie fell into an afternoon nap with a smile on his face.

The perfect day. No divorce stories. No suspects. No little anchors to be found.

Francine carefully lifted Charlie's snoring head and had just walked into the kitchen to do the dishes when the phone rang.

"Hello?"

"Hi. It's me. Bruno. Um, you don't have to say anything if you don't want to, but I hope you'll listen. I want to say I'm sorry for some of the things I said last night. I regret saying them, and I want you to know that. You were right that this investigation means a lot to me, and I can't change that, but I also shouldn't let my emotions take over. I definitely shouldn't have let them come between us. What you've been doing, meeting with Gerber, can't be easy. It's something I couldn't do myself. I'm not trying to ruin his life. I'm just trying to give Ida the closure she deserves, and that made me lash out at you and the opinions you're more than entitled to have. I'm really sorry, Francine."

Ben had never said he was sorry. Not once. Not when he begged to be taken back, not when he magically matured after the divorce, not even during the recent phone call he'd graced her with. To have her pain acknowledged for once felt nice to Francine. Really nice.

"I'm sorry too," she said. "I went about things the wrong way and I can't blame it all on the absinthe." She bit her lip in indecision. "But we both said such nasty things so quickly, it makes me wonder if we're doing the right thing by being together. It doesn't help one drowning person to grab onto another, you know? I hope we can finish the investigation the right way, but maybe it would be best if we ease up a little on the personal stuff. You know, between you and me."

"You might be right," he conceded.

It seemed like they were both waiting for the other to argue against the idea, but neither did.

"Will I see you at the parade tomorrow?" she asked.

"Yeah, but I was also calling because I wanted to see if you'd come to dinner tonight."

"That's not exactly easing up, Bruno."

"I know. Ida's coming."

"To Hawthorn Woods? Really?"

"I always bring her up to date on the investigation, and when I told her how things went last night, she insisted on coming to cook dinner. I didn't give her any private details," he assured Francine quickly. "But she could tell things were off. So yeah, she's gonna make dinner, then she's got a redeye back to New York. We don't have to talk about you and me. We don't even have to talk about the case. She said she'd prefer it if we didn't, actually. Ida's just…a person I think you'd enjoy meeting. I hope you'll come if you can."

"I'll think about it, Bruno. Thanks."

"Okay. Bye."

Francine hung up and twirled the cord in thought. Then she picked the phone up again and dialed.

"Hello?"

"Roland, it's me. How's he doing?"

"Francine. He is recovering well. I am so grateful for Del and Hollis and their quick actions." He paused, and Francine heard what sounded like a soft sob. "And for you. Ajax is alive, thanks to you, Francine. I was so overwhelmed this morning, I neglected to thank you. There is no question that you saved his life. I am forever grateful."

Francine fought to keep her own voice steady. "It was nothing. I'll come by later to check on you two, okay?"

"We look forward to it."

She hung up again and stood still in indecision.

Dinner at Bruno's would help bring the investigation to a proper finale, even if her answer wasn't one Bruno and Ida wanted to hear. Then she could say goodbye to Roland and Ajax, get a good night's sleep, watch Laura Jean's parade the next day, and pack for San Francisco. She might be leaving Hawthorn Woods by herself, but could still leave it the right way.

CHAPTER 37

I can stand as much pain as others can.
[   ] TRUE   [x] FALSE

Francine walked to Bruno's under an evening sky that sagged with humidity. Cheated by the previous day's paltry shower, the clouds looked like an ever-filling water balloon hovering above the neighborhood, waiting for a pinprick.

Dennis Asperski seemed to sense the same thing, as he dragged padded furniture off his back porch. Francine could see Eric had told the truth about one thing: Dennis had a dark circle around one eye. Had Lori really punched him? How he remained married to that woman might have been the biggest mystery Hawthorn Woods had to offer, but for now, Francine focused on the task at hand.

She rang Bruno's doorbell, second-guessing her outfit for the eightieth time. What did one wear when defending a suspected Nazi to a Holocaust survivor? Hopefully the yellow daisy sundress wouldn't fail her now.

The door flew open.

There stood Ida Nussbaum, short and round, her eyes shining as if Francine were a dear friend she hadn't seen in ages.

"My God, you are just as he said," Ida breathed.

"Hello." Francine held out a hand.

Ida pulled her into an enthusiastic hug. "I know, I'm too much too fast, but I cook good. Come in, come in."

Ida's accent was a lively mix of Eastern European delivered with East Coast brusqueness. Her wide hips and bosom gave her the look of a snow-woman wrapped in a plain brown dress, and she seemed absolutely over the moon at the idea of cooking dinner for a total stranger.

Rushing across the kitchen floor, she relieved Bruno of his pot stirring duties at the stove. "Bless you, Michael, you've done a number on yourself already."

She wiped spackles of sauce from his burgundy tie. He'd clearly attempted to iron his plain white button-up and brown corduroys, but succeeded only in adding long crease lines to the wrinkles. The kitchen's research debris had been temporarily confined to a single, dauntingly tall pile in the corner, leaving plenty of open space for an abundance of freshly-bought groceries. There was plenty of space, too, for the awkward uncertainty between Francine and Bruno.

They'd traversed the entire trajectory of a relationship in under two weeks, like a pair of grade schoolers: she didn't like him, yes she did, he didn't like her, yes he did, but there was a problem, now the problem's gone, yay things are great, oops they had a big fight, they stopped talking but then they kinda made up. And now...

"Hi."

"Hi."

Ida watched them with a wry smile. "How are we for drinks, Michael?"

Bruno produced the trusty bottle of Cutty Sark that by this point was basically an equal partner in the investigation. He poured the last of their colleague into three glasses and Ida, stirring dinner with one hand, raised a toast with the other.

"To my intrepid angels. *L'chaim.*"

They drank down the scotch.

"Now tell me about yourself, dear." Ida said, after tasting a sauce with her finger.

"You want to know about me?" Francine said.

"Absolutely. I know some of Michael's life, and all of my own, but shamefully little of yours."

Francine had been prepared to defend her thesis of Gerber's innocence, not tell the class a little bit about herself.

"Okay, um, I was born and raised here in the Midwest. Got married and divorced in California. I'm a hairdresser—"

"Come, dear, you're not a baseball card. What about your life lately?"

"Well, my biggest focus as of late has been helping Bruno with the investigation."

Ida scooped food from the pans onto teddy bear plates. "Ah, we needn't talk of that business."

But Bruno had already lit up. "Ida says the goat was killed kosher."

"Really?" Francine looked at Ida expectantly.

"Oh, all right." Ida surrendered. She handed them each a full plate. "If we must talk about the case, we're going to eat while we do so."

Ida was definitely right about one thing: She did cook well. Her lamb medallions, cabbage rolls, herb-dusted potatoes, and pierogi were some of the best Francine had ever tasted, and she was relieved she hadn't volunteered to bring over Puppy Chow.

"It is, of course, hard to say," Ida began, "but from Michael's description and photographs, the goat's slaying sounds like *shechita*, which is the butchering of animals according to Jewish law. Goats are permitted animals, and the cut, one clean slice across the neck"—she mimed the motion—"is in line with the law as well. Not a certainty, but a consideration, perhaps."

Bruno chewed thoughtfully. "I still can't figure out why Lischka would do something so reckless. And why he, of all people, would do it kosher."

"I thought we were still calling him Roland," Francine said softly. She turned to Ida and asked uneasily, "Have you…seen him since you've been here?"

"No," Ida said. "This visit is not to make my own inquiry. I have the utmost confidence in Michael, and with the addition of your talents, I am further reassured."

"If I thought he really did all those terrible things, I think I'd be at his door with a torch," Francine said. "Not that I could ever understand," she added quickly. "Sorry, the scotch is making me brave. What I'm trying to say is, I'm impressed with your restraint."

Ida set down her knife and fork. "Oskar Lischka took a great many things from me. Whether this neighbor of yours is him, I do not yet know, and it is certainly nothing I can control. Because I have a mind for justice, I have never given up my pursuit. But if I let Lischka's actions twist me into a bitter huntress, fed by fantasies of revenge, his hate will have continued through me. Evil begetting more evil. I have no intention of letting guilty parties go free, but neither is it my life's work. I made a choice, long ago, to be a person. To live with values inverse to Oskar Lischka and those like him. He gets a portion of my free time only, alongside bridge and crochet. I'd rather speak of the beautiful family I've raised, the business I ran with my husband, the influence I've strived to make on the world." She reached over and squeezed Francine's hand tenderly. "I've waited for decades. I can wait a little longer. Now have some more lamb, dear. Hitler was vegetarian."

Francine laughed. She was in awe of the woman, unable to recall ever meeting a person with such immediate and remarkable grace—much less one who had narrowly escaped annihilation at the hands of a monster.

✳   ✳   ✳   ✳

The three of them ate and talked for hours. Not about the goat or the case or Lischka, but about their lives.

Ida had worked as a chimney sweep and later sold computer parts, a rare Venn diagram of professions. She'd briefly dated one of the Yankees, though wouldn't say which one. She insisted travel was a requirement for personal growth, and had visited every continent at least once, but warned, "Antarctica's mostly snow and penguin shit and the commute is murder, don't waste your time." They all laughed at Francine for not being suspicious about Santa Claus until she was thirteen, and at Bruno for being winless against his students in ping pong for three years running. Ida grew quieter and quieter as the night progressed, letting the two sleuths banter with each other well past their honey cake desserts.

At length, she checked her watch. "Ten already? My taxi is due soon. Michael, wait outside for the driver, would you? Francine and I will see to the dishes."

"Ida, you don't have to—" Bruno began.

"Oh, don't grow manners on the spot. These dishes will soak for a month if I don't do them. Plus, we're going to talk about you, so scram."

With a grin in Francine's direction, Bruno wisely scrammed.

Francine carried plates to the sink, where Ida was already busily scrubbing.

"He's got stars in his eyes for you. You see that, yes?"

Francine felt herself blush. "Maybe. I don't know. It's complicated."

"I hope Bruno's favor to me hasn't been a negative influence."

"No. The investigation is basically what brought us together in the first place. We had a…strong disagreement last night." Francine put down the plate she was drying. "Ida, I don't think Mr. Gerber is Lischka. I can't imagine how disappointing that must be to hear, but when I talk to him, I just can't imagine he's a person who could've done all those horrible things. I understand if you hate me."

"Hate you? Never, dear. Michael's heart is in the right place, but he badly wants to deliver me a certain result. Perhaps you can ensure it's justice he's chasing, and not something else."

"Cab's here," Bruno called from the front door.

"Give him some small talk," Ida yelled back. "We're almost done."

"I really do want you to find closure," Francine said.

Ida turned off the faucet. "Finding Lischka and delivering him to justice would be a sweet digestif to my life, but if it doesn't come to be, I won't let it spoil a meal I've loved so very much." She picked up her purse. "I know you and Michael have both experienced hard times. If I had the power to will an outcome in all of this, it would be for the two of you to find vitality. Perhaps together. Ah, I almost forgot."

She dug around in her purse and came up with two brass earrings shaped like scrolls.

"If you've no aversion to Jewish iconography, I made these when I heard you'd joined the effort. Mezuzahs. We normally put them on our doors for protection, but I think they might do just as well on ears."

"They're beautiful, Ida. Thank you."

Once they were outside, Ida got into the back seat of the cab and cranked down her window.

"Francine, I am enchanted, just as he said I would be. Michael, you're still too skinny, but your taste in women is pristine. And now, the both of you remember this, please. The world is concerned with your usefulness. Your fulfillment is up to you. Good luck. Okay, let's go."

She slapped the cab door and the driver backed out of the driveway. A few seconds later, the benevolent force-of-nature called Ida Nussbaum was a pair of vanishing tail lights.

"Wow," Francine said. "She inhales smoke and breathes out fresh air."

"I thought you'd like her." Bruno smiled. "Can I walk you home?"

She nodded, and they sauntered around the block.

With the refreshing injection of Vitamin Nussbaum, Francine's mind returned to the near future that intended to send her and Bruno in opposite directions.

"Bruno, can I ask you something?"

But he wasn't listening. She followed his gaze and saw an envelope tucked into Ellie and Pete's front door.

"Francine, wait."

But she had already raced through the door and up the stairs to the master bedroom, where she breathed a sigh of relief. Charlie slept peacefully in his parents' bed. After gently closing the door, Francine hurried back downstairs.

"Charlie okay?" Bruno asked.

"Yeah. What's the letter say?"

He handed it to her.

Ms. Haddix and Mr. Bruno,

I should like to host the two of you this evening, however late the hour. All that is required is your company, which I await with eager curiosity.

Yours,

Roland Gerber

"He knows," Francine said.

"That's not for sure." Bruno sighed. "But it's definitely possible. What should we do?"

Francine gazed down the street at the unassuming line of spruce trees, then pinned the Mezuzahs in her earlobes.

"We oblige his curiosity."

CHAPTER 38

Sometimes in elections, I vote for people
about whom I know very little.
[x] TRUE   [   ] FALSE

Francine's mind hadn't decided on a clear emotional state just yet, keeping her on the knife's edge of a dozen different feelings as Roland answered the door.

"Mr. Bruno." He held out a hand.

Bruno shook it, his manner polite but reserved. "Mr. Gerber."

"Thank you for accepting my invitation. And Francine. You promised you'd visit and here you are. True to your word."

"How's Ajax?" she asked.

"Fine, thank you. If you would please show Mr. Bruno to the porch. You remember the way, I think." He stepped aside to admit them, and she could tell his manner was off. Maybe only by a single percent, but there was definitely a slight chill to his words and actions.

She led Bruno to the porch and they sat on the house-facing loveseat. Bruno stared straight ahead with a resolute expression Francine had never seen in him before.

Roland walked in with a tea tray. No cookies this time. Apparently their business was to be something a little more formal.

Ajax, neck cleanly bandaged, passed skittishly into the kitchen to lap some water.

"What happened to your dog?" Bruno asked.

The last twenty-four hours had been such a whirlwind, Francine hadn't yet shared the story of Ajax's harrowing night in the pipe.

"Ajax was attacked by a local hoodlum. He is distrustful at the moment, and best left alone."

"I was hoping he'd be up and walking," Francine said. "I'm glad—"

"Enough games." Roland had interrupted Francine for the first time since she'd known him. "I believe there are more urgent matters to be discussed." He poured them each a cup of tea, then pulled a pack of European cigarettes from a drawer in the coffee table. She had never seen him smoke before, either. "It has come to my attention there may be something you wish to ask me, Mr. Bruno."

Francine glanced at Bruno, wondering if he would play dumb a little longer. She could tell by the look in his eyes that the time had come.

"I'm here on behalf of a third party who believes you to be a man by the name of Oskar Lischka."

Francine's eyes flashed back to Roland. Her lungs forgot how to pull oxygen from the air while she waited for his reaction.

Roland displayed only a look of disappointment, maybe even boredom, as he took a long drag on his cigarette. "This man you speak of is no doubt a member of the Nationalist Socialist German Workers' Party."

"Correct," Bruno said.

"Mr. Bruno, while your intentions may be noble, I'm sorry to say they are in no way original. As I have explained to your associate, I am a man of a certain age, who emigrated here from a certain part of the world, following a war everyone loves to remember. I speak German. I have little documentation to support my life's events because the world was not as formalized back then. This suspicion has been cast upon me before, albeit in a more direct manner."

He looked patiently at Francine. She focused on her cup of tea, her face warm with shame.

Roland turned back to Bruno. "Instead of accusing me of something, why don't you ask me something instead?"

"You go by the name Roland Gerber," Bruno said.

"Is that a question? Yes, I go by my own name, which is indeed Roland Gerber. I hail from the region of Engadin, Switzerland. All of my immediate family is deceased, I am a naturalized citizen of the United States, I pay my taxes in full and on time, and I'm a card-carrying member of the county library. No late fees outstanding."

"What year did you leave Europe?" Bruno continued.

"1949."

"Why?"

"The war had depressed the entire continent. I had long wished to come to America, and when the opportunity presented itself, I did so."

"Traveling on *Die Spinne*?"

"Ah, yes, an exotic escape afforded to the highest of Nazi officials. No, I'm sorry to say my mode of travel was much less fantastical. I came by commercial airline, but never one for scrapbooking, I've since misplaced my ticket." He sipped his tea. "I believe it was an aisle seat."

Francine had never seen Roland so bitterly sarcastic, or Bruno so steely and coarse. The change in both men was a touch frightening.

"Why don't you tell me my alleged story, Mr. Bruno, since you know it so well?"

"You went to Argentina in early 1945, afforded travel by your status in the German military. To avoid capture, you murdered a man and fled north. A few of your compatriots had found employment in the American government, but since they wanted rocket scientists, not exterminators, you were forced to forge a Swiss passport and assume a Swiss name. Roland Gerber immigrated to the United States, found a quiet place to settle, kept his head down, and lived a modest life. And your escape was successful, from the moment you fled until this moment now."

Roland dragged on his cigarette and tapped the long finger of ash into the tray. "I must commend you on a robust imagination. But factual merit? I'm afraid not."

"Most of the tall poppies got cut down at Nuremberg," Bruno said. "Mossad's been working their way down the chain of command ever since. These days they get excited for scraps, for men who followed orders. But a man who *gave* them? You'll be a sensation."

"Your ability to generate hysteria, I do not doubt. The veracity of your claims, however, is another matter." Roland neared the filter of his cigarette. "What is your profession, Mr. Bruno?"

For the first time, Bruno faltered. "I'm a cold case investigator—"

"Not the capacity in which you are interfering in my life. What is your actual employment?"

"I'm a history teacher."

"Ah. Perhaps this explains a few things." Roland inhaled the last of his cigarette and crushed it in the ashtray. "If I suspected you of a crime— or rather, someone made it in my interest to suspect you—and I made these baseless suspicions known to the world, when would you feel the judgement of others? Perhaps before a jury had decided your fate, yes?"

"If I committed a crime, I'd deserve the judgement."

"And if you hadn't?"

Bruno shook his head. "That's not—"

"*If* you were a professional," Roland said, taking control of the exchange, "and *if* you had hard evidence won from a thoroughly conducted investigation, I might now be suffering the confines of a jail cell. But you

are not a professional, Mr. Bruno. You are a hobbyist, recklessly attempting an investigation, perhaps as you've seen in the movies. You are not a
law enforcement officer, nor a licensed private investigator, nor anyone
qualified to pass the judgements you now cast upon me. An accusation of
the sort you are suggesting is not a flag to be neatly removed upon a ver-
dict of not guilty. It is a dousing that will stain, whether or not the intention was in good faith. Your delusions are no doubt motivated by many
things, but not by evidence. Yet you are intent on slandering an honest
immigrant who has lived in this country longer than you've been alive. I
fear your imagination has rendered you delusional." Roland's brow furrowed as he nodded toward Francine. "And in your delusion, Mr. Bruno,
you've taken advantage of a vulnerable soul, drawn her close, and whispered words that are dangerously untrue. Shame on you."

The inclusion of Francine seemed to incense Bruno, and he returned
to the offensive.

"My client has authorized me to extend you the opportunity to turn
yourself in. Confess to us what we know to be true. That you were a rank-
ing member of the Schutzstaffel. That among numerous other crimes, you
ordered and personally participated in the massacre of civilians in Trnów,
Poland in 1943. And that you fled judgement in order to live a comfortable life under the false name of Roland Gerber. Failing these admissions,
I will have no choice but to notify Mossad, the US Office of Special In-
vestigations, the local police, and any organization with a passing interest
in justice. Confess, Lischka, and you end an otherwise disgraceful life
with a small bit of dignity. Or you can let news vans brown the grass of
your lawn for the rest of your days, until you die as the cowardly murderer
you are."

"I murdered no one!" Roland was on his feet, matched quickly by
Bruno. "How *dare* you come to my neighborhood, my home, and speak

to me this way! I will not have you call me by some criminal's name and visit his sins upon me."

Roland poked Bruno hard in the chest. Bruno grabbed at his blazer.

Francine knifed an arm between them. "Stop it! Both of you! A fist fight won't help any of us."

Bruno held up his hands and backed away.

"Your welcome in my house has ended, Mr. Bruno," Roland said, his face stony and dark. "Francine, I'd ask you to remain a moment longer."

"No," Bruno said.

"It's fine, Bruno," Francine said firmly. She'd let him take the lead in the conversation, but she was starting to feel like a ball being hit back and forth. "I'll be out in a minute."

Bruno glared at Roland, then banged open the porch door and loitered just beyond the screen.

Roland lit a new cigarette and stood facing away from Francine. "I regret that our acquaintance has been under false pretenses, but I value the time we've shared nonetheless."

"How did you know?"

"I heard the two of you arguing last night. Heard my name mentioned. Curious, I followed you to your dinner this evening, and once again heard my name. The woman you dined with, I presume she is your client? Who is she?"

"I'm not going to tell you that."

He turned to face her, and his face showed no sign of anger. The uncharacteristic armor and aggression had melted away. He was Roland once more.

"All of your actions up to and including this very moment have been noble. Had I been in your position, and told the things you've been told, I'd like to think I would have the courage to do the same. For you to even entertain the idea that I am this…Lischka, I must not have been a man well met. For that, I apologize."

He carefully placed the tea cups back on the tray.

"I believe Mr. Bruno is compromised and confused," he went on. "What I ask, and I believe it is only of you I may ask it, is for a judgement free from influence, be it his, mine, or that of this unnamed woman. You have a sound mind and a good heart, Francine. And I trust in them both. Good night."

Without waiting for a response, he went back inside the house.

Francine joined Bruno in the backyard.

"What'd he say?" Bruno asked as they left the driveway.

"He said he's sorry he let me down, but that he understands why I'm doing this. And he said I'm the only one who could see everything clearly. Without being influenced."

They walked in silence for a moment before Bruno shook his head in frustration. "Goddammit."

"What?"

"He's not wrong."

"*What?*"

"This is about justice. Ida says it every time we talk. Justice is objective."

"None of us is objective. We're all mixed up in this in different ways."

"But you have the best view. You, Ida, and I all know Lischka in our own way. You're the only one who knows Gerber too."

"Bruno, I hate picking restaurants. You can't lay something like this on me. We're supposed to be partners."

"We are." He thought for a moment. "How about this? I think Gerber is guilty. If you think he's guilty too, I'll be the one to turn him in and accept whatever consequences come with it. But if you really think he's innocent, if you think he's Roland Gerber and no one else, then I won't do anything. I trust you, Francine."

She sighed, forcing herself to consider the possibility that the decision somehow fell to her.

"This is the worst fucking vacation."

"So you'll do it?"

"Yes. But I need time."

"We don't have much—"

"I know. Just give me the night to think it over. I'll have an answer for you in the morning."

"Do you want me to stay up with you?"

"It's okay. I need to do this on my own."

Bruno looked over his shoulder. "Think he'll try and run?"

"No," Francine said confidently. "Not unless he knows for sure he has to. If Roland Gerber's not in Hawthorn Woods, he's nowhere."

CHAPTER 39

```
I have habits that are really harmful.
      [ x ] TRUE   [   ] FALSE
```

Charlie crawled carefully across the upstairs landing and peeked into the guest room.

Aunt Francine was still awake, an hour after she'd come home. She was just walking back and forth, sometimes drinking coffee, sometimes just sitting on the bed and thinking.

It was true he had promised not to go outside, but even though he'd helped her with Ajax, they still hadn't fixed everything. They were close, Charlie could feel it. They just needed a little something more.

Out on the roof, he soft-footed across the shingles, tied knots around the weather vane, and shimmied down the frog sheet to the yew bush. His feet made quick work of yards, front and back, as he looked for the answer everywhere he could think of. In the Cunninghams' oak trees. On the side of Mr. Merlin's garage. In the glow of Diana's bedroom. The Asperskis' house. The Durhams' house. But there was nothing to be found in any of those places. Of course there wasn't. He'd been to all of them before.

Then he saw something new: a pale blue pickup truck, parked around the corner from the Banderwalts' house. A huge forearm rested on the driver's side door, and every once in a while, a stream of brown spit flew from the open window down to the asphalt. Charlie walked closer to better see inside the cab. He recognized Eric and Diana's dad, sitting in the low light of the dashboard.

Mr. Banderwalt didn't seem to be doing much, just watching the yellow house and spitting every now and then. Then he noticed Charlie standing in the grass. He didn't look surprised or scared. It was almost like he thought it was funny. He started up his truck and shot a finger gun in Charlie's direction, then drove off without waiting for a response.

Charlie started to walk home, disappointed he wasn't going to find anything. Then he realized there was one last person, one last house he hadn't been to yet.

He ran past a line of spruce trees and a hammock swinging gently in the wind. The door to the screened-in porch was unlocked, and so were the double doors inside.

CHAPTER 40

I resent having anyone trick me so cleverly
that I have to admit I was fooled.
[x] TRUE   [   ] FALSE

The clack of the kitchen's screen door closing jolted Francine awake. Pete's clocks told her she'd gotten maybe an hour of sleep, bringing her grand total in the last two days to…an hour.

But it had been worth it. She'd weighed every word of research, every ounce of evidence, every second she'd spent with Roland. And finally, around the first birdcalls of dawn, she'd reached her decision.

Stomach churning and head pounding from exhaustion, she trudged down the stairs to call Bruno and give him her answer. They were either going to bring long-overdue justice to one of the greatest travesties in recent history or condemn an innocent man to a waking nightmare for the rest of his days.

Francine walked into the kitchen and screamed.

Roland Gerber sat at the table under the soft ambience of the Tiffany lamp. He made no other move other than to hold up his hands in the scant daylight.

"I didn't mean to frighten you."

"Roland. What are you doing here?"

"I didn't mean to frighten you," he repeated.

"*What are you doing in this house?*"

"I was hoping we could speak a moment."

Francine considered making a grab for the phone, or simply running out the door. But she didn't know if Charlie was still upstairs. She couldn't risk leaving him alone in a house with this man.

"Speak," she said.

Roland nodded his thanks. He appeared to have aged a decade overnight. Deep shadows hung below his eyes, and his chest was sunken beneath the normally well-fitting blazer.

"It seems you've had a long night of contemplation," he said.

She didn't answer.

"May I ask if you've come to any conclusions?"

"I haven't made a decision yet, Roland."

"At least you're still calling me Roland." He tried a smile, but when Francine stayed rigid, the smile vanished. "Very well. I was hoping I could stay uninvolved."

"Uninvolved?"

"I am not a Nazi, Francine. But neither am I someone who will idly allow his life to be destroyed by a mistake in judgement. I provided you an opportunity to reflect and realize the plain truth for yourself, yet you linger in uncertainty. So I will make the decision easier. Tell Mr. Bruno, and whatever third party bribes you in earrings, that you do not believe me to be this Oskar Lischka. Convince them of the same. Mr. Bruno will listen to you, I have no doubt. I want only to be left alone, but as you know, I am a survivor. You alone can keep me from any extreme acts of self-preservation."

The slowly hinging rays of sunlight caught one of the empty root beer float mugs from the day before, and Francine suddenly felt it imperative to know where her nephew was.

"Tell me when it's done," Roland said. He stood, fixed her with a withering glare, then left through the back door.

The second he was gone, Francine tore out of the kitchen and vaulted up the stairs two at a time. She'd find Charlie sleeping, rubbing his eyes and asking who she'd been talking to. She would make him breakfast and—

The bed was empty.

A fire engine roared outside. The Fourth of July parade. That's where she'd find him.

She ran full stride down the block in her daisy sundress, and looked with dismay at what must have been at least a hundred people lining the parade route.

Freshly washed fire trucks rolled slowly down the asphalt with every light oscillating and every siren whining. The first responders inside tossed handfuls of colorful candy to legions of children scampering along the edge of the street, stuffing their pockets with as much loot as they could fit. Girls in gymnastics leotards turned cartwheels in front of a tractor towing a fence-lined flatbed of kids dressed like Tom Sawyer. Even Diana Banderwalt was there, waving a brilliant white sparkler, its glittering light extinguishing at the feet of her brother, who followed close behind, keeping a wary eye on the crowd.

None of the happy faces belonged to Charlie.

A drop of inky-black dread fell inside Francine's heart and began to leach outward. She had to outpace it, had to keep ahead of the ridiculous notion that her nephew was missing.

She ran past the lawn chairs and picnic blankets lining the parade route, dodging pinwheels and American flags as the parade snaked between the three ponds. At the finish line of the barn parking lot, carefree parents put Band-Aids on skinned knees and daggered straws into juice boxes. Francine navigated around bandana-wearing dogs and face-painted toddlers, the dread inside her growing stronger with each step.

"Francine!"

Bruno waved to her from across the crowd, just as Laura Jean stepped up to a podium.

"Morning, everybody! Thanks for coming out and helping make this a day to remember. They're forecasting rain today, but we're gonna have fun while we can!"

Francine pushed her way through the crowd and finally got to Bruno.

"Hey," he said. "I went to your house but—"

"I can't find Charlie."

As she said the words out loud, the black dread filled her completely. The nightmare was real. Ellie and Pete had left Francine with their only child, and she had lost him.

"Okay," Bruno said. "No problem. We'll find him." He cupped his hands to his mouth. "Charlie? Charlie?"

Laura Jean noticed their distress and abandoned the podium. "Francine? What's wrong?"

The cloud of panic in Francine's mind thickened, making it hard to think and form words. She just needed Charlie back. To see him. To hug him and keep him safe. All her other problems would be nothing if she could just hold him again.

"I can't find him!" she said. "*I can't find him.*"

The crowd around them began to quiet.

"Mark!" Laura Jean flagged down her husband who arrived at the same time as Chief Durham.

"What's wrong?" Mark asked.

"Everything okay?" Chief Durham put a hand on Francine's shoulder, but she brushed it away, reaching for Laura Jean's instead.

Laura Jean was Ellie's best friend. She would know where Charlie was. She would know what to do.

"Who's missing, Francine?" Laura Jean asked clearly.

"Charlie."

Laura Jean looked at the others, then back at Francine.

"Who's Charlie?"

CHAPTER 41

When I am with people I am bothered
by hearing very strange things.
[x] TRUE [ ] FALSE

"My nephew, Charlie," Francine said impatiently.

Why was Laura Jean staring at her? Why was everyone else's face just as blank?

"Charlie!" she screamed, as if they hadn't heard her.

Laura Jean looked to Chief Durham for help. "I don't..."

He crouched down. "Francine, look at me. Breathe for a second. I want you to very slowly tell me what's wrong."

"I can't find Charlie," she enunciated. "My nephew, Charlie." The name got heavier every time she said it.

Chief Durham turned to Laura Jean. "Pete and Ellie have a child?"

"No," Laura Jean said.

Then Francine saw Diana, a burned-out sparkler hanging from one hand as she watched the scene.

"Diana! You know Charlie," Francine said. "He told me he brought you batteries."

Diana cowered behind her brother's legs.

"Did a boy bring you batteries?" Eric asked her.

Diana's voice came out in a squeak as she pointed at Francine. "She did."

Francine's head felt like a balloon someone had let go of.

The next thing she knew, she was being carried into the police station, through a tunnel of staring faces and melting popsicles, until the world itself began to melt, and everything went away.

CHAPTER 42

There is something wrong with my mind.
[x] TRUE   [   ] FALSE

Her eyes opened to the porous white grid of a dropped
ceiling.

She was on a couch in Chief Durham's office.

Her head was cold.

Something had happened…something with Charlie. He was missing.

She sat up, spilling an ice pack from her forehead.

"Leave it on, honey. You were burning up." Laura Jean, her eyes red
from crying, eased Francine back down onto the couch.

"Did you find him?" Francine asked.

Laura Jean bit her lip. "Do you and Ellie have another sibling?"

Francine shook her head.

"Is Charlie a relative of Ben's, or someone back in San Francisco?"

Francine shook her head again. "He's my nephew. Ellie and Pete's
son."

Laura Jean winced. "Francine, I've lived next to Ellie and Pete for
years. They don't have a son. I'm sorry, but they don't. I promise you."

Francine tried to make sense out of the impossible idea that she'd
created a person out of thin air. A person with brown hair, blue eyes, and
freckles…just like her, who lived a life free from the tortures of adulthood…just like she wanted. Then she thought about imaginary friends
who'd lingered a little too long, and fuzzy identities, and becoming a

whole other person for one night in San Francisco. Maybe the idea wasn't so impossible after all.

She sat up again, reassuring Laura Jean with a steady hand. "I'm all right. I…I haven't gotten much sleep lately. I got confused."

"Well, that's all right," Laura Jean said, with a pained smile. "We all have our moments."

Francine stood shakily and opened the door to find Bruno, Mark, and Chief Durham—each face rife with sympathy. Sympathy for someone who had gone mad.

"I'm going home," she told them.

"Francine, you should rest here," Chief Durham said. "While we figure out—"

"Did I do anything illegal?"

"What? No."

"Then I'm going."

"Hon, the storm's gonna be bad," Laura Jean tried. "I think if we stay here together, we'll be safer. We can figure all this out."

"I know, I'm sorry, I just…I have to go." She pushed through their concerned looks and left the station, stepping into an afternoon dark with storm clouds.

In the parking lot, Lori barked orders at arriving families.

"Check in here for cot assignment. No unauthorized guests will be permitted in the storm shelter. No exceptions."

Francine fled Lori's magnified voice and the staring faces of the Hens, keeping a brisk pace all the way to Ellie and Pete's back door as the rain began to fall.

She stepped inside and closed her eyes. Her hand gripped the door-frame, finding the divot she'd dug with her thumbnail the first night. At least that much was real.

Then she called out, not knowing what she dreaded more, silence or a response.

"Charlie?"

Under the din of heavy rain, all was quiet and still.

Francine threw open cabinet doors, looking for a juice box, a sippy cup, an old baby bottle.

Nothing.

An infant's picture in the dining room, a little pair of shoes by the front door, a trove of Disney movies downstairs?

Nothing.

No sign of Charlie in the master bedroom or the guest bedroom. No sign in Charlie's bedroom either, because it didn't exist.

Dizzy, Francine sat on her bed, and noticed the papers peeking out by her feet. She grabbed the MMPI packet and flipped through the questionnaire she loved to hate, all the way to the final page with the scoring chart she'd never quite looked at before.

D, Hy, Pd, Pa, Pt, Sc.

Astrological signs? Cutesy personality types? No. Only now did she see the definitions below: depression, hysteria, psychopathic deviate, paranoia, psychasthenia, schizophrenia. It wasn't a personality quiz. It was a mental health assessment.

How had she never noticed? *How had she never realized any of this?*

The answer was simple.

Because she didn't want to.

It had been Francine who didn't invite people over to the house, and only mentioned Charlie to those who wouldn't know him. Francine, who, yearning for the purity of a child in summer, had spent night after night exploring Hawthorn Woods with its easy joys and alluring secrets. The batteries on Diana's windowsill, the eavesdropping on Bruno, the secret in Eric's shed. All of Charlie's memories unlocked and shuffled, one by one, into Francine's mind like a second deck of cards.

Still holding the stack of papers loosely in one hand, she walked numbly out of the room, not knowing where to go. The tub in the bathroom still held water from the day before. An incredible day, an incredible lie, all invented by her broken machine of a brain.

Her toes pierced the soap film on the water's surface, sending it into swirling eddies as she climbed in, submerging her daisy dress and the troublesome papers alike, the questions bolding, then fading as they sank.

Most of the time I fee*l b l u e*

My sleep is fitful a*nd d i s t u r b e d*

I often feel as if things are *not r e a l*

I am afraid of losing m y *m i n d*

Francine looked closely at her thumb, slightly swollen by the nail at the spot where Charlie had pulled out the sliver. She dug into the healed-over skin with her teeth, drawing blood until she bit down on the needle of wood. Charlie hadn't pulled it out. He hadn't done anything, because he'd never existed in the first place.

She spit the sliver into the blood-pinked bathwater, eyelids sagging as the questions continued to disintegrate around her. The lights flickered once, then died, as a dropped-mountain boom of thunder shook the house.

The approaching storm was opening wide to swallow Hawthorn Woods, but Francine couldn't find a way to care.

CHAPTER 43

There is something wrong with my mind.
[   ] TRUE   [x] FALSE

Francine's eyes opened as someone knocked on the door downstairs. The sky outside the bathroom window was pitch black. The whole block must have lost power.

Between overlaps of thunder, she heard the front door creak open.

Footsteps wandered around the house, eventually climbing the stairs to the creaky landing and the door to the bathroom.

"Francine!"

Bruno ran in and dropped to his knees, setting a camping lantern on the rim of the tub. He pulled her arms from the pink water and felt at her wrists, exhaling with relief when he found the blood had come from her thumb alone.

"Hey, Bruno," she said dreamily.

"The storm's getting worse. I tried to give you as much space as possible, but it's time to go. Let's get you out of the tub."

She pushed her fingers into his chest. Solid. Real.

"Your name is Michael Bruno."

"Yes."

"I'm Francine Haddix."

"Yes."

"Is Roland Gerber real?"

"Yes."

"And the investigation?"

"Yes."

She sighed. "I was kinda hoping that part was made up."

"Francine, we called Ellie and…it's only Charlie. Everything else is real. You live in San Francisco, Ben is real, your divorce, all of it. Ellie's never heard of Charlie. You must have made him up when you came to Hawthorn Woods."

"When Magdalena threw that drink, I think I realized Hawthorn Woods wasn't going to be some magic oasis," she said without enthusiasm. "It's just California without the mountains. But it's different for Charlie. He doesn't have problems. Or fear. Or hatred. Or regret."

She winced and put a hand over her mouth, knowing if she started crying, she'd never stop. "I got all his memories. Except they're different. I see myself doing everything I thought he did."

"I can't imagine what you're feeling right now, but we have to get to the barn. Then we can talk about everything. Or nothing, if that's what you want."

She looked Bruno in the face. "There's something I didn't want to tell you. Something I told Roland after the microphone went out. I've had confusion like this before. Little things here and there, but it's never been this bad. I'm moving farther and farther away from reality, inventing entire people." Her voice was paper thin, the words barely holding together. "I'm fucking crazy, Bruno."

"You're not crazy."

"I am."

"*You're not crazy.* You just need to get out of that water."

"No," she said. "I think I should stay. In Hawthorn Woods. In Charlie's world."

"Francine."

"Yesterday I had one of the greatest days of my life, just playing with him. He wears capes and builds pillow forts and just wants to run and be free. I'd forgotten this, but if you go really high on a swing, there's a moment at the top of the arc where gravity forgets you. The chains go slack and you're just floating. That's how his world feels, all the time."

"But he isn't real."

"I know. But his joy is. We all try to fall back asleep after a really good dream. Try to fool ourselves a little longer. So what's the harm if I stay? I can live here as Ellie's harmless and happy sister that walks around barefoot and pretends she's a kid."

Bruno shook his head. "But there's no weight to that." He thudded his fist on the tub. "*This* has push and pull. Ups and downs. That's how you know one from the other. The dream world you're talking about, Charlie's world…you'll go hungry there."

"You don't have to feel bad about leaving me, Bruno. It's happened before. I'll be fine. I promise."

He huddled closer to the tub. "You used fantasy to get through trauma. That's not unreasonable. It's not even uncommon. Everyone endures stress and deals with it in different ways. Some people drink, or hurt themselves or others. You imagined a happy person in a happy place. You can come back from this."

"How?"

"We'll get you help. Real, professional help. It won't be perfect or easy, but I'll be with you every step of the way. You don't need all the answers right now, you just need to be willing to look for them."

He held her hand and waited in silence as the storm roiled outside.

After a very long time, Francine stepped out of the water.

Bruno helped her out of the cold sundress and into a sweatshirt and some jeans. Once she'd warmed up, he lit her a cigarette, and they sat by the guest room window in the light of the camping lantern, watching the wind push curtains of rain down the street.

After a very long time, she spoke. "I want to go to New York. With you. Would that be okay?"

"Yes."

A knock sounded on the front door.

$$\ast \quad \ast \quad \ast \quad \ast$$

"Wait here."

Bruno took the lantern and left Francine sitting by the window.

She heard him creak across the landing and down the stairs. The front door opened. Voices. A woman's, maybe, though it was hard to tell under the snarls of thunder.

The phone rang. Francine had forgotten they still worked without power.

She felt her way to the handset in the dark.

"Hello?"

"Francine. Hey."

"Hi, Ben."

She didn't stutter or lapse into an involuntary silence, just waited for him to speak, lightly curious.

"Sounds like a storm there."

"Yeah."

"Okay. Well listen, I didn't call to dig up the past again. I was wrong to do that last time."

"I was upset," she said. "But I'm getting better. And I'm actually kinda glad you called."

"Oh, yeah?"

"I learned a little more about myself recently. I've always looked back at our time together in a certain way. And knowing what I know now, I might have misread, or even misremembered, a few things."

"That's great. Look, I uh, well, there was something I wanted to ask you last time I called, but you hung up so fast I didn't get the chance."

Was this an apology years in the making? Proof she'd misjudged him for years?

"Go ahead."

"I want everything to be right the second time around, you know? With the new wedding, the kid, all that. But right now, I'm still not technically married. So I was thinking, if you want to sleep together one last time, I could do that. For you."

Francine smiled to herself. She'd been wrong about Charlie, but very right about Ben.

"Francine?"

"That's very sweet of you to ask, but I'm not interested."

Apparently she'd failed to keep the amusement out of her answer, because Ben's voice rose a little. "Hey, listen, I went through all the trouble to find you and call. Do you think it was easy to find the time to do that? I didn't have to make this offer."

"I'm not upset anymore," she said, and meant it. "It's just that one of us is incurable, and I used to think it was me. Goodbye, Ben."

He started to say something not nice, but Francine calmly hung up. She felt at her wedding ring, a bandage covering a now-healed wound. She took it off and immediately felt lighter, in every way possible.

Then she realized the voices at the front door had stopped.

And Bruno hadn't come back.

CHAPTER 44

At times my thoughts have raced ahead
faster than I could speak them.
[x] TRUE   [   ] FALSE

Francine edged slowly down the stairs and found a woman standing in a small pool of water. Bruno's camping lantern lit her face as she dried herself with a dishtowel.

"Thank you," Magdalena said, handing the towel to Bruno.

"What's going on?" Francine stepped uncertainly from the stairs.

"I was just about to come get you," Bruno said. "She wants to tell you something."

Magdalena looked shyly at Francine. "I don't know exactly how to say so much, but I will try. Hollis has told me about himself. About who he is attracted to. He has told me this, because you have asked him to. Because you understand how I was feeling."

"Oh."

"I always believed Hollis loves me, in his heart. But when he was not attracted physically, I thought this meant his love was gone. I was sad and angry. I thought I had done something wrong." She stepped toward Francine. "I am far away from my old home. Hollis is all I know here. And then you come, and you are so beautiful, and I am scared you have come to make everything worse. To take Hollis from me. Now I understand he does love me, in his own way. And though this does not fix everything, I am no longer angry, because he no longer lies." She hung her head. "I was cruel to you, many times. I have come to tell you I am sorry for this, and to see if you can forgive me."

It took Francine just a moment to process the new Magdalena. "Of course."

Magdalena lunged forward and pulled Francine into a wet hug, then stepped back, smiling behind her pixie cut. When she wasn't throwing cocktails or right hooks, the woman could be pretty endearing.

"I couldn't wait to say these things, even in this storm. Thank you for listening," Magdalena said. "Also I will say I love your earrings. I did not know you are Jewish."

"I'm not," Francine said. "You know what these are?"

"Mezuzahs, yes?"

"How did you know that?" Bruno asked.

"Because I am a Jew," Magdalena said, as if it were obvious. "See?" She reached inside her shirt and pulled out her necklace. It held the same star pendant Francine had noticed the first night, right before Magdalena had thrown the drink in her face. It was a Star of David.

"Roland saw you throw the drink on me," Francine thought out loud.

"I am still sorry for that," Magdalena said.

Francine turned to Bruno. "He thought I left Laura Jean's barbeque because of her too. He drank too much that night. That was the night Brownie got killed."

"Mockingly kosher," Bruno said, slowly. "At the bottom of Magdalena's driveway. 'Get Off Our Block.'"

"It wasn't an unfinished police star he carved into Brownie." Francine pointed to Magdalena's necklace. "It was an unfinished Star of David."

"Gerber is Lischka," Bruno said, almost sounding surprised.

"Gerber is Lischka," Francine agreed.

"Gerber is who?" Magdalena asked.

But Francine didn't have time to explain. "Bruno, he came here."

"What? When?"

"This morning. He said if I put you off the case, he would stay uninvolved."

"Uninvolved how?"

"I don't know." Francine turned to Magdalena. "Where's Hollis?"

"He has gone back to the police station. To help people sheltering from the storm."

Francine stepped into the kitchen and dialed 9-1-1. Bruno followed her.

"When I focused on the goat killing for too long, Roland got nervous," she said to Bruno, while she waited for someone to pick up. "He tried to make it look like Eric hurt Ajax so we'd think Eric killed Brownie. There's a problem though. Roland was with Del the night Ajax was attacked."

Bruno scratched his chin. "Either they did it together, or Del was an unknowing alibi, and Roland had someone else do it for him."

Then Francine remembered the beers she'd seen on Lischka's porch. Del didn't drink. So who was Roland's visitor?

"Police," Lori's voice crinkled over the phone.

Christ, just what she needed.

"Lori, it's Francine. I need to talk to Chief Durham."

"Francine, how you feeling, sweetie?"

"I need to talk to the Chief now."

"Chief Durham is currently occupied. If you fill me in, I can determine whether—"

"Roland Gerber is a Nazi and had someone stab his own dog, is that urgent enough?"

There was a long pause.

"What makes you say that?"

"I don't have time to explain everything right now."

"Francine. A nasty rumor like that could—"

"Give me the Chief, you bitch!" Francine shouted.

Another pause. "You sound a little hysterical. It's possible you're having another episode. We're very busy here with the storm. Please don't call again."

The line went dead. Lori had hung up on her.

The woman wasn't spooked by a speeding pickup truck, fine, but why would she try to downplay a real emergency? Then Francine realized why—at the same time she realized who Gerber's conspirator was.

Dennis Asperski smiled at her through the screen door. "Hello, neighbor."

Francine ran from the kitchen, pushing Bruno and Magdalena toward the front door until it opened and a man stepped in, wearing a blue blazer and carrying a rifle.

His name was Oskar Lischka.

CHAPTER 45

My thoughts these days turn more and
more to death and the hereafter.
[x] TRUE   [   ] FALSE

Bruno, Francine, and Magdalena sat on the couch down in the family room. Other than the occasional fork of lightning that briefly whited out the room, the only light came from the camping lantern in Francine's lap.

In the opposite corner, Oskar Lischka sat contemplatively in the rocking chair, the rifle laid across his lap.

She'd looked in his closet, under his mattress, in every nook and cranny of his house. How had she missed the rifle?

Dennis paced relentlessly around the carpet, his manic energy a sharp contrast to Lischka's mousetrap calm. Francine didn't need the dynamic to be spelled out for her. Dennis's hunched posture and mousy demeanor told of a life lived under the thumb of everyone he met. This was a frustrated man who'd felt ignored, left behind, and irrelevant. Somehow he'd learned of Lischka's past, maybe during some other summer barbeque when Lischka drank too much. Suddenly Dennis was treated with a philosophy, a mode of thought that explained why. Why his life didn't satisfy. Why others had what he did not. Why a certain group of people were responsible. Dennis got an explanation for his failure, and Lischka got an outlet for his hate.

"You put up the flag," Francine said to Dennis.

Dennis's eyes, one still ringed in a purple bruise, lit up. "That's right." He sneered and pointed at Magdalena. "This Jew walking around my yard, touching *my* things. All I had to do was slip away. No one ever notices where I go or what I do. But you noticed the flag, didn't you, Jew? Got a little scared, I bet."

"Hold your tongue." Lischka said it softly, but Dennis immediately backed down. "That flag was the most foolish thing you've ever done. I should've blacked both your eyes."

"Instead, you had him try to kill Ajax," Francine said icily.

Lischka's lamplit eyes flashed to her. "Ajax would have been a costly sacrifice. I never wanted him to suffer. There's nothing I won't do to survive. You know this about me."

"I know nothing about you. Because everything you told me was a lie. You're the most vile person I've ever met."

"Your disapproval I will learn to live with. However, I think this should be the least of your concerns. I waited all day to hear from you, Francine. When I could wait no longer, I returned. What do I find? You conspiring against me, with him and *her*."

"What are you going to do with us?" Bruno asked.

Lischka nodded, as if that was indeed the question. "Nothing you haven't brought upon yourselves."

A flash of lightning briefly lit the room.

Dennis scurried over to the rocking chair. "Please, Oskar. Let me hurt them. I've been patient. I want to demonstrate my power."

"You couldn't even kill a dog. Only the superior can kill the inferior." Lischka's gaze roamed across Bruno, then Francine, then Magdalena. "You are superior to the Jew, at least."

Francine's stomach turned at hearing the horrific words coming from someone she had once treasured. But she also noticed how much

Lischka's disapproval had wounded Dennis, and it gave her an idea. She'd never get to the rifle while it was still in Lischka's lap. But if she could get Dennis even more worked up than he already was, maybe he'd pick up the gun on his own, and come close enough for her to grab it. It was a risk, but the look in Lischka's eyes told her he had no intention of letting anyone on the couch leave the room alive.

Dennis was staring at Magdalena, who still hadn't said a word.

"Oskar told me the truth. He told me why my life was shit. Why I never get what I deserve." Dennis's voice quivered as it rose. "It's because of people like you. Oskar told me how life used to be. The great days. When a man could be someone—"

"You could be someone today if you weren't so pathetic," Francine said.

Rain battered the windows.

"W-what did you say?" Dennis stammered in disbelief.

"Your Nazi mentor is just as disgusting and evil as all the others of his time. But you don't live in a destitute country. You don't have a silky speech giver tricking angry masses into hating people you can blame all your problems on."

Dennis' face reddened with each word.

"Shut up," he mumbled. "Oskar killed for you. Killed that goat to defend your honor. His honor was his loyalty, and you don't even appreciate it."

"He's an old murderer who got drunk and forgot to disguise his ugliness. But he got the job done, didn't he, Dennis? Brownie is dead, but Ajax is still alive. That was your job, wasn't it?"

Dennis was shivering with rage.

"We all see your inadequacy, Dennis," Francine went on. "And we know inadequacy breeds hostility. So why don't you prove what we already know? Why don't you show us just how inadequate you really are?"

Dennis sprang into action, ripping the rifle out of Lischka's hands and swinging the barrel toward the couch. Francine and Bruno reached for it at the same instant.

Maybe they would've gotten to it in time, maybe not. It didn't matter—because Magdalena moved faster than anyone.

Her shriek filled the room as she swung the lantern into the side of Dennis's face. The glass exploded, the light died, and the room was plunged into total darkness.

Francine, the only one who knew the room, pulled Bruno and Magdalena toward the stairs.

"Someone has to get to the barn," she said as they scrambled awkwardly up the steps.

They were almost to the front door when Francine's bare feet slipped on the rain-slicked tile, and she fell.

A sequence of lightning revealed her surroundings. Bruno had slipped, too, nearer the front door. Magdalena was feeling her way into the kitchen. Down in the family room, Lischka stepped over Dennis's crumpled form. He had reclaimed his rifle, ready to hunt. She was the prey he wanted. Maybe she could give Bruno and Magdalena just enough time to escape.

Darkness returned.

"Come and get me!" Francine shouted, slapping the banister as she ran upstairs. "Come and get me, Lischka!"

Dashing into the master bedroom, she tried to wrench open the window, but the heavy moisture in the air had swollen the wood.

A creak sounded on the landing at the top of the stairs.

Francine pulled as hard as she could, and with an angry groan, the window slid upward.

Climbing out onto the slippery shingles, it was all she could do to stagger wildly across the roof, waiting to be shot in the back at any moment. When she was close enough to the weather vane she leapt forward, shingles tearing at her hands as she landed. Momentum took her legs over the edge of the roof, but she grabbed the frog sheet just in time, the knot around the weather vane shivering as her weight registered.

A burst of lightning showed her Oskar Lischka, standing in the bedroom window. As he raised the rifle, the knot finally failed and Francine fell, hearing the whistle of a bullet pass just above her head.

CHAPTER 46

At times I feel like picking a
fistfight with someone.
[x] TRUE   [   ] FALSE

F rancine landed hard in the bushes. Broken branches clawed at her
as she rolled out onto the soggy lawn, fully soaking her sweatshirt
and jeans.

She looked up at the roof, wondering if Lischka had come out after
her. But there was no way he'd be able to navigate the rain-slicked shingles. Was he running down the stairs to chase after her? Or was he still at
the window, waiting for her to walk into his rifle sights?

Keeping as close to the house as she could, Francine jumped over
fallen tree branches and deepening puddles, hoping to run into Bruno or
Magdalena out in the driveway. But there was no sign of either of them.
Hopefully they were both well on their way to the barn.

Then she saw a light next door. Candlelight, playing along the flanks
of a Roman Red convertible. The best cure Francine knew for a Nazi with
a rifle was a Marine with his.

She sprinted through the blinding rain and into the garage. Del wasn't
there. Francine brushed wet strands of hair from her face and opened the
door to the house. "Del? *Del?*"

She heard a strange, snoring sound coming from the other side of the
Corvette. Rounding the front bumper, she found him: sprawled out on the
floor, a black and blue welt swelling the side of his head.

"Oh, Jesus." She carefully leaned him up against the wall into a more natural position. His breathing normalized. "Del, can you hear me?"

He eyelids fluttered. "Francine? I don't…Gerber hit me," he slurred. "Bastard just came in and hit me with a rock."

Francine saw the rock, lying next to a fractured padlock on the ground. The hooks above the workbench were empty. She hadn't missed a rifle in Lischka's house, he'd just taken Del's.

"Listen to me, Del. Gerber isn't who you think. He's a Nazi that's been hiding here since the war. Bruno and I found out and he took your rifle to try and keep us quiet."

"What? Are you serious?"

"I have to get to the barn and warn everyone. Can we take your car?"

Del pulled sloppily at the keys on his belt. "You take it. I'll be okay here."

"Are you sure?"

He pressed the keys into her hand. "Bring the cavalry. And some aspirin."

She cupped his cheek. "I will."

She jumped into the driver's seat of the Corvette, hoping Del's ten million hours of maintenance hadn't been in vain.

The engine roared to life, magnified in the close confines of the garage. Francine hadn't driven a stick shift since high school, but hopefully it was like riding a bicycle. A three-hundred horsepower bicycle.

Headlights. Clutch. *Gas.*

The car lunged in reverse down the driveway. Francine was almost to the street when she saw the pickup coming and jammed on the brakes with both feet.

The passing truck killed one of the Corvette's taillights as the vehicles glanced one another, spinning the Corvette in a full circle. Francine watched the pale blue truck continue on its way, barely slowing down as it headed for the other side of the block. The side the Banderwalts lived on.

A forgotten crisis pushed its way to the front of Francine's mind. Mr. Banderwalt had come back, just like he said he would. Probably blind drunk from some rained-out barbeque, looking for trouble. Or payback. And this time, Chief Durham wasn't there to stop him.

Francine gunned the Corvette's engine, shifting from first to second to third. The powerful back wheels fishtailed as she took the first corner, but she managed to stay on the road. She swung onto the other side of the block, desperately hoping Eric had taken his sister and mother to the storm shelter. But above the relentless howl of the wind and the pickup truck idling in the gravel driveway, she could hear screams coming from inside the house.

She slowed to a stop, rain pooling on the seat next to her as she thought. Del was injured and bleeding, Bruno and Magdalena might be almost to the barn, and Lischka was God only knew where. One thing alone was certain: Violence had come to the Banderwalt house, and no one else was coming to help.

Francine hooked the Corvette into the driveway, blocking in the pickup. Gravel dug painfully into her feet as she ran up the driveway. The shed doors had been wrenched open, nearly off their hinges, so that the pickup's headlights reflected off an empty rear wall. The pile of animal skeletons had been flung out onto the flooding lawn. Mr. Banderwalt was looking for Diana, but judging by the roars of anger from inside, he hadn't found her yet.

Then came the meaty sound of someone being hit. Mrs. Banderwalt wailed. Eric shouted. Another meaty hit.

A lead-up of thunder, like an entire glacier cracking in half, ended in a boom Francine felt deep in her guts. Someone was going to die here. The instincts that had so maddeningly abandoned her were back, and this was the message they brought.

She grabbed the biggest animal skull she could find and ran for the front door, not knowing what she was going to do—only that she had little time to do it.

✶　　✶　　✶　　✶

F rancine found the Banderwalts' living room in shambles, tables cracked in half, lamps shattered against the wall. Sounds of destruction came from the bedrooms as they, too, were trashed in Mr. Banderwalt's search.

Eric lay in one corner, half of his face wet with blood, holding a protective arm across his mother, who had been thrown out of her wheelchair. The teenager had obviously been putting up a fight, but he didn't look like he could do it much longer.

Mr. Banderwalt marched back into the room, squinting in the truck's headlights. He looked even larger than he had the last time Francine had seen him—the veiny arms beneath his desert camouflage t-shirt bulging like he'd grabbed onto something electrified. His eyes, pink with inebriation, blurrily focused on Francine.

"You. You're the bitch that called the cops on me."

"Yeah. And I did it again. Chief Durham's on his—"

Mr. Banderwalt lurched forward and grabbed Francine by the hair. She punched the animal skull into his face, breaking it on the closest cheek. Mr. Banderwalt grunted in pain, and Francine smelled alcohol. She felt her hair twist as he swung her hard into the wall, and she collapsed next to Eric and his mother.

"*Where's my Diana?*" Mr. Banderwalt roared.

Francine tasted blood. In her wavering vision, she saw Eric pull something lime green from his pocket. The boy got to his feet and lunged, his pocket knife slicing a long red line down Mr. Banderwalt's veiny forearm.

But the giant barely noticed. He twisted Eric's wrist until he dropped the knife, then wrapped a huge, bloody forearm around his neck, lifting until the boy's sneakers dangled above the carpet. "I've had enough. Tell me where she is, or I'll kill him. I'll kill him right now."

His glistening red forearm viced tighter around Eric's neck. He gurgled.

"The window well!" Mrs. Banderwalt wailed. "Out front."

Mr. Banderwalt smiled, blood dribbling from the shard of animal bone Francine had lodged in his cheek. He dropped Eric and went out into the storm.

"Can't...let...him take her," Eric rasped.

Francine got to her feet, her legs feeling like they were made of concrete. She staggered dizzily across the room and ran into the doorframe. Leaning outside, she saw Mr. Banderwalt fling a plastic shell weightlessly into the yard. A yellow-orange glow rose from the window well. He'd found her at last.

One of his huge, bloody arms reached down into the well and effortlessly pulled up his daughter. Diana's toes dragged along the smooth, corrugated metal in a final effort to stay. The Glo Worm fell from her hand as Mr. Banderwalt carried her toward the pickup.

Francine stumbled down the ramp and picked up the toy by its pajama tail. She caught up to Mr. Banderwalt and swung it as hard as she could into the side of his face, driving the shard of bone deeper into his skin.

He screamed in pain and dropped Diana in a puddle. Then he rounded on Francine, pink eyes wide with rage.

"Okay, bitch. You want it?" In one step he had his hands around her neck.

They fell together onto the lawn, his weight squeezing the air from her lungs as they sank into the watery grass. Diana screamed and ran inside the house.

Spots of color popped in Francine's vision as Mr. Banderwalt's hands pressed tighter and tighter. The simplest thoughts came with more and more difficulty.

He was hurting her. She was going to die. The monster was going to kill her.

Then she saw an even bigger monster stalk past the headlights of the pickup.

Lischka's command came low and deadly. "Off her."

The grip on Francine's neck loosened and she inhaled hard, gulping burning air down her ravaged throat.

Mr. Banderwalt stood slowly, half-smirking at the elderly man before him. "What is this? What do you think you—"

The tip of the rifle flared white in the darkness. A pillar of light passed straight through Mr. Banderwalt's head and into the graveyard of bones below. He fell sloppily to the ground, and the deafening sound of the gunshot faded, letting the rain and thunder back in.

Lischka spat on the corpse. "A man like my father. And so he enjoys the same fate."

He turned his attention to Francine, pressing the still-hot barrel of the rifle into her cheek.

Francine looked up at the man she'd once trusted, once revered like a father. Rain plinked off his blue blazer and the gold frames of the readers clipped to the breast pocket.

"Your reader glasses." She croaked a bitter laugh. "They were Ida's father's. You did keep something."

Lischka glanced down at his pocket, realization coming to him slowly. "The hotelier in Poland? His daughter. She escaped."

"Yes. And she found you." Francine's voice was raspy, but satisfied. "No hammock for your twilight years. No happy poem on your gravestone. You'll be captured, or die in an unfamiliar place, under a new meaningless name. But you'll always be Lischka to me."

Lischka tapped the glasses down in his pocket, and smiled. He knelt close to her, still holding the hot rifle barrel to her cheek. "I was superior to my father, to the Jewish disease of Europe, to my pursuers in South America, to this pile of filth on the lawn. And now, to you as well, Francine. Goodbye—"

His eyes caught on something at the front door.

Eric Banderwalt, walked slowly out into the storm, his BB gun pointed at Lischka's head. In the darkness and rain, the rifle looked real enough.

"Put it on the grass," Eric said, as rain dappled the mask of blood on his face.

Lischka slowly withdrew the barrel from Francine's cheek. "Easy, boy. Easy…"

"*Put it on the fucking grass!*" Eric shouted.

Lischka dropped his rifle and walked carefully backwards, stepping through the scattered bones until he reached the idling pickup.

"Can't let him leave," Francine rasped to Eric, but he didn't seem to understand.

Lischka reversed the truck into Del's Corvette, inadvertently pushing it sideways and blocking the driveway. He threw the pickup into drive and fishtailed across the lawn, sending a wave of mud and bone over Francine as she picked up Del's rifle.

Wiping the sludge from her face, she aimed at one of the truck's rear tires and pulled the trigger. The recoil hammered her shoulder so hard, it was impossible to see if she'd hit anything. When she tried to fire again, the gun jammed.

As the pickup hit the ditch between the yard and the street, it slowed just long enough for Francine to run forward and jump in the back.

CHAPTER 47

At times I feel like smashing things.
[x] TRUE   [   ] FALSE

She landed hard in the truck bed and lost the rifle in a sloshing pool of rainwater. A moment later, everything shifted in a surge of energy as the truck's front tires gripped the road. Francine was thrown into the truck's back gate, but mercifully it didn't buckle.

She watched Eric shrink behind them as the truck accelerated down the street. The sky beyond the Banderwalts' house glowed orange. Accelerant-fueled flames battled the rain as the roof of Lischka's cottage began to fold in.

Lischka took the next turn hard and Francine fell into the side of the truck bed. She tried and failed to find her footing on the slippery metal, fighting against every one of Lischka's attempts to throw her out. Finally, her fingers dug into a seam on the cab, and she pulled herself to a standing position. The truck gave its biggest lurch yet as the rear tire Francine had apparently hit earlier tore apart under the stress of the last turn. Chunks of rubber and yellow sparks spit up behind the truck as Lischka approached the three ponds.

Then something in the water bumped against Francine's leg. The rifle.

She grabbed the weapon by its barrel and arced it high over the roof of the cab. The shoulder stock smashed into the truck's windshield, spidering fracture lines across the glass.

Lischka cursed, leaning to see through the ruined windshield just as something white dashed across the road ahead.

He automatically jerked the steering wheel to avoid Ajax, and the truck left the road, veering wildly toward Haunted Pond. They hit a berm in the grass and Francine was thrown clear, ground and sky becoming a spiral of color until her feet caught the pond's surface and she plunged underwater.

Headlights stabbed into the darkness a half second later, yellowing the water as the truck sank toward the silty bottom of the pond, pulling Francine down along with it.

She fought with everything she had left, working against her heavy clothes, the sharp pain in her neck, and the fiery exhaustion in every muscle. She kicked and kicked until her hands clawed the bank of the pond.

She lay there, gasping in the euphoria of escaped death. Then she saw them, running toward her from the direction of the barn as the storm continued to rage. Bruno in the lead, Laura Jean and Magdalena behind him, Chief Durham and Mark behind them.

The rain was practically horizontal now, tree branches bending and breaking as a tornado siren screamed somewhere in the distance.

Bruno slid to Francine's side and shielded her from the flying debris as best he could, careful not to move her. A moment later, Laura Jean and Magdalena were on her other side.

With great effort, Francine tilted her head up to watch Chief Durham and Mark pull a blue-blazered figure from the water and put him in handcuffs. It was over.

Unable to hold her head up any longer, Francine lay flat against the grass. The sky above was green and black, but calmer now. Maybe the eye of a storm. Maybe the remnants of a storm now passed.

She felt Bruno's hand slide into hers. He squeezed, and she squeezed back.

CHAPTER 48

I have had a tragic loss in my life
that I will never get over.
[   ] TRUE   [x] FALSE

"Shall we?" Ellie asked.

Francine nodded at her sister as much as the neck brace would allow, and out they went.

Down by the mailbox, Laura Jean and Magdalena applauded their arrival.

"I went for walks with Francine before it was cool," Laura Jean announced. "I just want that on the record."

Magdalena offered Francine a pack of Camel 100's. "I brought the cigarettes you like. But Laura Jean says she does not allow this."

"The doctor doesn't allow it." Laura Jean stuffed the cigarettes inside the mailbox. "But I agree. It's a bad look for a national hero."

The four of them started a slow walk around the block, the topics of conversation as numerous and wide-ranging as breath would allow: Laura Jean's ideas for the Halloween parade, Magdalena's plans to visit her brother in Indiana, Ellie's favorite cafés in Paris.

Francine participated, but couldn't keep her mind off the slow scroll of people and houses they passed, wondering what the future might hold for each.

The Cunninghams' home was blessed once more by the twins, who'd decided to come back from Notre Dame and spend the rest of their summer in a neighborhood that wasn't quite as dull as they'd thought. Laura

Jean was delighted to have them, as well as the ten pints of rum raisin ice cream gifted by Francine.

A moving truck shaded the driveway of the mint-colored ranch on the other side of the block. The new residents, busily throwing out teddy bear knick-knacks by the bagful, had heard about the recent events in the neighborhood, but were unaware that their very own kitchen had been ground zero for what had turned out to be a very effective, improvised detective agency.

The storm had finally erased the bloodstain marring the street in front of the Durhams' house. There was still much to be worked out between Hollis and Magdalena, but in the afterglow of full disclosure, both had decided to try and make the situation work. They'd requested the matchmaking services of Laura Jean for outside dates, while continuing to maintain total honesty in what was proving to be quite the modern marriage.

The Colonial next door was uncharacteristically humbled: every window closed, every blind drawn. Aiding and abetting a kidnapping meant Dennis wouldn't be back to Hawthorn Woods for quite some time—assuming Lori stayed herself. It was unclear exactly how much she had known about her husband's unwholesome hobby, but she'd been notably absent from the opening of his court case, and from every neighborhood event since.

An opposite change had taken hold in the next house. Mrs. Banderwalt was seated in the shade of a leafy maple, her face clear and smiling as she watched her daughter play with Ajax, the family's new pet. Eric's shed had been cleaned out and converted into a giant dog house, leaving plenty of room for a cushy dog bed and the windfall of toys gifted by the rest of the block. Del Merlin crouched in the gravel driveway, helping Eric fine-tune the engine of his dirt bike. Aside from a baseball-sized lump and a week of headaches, he had emerged from the ordeal unscathed, though the same couldn't be said for his truck-smashed Corvette. But the mechanical enthusiast had waved away Francine's apologies, thrilled his car needed actual repairs for once. He was excited to do the work, and his new assistant, Eric, was excited to learn. The shocking death of Mr. Banderwalt hadn't exactly been celebrated by the boy, but it seemed the cloud of dread that had long fogged his family had lifted, allowing them a chance to start their lives again.

The charming cottage nuzzled in the spruce trees was still picturesque, save for the yellow ribbons of crime scene tape crossing off every charred door and window. Everything inside that hadn't been turned to ash had been relocated to police lockups. Oskar Lischka was in a jail cell somewhere downstate, awaiting a distant trial. He'd become the rope in a legal tug of war between a dozen different governments, all of which were thoroughly reviewing the findings of an overly dedicated history teacher and a vacationing hairdresser.

Francine and her friends stepped back into Ellie and Pete's driveway. Once the honeymooning couple had gotten over the incredible events that had taken place in their absence, Francine had noticed a mild glow to her sister, and a more chipper attitude in Pete. She had a feeling, just a feeling, that Ellie had gotten pregnant in Paris. If it was true, Francine would be genuinely ecstatic for them, as long as they picked any name other than Charlie and used any baby food other than Gerber. She would be a great aunt. She'd had the practice.

Everyone they'd seen on their walk slowly converged in the driveway, where Chief Durham and Pete chatted with Bruno next to a car now packed with one more suitcase than it had arrived with.

The thirteen-hour drive to New York in a neck brace wouldn't allow for much sightseeing, but Francine didn't mind. She'd count down the highway exits to her new life with anticipation. The first thing she was going to do when they got to the city was check out the referrals given to her by her recently-acquired therapist. Francine had learned a lot about something called dissociative identity disorder, and the alternate personalities that sometimes emerged out of it. She hadn't seen or become Charlie since the night before the storm, but she was ready to deal with it if she did. Her therapist was confident she'd continue to make progress with the right kind of support, both professional and personal.

She and Bruno were going to pick up where they'd left off, now free from the incredible stresses of their investigation. Unless, of course, they opted to embark on a new case together, becoming summer sleuths who solved mysteries between May and September. Maybe they'd swap research and field work while they waltzed to classical music in the kitchen of their new apartment, somewhere not too far from Bruno's old one, so they could still have dinner with Ida from time to time. Francine was looking forward to all of it. The easy times that would bring joy, and the difficult ones that would bring perspective.

After a flurry of hugs, well wishes, and promises to call and visit, she and Bruno were alone in the car, waving goodbye to the grateful residents of Hawthorn Woods through the windshield.

Bruno put on the "New York or Bust" tie Laura Jean had made for him, then handed Francine a map from the glove compartment. "Ready?"

She smiled. "Absolutely."

ACKNOWLEDGEMENTS

Thank you to these people, whose generously shared childhood memories helped detail the book's setting: Nick Canning, Amy Jackson, Becca Mandru, and Jess Palakshappa.

And thank you to these immensely brave individuals for reading and critiquing early drafts of the story: Bett Canning, Justyna Canning, Terry Canning, Katie Contri, Sachi Georgieva, Jess Gittler, and Sarah Novak.

PATRICK CANNING is the author of *The Colonel and the Bee,* and *Cryptofauna*. He currently lives in Los Angeles with his Australian Shepherd, Hank, considered by some to be the greatest dog of all time.

For more of his work, please visit

www.patrickcanningbooks.com